DEVOUR

Jacob Russell Dring

"People sleep peaceably in their beds at night only because rough men stand ready to do violence on their behalf."

George Orwell

1

The conference room was a commotion of applause and overlapping voices. Even at their calmest, the men and women around the table, dressed in their finest suits and wearing big grins, were bubbling on the inside, with excitement. With greed.

Farooq Meskin was more than halfway through his orientation of the new AMF *Mastodon*. Ten months ago, the Mech model went into mass production. Since, it had made trillions worldwide, billions alone for the designers and AMF executives in the United States.

Farooq had been named the youngest AMF architect four years ago, when E&D signed his contract. Fresh out of cadet school, too.

He had anticipated the orientation to be finished by now, but his hologram presentation was only sixty-percent through. The executives around the table were more enthusiastic than he anticipated. He couldn't help but wonder, in the back of his mind, if they were trying to kiss-ass for some sort of bonus.

As if Farooq himself was the boss.

In mentioning the *Mastodon*, he might as well be; the lead designer, or Mech Architect as they were casually called, he received revenue for each unit sold.

It was "only" three figures, and he wasn't the sole person responsible for the *Mastodon*'s design, let alone its marketing, but the numbers rapidly added up.

At just twenty-six, Farooq had become a sort of business celebrity over the last year.

Before he proceeded to the next stage of his hologram presentation, the device sitting at the head of the table to his right, one of the eight executives raised her hand.

"Yes, Mrs. Werner?" Farooq pointed.

"Is it true that your father was among the first to test-pilot a *Mastodon*?"

He tried to suppress his pride, to not let it shine through so exuberantly. This was difficult. Especially with the sun's brilliance coming through thin clouds above the skylight on the roof of the building, the conference room its top level.

Illuminated by the late-morning sun—protected by the UV film on the glass—Farooq's true feelings couldn't hide. His expression of pride was undeniable.

Four years ago, when he graduated cadet school and was contracted by AMF Engineering & Design, Farooq feared that his Mech-jockey father would be disappointed in him, for not pursuing a pilot's career.

It had been the opposite. His father was proud and had high hopes for his son's future.

"An AMF office is a different kind of helm than a Mech cockpit," he had told 22-year-old Farooq, "but it is a helm nonetheless. And a necessary one, for without it, I'd have never become a pilot in the first place."

The words, among others, had stuck with Farooq over the years. They were the only inspiration he needed.

In addition to the fact that his mother had been a civilian casualty of the Great Mech War, which spanned from 2049 to 2053. A global conflict between warring nations, insatiable with the power of what was, at the time, revolutionarily new technology.

So in many ways, it was a personal endeavor to design Mechs. He was not traumatized by their existence due to his mother's death. He had been a young teenager at the time, and the memory of the attack was immortal, like scar tissue that never healed.

His father, called to arms. But rushing to find them. A San Diego invasion, as only coastal cities were attacked. They were being evacuated, but it was too late.

The guilt his father lived with, Farooq couldn't fathom. Still, he had moved on and fought harder than ever. His dedication as a Mech pilot was unwavering; his devotion as a father was pricelessly admirable.

So, Farooq had history.

The Alliance of Mechanized Forces, established after the war's concession in 2054, united to build one superpower. Through the horrors of war, humanity unearthed peace.

Farooq came to embrace this, and he would defend it against anyone who stated otherwise. The AMF had hordes of enemies in the public, yet despite continuous Mech design and production, Mech combat exercises and cadet schooling, it was now 2066—

Twelve years of peace.

This could not be argued.

The consistent development and training within the AMF was a design of reassurance. To the people of every

3

nation, a statement by their government that they were protected, no matter the threat.

The global unity was an unspeakable and unprecedented epoch in humanity's history.

Something everyone could be proud of.

Even, if not especially, Farooq.

"Yes, ma'am," he replied, nodding and sustaining a small smirk. "My father was not only among the first to test-pilot the new *Mastodon*, but is currently an active operator of one."

Some gasps and impressed murmurs around the table. Meanwhile Farooq's smile spread a little and he nodded, hands clasped in front of his suit.

A finger was lifted into the air by another executive. A very young man.

"How, uh, old is your father? If I may?"

Farooq chuckled. "He'll be forty-seven this September." Some minute gasps and expressions of awe. Farooq continued: "Yes, but still a capable pilot as ever. One could even go so far as joking that the *Mastodon* is a perfect fit for him."

It took some of them longer than others to get the prehistoric reference, but the end result was nonetheless copious laughter. Perhaps over-exaggerated, Farooq enjoyed it nonetheless. He couldn't imagine how much his father was the butt of that joke among his fellow pilots, which amused him, as he was aware of how juvenile some of them could be.

"In all seriousness, though," Farooq continued, tacitly hushing the room, "the *Mastodon* has no correlation to the antiquity of its namesake, only the brute size and power of such a beast."

Reclaiming his surprisingly commanding voice, which could seize the attention of hundreds in an auditorium, and had at cadet schools over the last few years, Farooq continued his presentation.

The hologram flickered and next displayed a moving depiction of a *Mastodon*. The Mech walked at various speeds, and even engaged its weapons with various targets, also portrayed through the hologram. It was a soundless presentation; Farooq was here to command their ears, and awe their eyes.

He slowly advanced the hologram, showcasing a diverse array of visuals representing the *Mastodon*'s design. These included external and internal components, from its Tungsteel armor to its spacious cockpit.

"Functioning on the largest fusion engine yet, developed exclusively by the AMF's partnership with Boeing, here in Chicago, the *Mastodon* is truly a force to be reckoned with. Fifty-two feet at its highest point, the *Mastodon* is the second-tallest Mech in AMF's roster. Standing in a perpetual hunch due to the weight it carries, particularly on its shoulders—"

Farooq paused to indicate the massive shoulder-mounted cannons on the vaguely humanoid Mech.

"—the *Mastodon* is nonetheless an imposing sight. In addition to the twin Autocannons, on its right arm alone is a dual Railgun configuration, the first of its kind."

Gasps all around. Mutterings.

A raised hand.

"Yes, Mr. Dominguez?"

"What is the tonnage of the *Mastodon*, compared to, say, the *Colossus* or *Tyrant*?"

Farooq nodded. He advanced the hologram, which depicted the *Mastodon* being stripped of its components in a suspended CGI model.

"Like the other two Mechs you mentioned, the *Mastodon* is also a Support Class model. Slower speeds, no hop-jet capability, limited torso pivoting, high heat output—these are all its cons. But its pros? The same as any other Support Class Mech: maximum armor, overwhelming fire-power, increased ammunition supply, superior balance, and, well, just look at it."

Delighted faces on the executives.

Farooq was bittersweet with what he saw: hope, in the faces of civilian business men and women, the funders behind AMF E&D here in Chicago. Hope and optimism, that they were building war machines with the prospect of no war.

It was an inarguably beautiful sight, especially beneath the skylight.

He also saw naïveté, though. Men and women oblivious to the true grittiness and terrors of operating Mechs in actual combat. Even the dangers of exercises alone, with or without the use of live ammunition. The heat in a cockpit, the weight of a coolant vest, the dizzying array of HUDs and alarms and warnings…

Farooq was only minimally experienced. Cadet school was just that—a school. For cadets. Trainees.

Veterans like his father were few and far between. It was largely a young man's career; the average Mech pilot was thirty years old, male. Women went through the

6

stringer at a lower quantity; thus any females that became Mech pilots for more than a few years were inarguably among the best, regardless of sex, given the strenuous physical stresses.

Farooq was, in many ways, grateful that E&D set their sights on him when they did. He had not even applied, but his grades in cadet school, where most pilots only barely passed, he did so with flying colors. And his consistent questioning and after-hours pursuit of knowledge in the engineering field rose some eyebrows.

Good eyebrows.

He had only ever been true to himself.

This was one reason why his father couldn't have been prouder.

"To answer your question, though," Farooq continued, "the *Mastodon* clocks in at an even hundred-tons. The eighteen heat-sinks are allocated in its upper torso, which bears the resemblance of an inverted pyramid. This promotes the stability of carrying such weight on its shoulders, without sacrificing as much movement speed as the *Colossus* and *Tyrant*."

Clapping all around the room.

Farooq smiled and nodded.

"The *Mastodon* has exceeded expectations in combat exercises around the globe over the last ten months, and has been favored by the Russian Federation. I want to thank you all for your support and confidence in our E&D branch here in Chicago. To wrap things up here, I actually wish to bring it back to my father, the great Walid Meskin. He made a public statement a few months ago during a press conference with the Ember Wolves of Sacramento. I'm sure all of you have seen it on the screen, or heard it on the airwaves, so instead of playing a recording on my hologram, I thought I'd reiterate a certain sentence my father spoke, of the *Mastodon*."

Everyone watched, waited, and listened with courteous respect.

Farooq cleared his throat and lifted his chin slightly, hands clasped before him.

He deepened his voice only a touch, nothing theatrical, just enough to indicate that he was impersonating his father.

"The *Mastodon* is an imposing giant—not of war, but strength. The strength to carry the weight of the world on its shoulders; the burden of protecting loved ones; the pride of perpetuating peace through preparation."

Farooq bowed his head and took a step back.

Applause swept the conference room.

Eventually it faded, and everybody stood. Farooq wove between chairs and people, shaking hands.

Exchanging pleasantries, and wishes of "good luck," "Godspeed," and even one woman who claimed that "fortune favors the bold."

Farooq was borderline speechless with each one. Grateful, nonetheless.

The shadow that came over the conference room, through the skylight above, disappointed Farooq more than the others. He was looking forward to a sunny day, crisp spring weather here in Chicago.

The omen of rain was not one he fancied, especially after spending so many hours a day in an office building. He long awaited his return home, to a suite six blocks away, where his fiancé likely held a surprise party to celebrate the *Mastodon*'s success.

He didn't know for sure; it was pure deduction.

Thunder followed, and now more than Farooq sighed with disappointment. Overcast was one letdown, but a storm could ruin everyone's day. Power outages were rare, at least, in the bigger cities.

And as high as the building was, they had nothing to fear within the room. A lightning rod protruded from the peak of the building's highest point. The conference room was the top floor, but not the true summit.

"A thunderclap to punctuate our own, Meskin," one of the executives said, an older man with a graying beard. He chuckled and shook Farooq's hand with both of his own.

"An optimistic perspective," Farooq smirked, nodding.

The crack of lightning startled everybody in the room. Some nervous laughter followed.

Gazes lifted up, through the skylight.

Clouds wafted, parting as if to give way to a greater force. The darkness overhead became more than a shadow. A sight itself—the sky fissuring, providing a glimpse into space, miles above them. And from the Earth's exosphere, a gaping slit. Impossibly wide, and unfathomably deep. Long, crescent, curving across the sky's farthest reaches.

From the men and women in the conference room, their perspective was only a particle of this.

Farooq had never felt smaller than in that moment. Microscopic, beneath the eye of God.

No…

Something else.

An object the width of the Chrysler Building, but at least five times the height, descended from the slit in the sky. Curved slightly, like a canine, and bone-colored. Tapering to a broad tip; sharp, perhaps, from the perspective of the Earth's crust. To a human, too immense to call a point.

The tip of the tooth-like structure drove into the office complex's top floor. The skylight and conference room were obliterated in an instant, plunging level after level until the enormous tip stabbed into the ground. Shaking the earth and shattering windows in a half-mile radius.

Farooq had not felt a thing.

Except fear, and disbelief.

The building's impaled sides crumpled in landslides of glass and steel.

Screams flooded the streets of Chicago, as similar structures descended in great whooshes. Each impact induced a destructive quake. Pedestrians were thrown from their feet, some suffering broken limbs in the process. Cars veered and wrecked, auto-driving interfaces scrambled and disoriented.

From the fissure in the sky above Earth emerged more violations, some larger than others and some smaller, spindlier.

Despite the enormity of the gaping jaw in space, the sun wasn't completely obstructed.

It appeared that Farooq's beautiful weather wasn't called off, afterall.

2

Jarring alarms didn't just wake him up. He was thrown out of bed, as if his mattress were a spring. Eddie Locke clambered to his feet from the bare concrete floor. Then his bunkmate, Luke Shaw, crossed the quarters in a hurry. They briefly collided and exchanged expletives before clasping each other's shoulders. Luke helped Eddie catch his balance, and vice versa.

Then they headed for the auto-door. Motion-sensor activated, like the others in the base. It slid open right-quick and they emerged into the corridor, bumping into other personnel.

"The hell is going on?" Eddie demanded from one of them. According to the young man's insignia, tank gunner.

"Touch-down, San Fran," the guy replied, his face all sorts of crazy.

Eddie didn't know how to respond. His expression said "what" in six different moods, but his mouth was too dry to articulate anything.

Among the horde of personnel rushing down the corridor, Eddie asked four people until he got a decent answer. The three previous were clueless, which he ironically found more comforting than the tank gunner's response.

And then he asked a woman who was gutting through the crowd as if a bat out of hell. Her blonde hair was a mess,

11

several strands clinging to her face, slick with sweat. Like most of the other personnel, she was still in her sleepwear. Given that it was an AMF base with unisex quarters, her attire was homogenous.

"Something from above," she said.

Eddie spotted no insignia. The tank gunner had donned the top half of his olive-green uniform. Most of these people had just been jolted awake.

It was half past eight.

"Space? Something from space?" A passerby asked, eavesdropping as they all hurriedly rushed down the corridor. He was fairly young, in a gray T-shirt and stark white boxers. He wore a look of unadulterated excitement on his barely weathered face.

"Don't be ridiculous," Eddie scoffed. "She means aircraft."

The woman didn't respond.

"Where'd you hear that?" Luke asked, butting between Eddie and the woman. "W-We just woke up from alarms."

"The airwaves are bustling," she said, and wiped her lips with the back of her hand. She shot them darting glances. "Frequencies scrambled, b-but I made out some words."

"Like?" Eddie pressed.

"Synonyms for "big," for starters," she said, and then grunted. "Excuse me."

She jostled her way forward, with greater drive than others.

"Aliens, I bet it's aliens," the eavesdropper said.

"Can it, Fox," Eddie snapped, shaking his head.

12

Felix Kowalski went by Fox because he hated his given name, claiming that it was too "feline." He figured that by replacing the E, L, and I with an O, he could have something more masculine.

At times like these, he wasn't too sure.

"These aren't drill alarms, Eddie," Luke said, his scarred face grim; the one cataract always gave him a fierce look, even when it wasn't his intention. "Been eons since I heard the combat intonations but I think this is 'em."

Luke often acted like he was older than Eddie, despite being two years younger. He had seen and endured rougher circumstances in the Great War, but shared the same amount of experience.

Eddie shook his head. "Bullshit. Probably another shuttle launch."

He looked over at Fox.

"Why can't you wingnuts keep your feet on the ground?"

Fox chuckled. "Says a Mech pilot. *Pilot*. You might be sitting on your ass, you might not have wings, but you're still, what, thirty feet off the ground?"

Eddie rolled his eyes and nudged Luke with his elbow. They picked up their speed and jogged through the crowd.

The end of the corridor split into two routes. The left went to the mess hall, restrooms, and showers. The right led to a series of more corridors that snaked through the base, branching off to the Mech bays, hangars, and tarmac.

The horde of alerted personnel divided in that moment. Most of them beelined for the mess hall, which housed the largest screen in the base. Others ventured in the opposite direction, likely eager to get outside and gather their information that way. Or increase the likelihood of bumping into an officer.

Fox started to veer right, away from the mess hall. Suddenly Luke grabbed his collar, almost ripping his shirt as he pulled him back.

"You think you're gonna hop in your jet and take off?" Luke said, brow furrowed. "Don't be stupid."

Although only five years younger than Luke, Fox often acted twice that. As if he were fresh out of cadet school. This of course didn't detract from his qualities as a flight pilot. If he had more discipline, Eddie had said in the past, he would make for one helluva Light Class Mech pilot.

Still, he was an Ember Hawk.

Nobody could take that away from him.

Except maybe his own rashness, if it went too far.

"Where are Brick and Charly?" Eddie asked Fox once he joined them in their trek to the mess hall.

"What do I look like, their babysitter?" Fox replied. He shrugged. "They're probably in the same bunk."

Eddie and Luke laughed.

"That'll be the day," Luke said.

"Who knows," Eddie said, "maybe they've been at it all these years. Too much sexual tension could ruin a Clan."

"You're one to talk," Fox smirked.

"Excuse me?" Eddie shot him a hard look.

Luke put an arm around Eddie, to keep him at bay.

"When are you finally gonna put the moves on Mal?" Fox stoked the fire.

"Shut your mouth," Eddie said simply, suppressing his

own rage.

"Hey!" Luke snapped. Aggressively enough to garner some glances from surrounding personnel, as they neared the mess hall. He cleared his throat and exchanged looks between the two men. "We're all Embers, gentlemen. It's a Clan, a *family*. When we're not on base, have at it. Here, we're AMF. The Ember Clan. Quell the bullshit."

Fox raised his palms. "Apologies." He nodded at Eddie. "No hard feelings?"

Eddie sighed and slapped Fox's shoulder, behind and across Luke.

"Not with any Clanner," Eddie said.

Fox appreciated the gesture, one could tell by the look on his face. Luke, too, for that matter.

They reached the mess hall double-doors, which operated like traditional galley flaps, as auto-doors were prohibited for safety reasons in high-traffic areas.

Carefully, but eagerly, the three men filtered into the large cafeteria, lightly jostling other personnel. The room had a high ceiling, a myriad of support beams crossing beneath the domed roof, a dozen long tables and hundreds of chairs, and mounted on the front wall, a massive screen. It spanned eleven by thirty feet.

"Nice speech back there," Eddie muttered to Luke, once they were clear of the main crowd. Most people flocked toward the front of the mess hall, wanting to be as close to the screen as possible.

As if it was needed.

What it depicted was…unmistakable, and yet…

Catastrophically puzzling.

Eddie was looking at Luke, waiting for a response. He

had taken himself out of the panic in hopes of fishing for some comedic relief. Luke didn't bite, though; he was too fixated on what he saw on the screen.

Finally, Eddie followed his teammate's gaze.

Hundreds of personnel filled the mess hall. Hundreds of jaws dropping. Hands over mouths. Upset stomachs. Weak constitutions of men and women who were, before now, fortified in every way.

Eddie felt himself crumble in an unexpected manner. His mind, his perception, and his emotions. The latter, at least, found some kind of balance while his adrenaline took the reins.

Slowly, he and Luke made their way toward the screen. Fox had long since leapt onto a table and advanced in that direction. A few other spry personnel followed suit.

The massive screen fed live video taken from broadcast aircraft in a city. According to the headlines, it was downtown San Francisco. What was happening in the video was difficult to perceive for any of them. For some reason the screen fed only visuals; the speakers were either malfunctioning, or the volume was low and nobody was trying to change it.

Everyone was too mesmerized.

Massive bone-colored structures had impaled skyscrapers and even the Golden Gate Bridge. There were maybe half a dozen of them scattered throughout the city. They appeared to be attached to something in the sky, and resembled colossal teeth. Video feeds panned up, displaying some kind of citywide crevice in the exosphere, gaping into blackness, and from which emerged these structures.

Among other things.

Glistening, wet, scarlet tentacles. More like exposed tendons in appearance than the limbs of octopi or squids. They nonetheless snaked through the sky, often in a helical fashion, before finding a home in tall buildings, as a worm would in an apple. These enormous, slithering tentacles were lined with what could only be described as teeth. Much smaller, arm-sized versions of the gigantic impalements from above.

Video changed to satellite feeds.

Each one offered a different view of the fissure in space, above Earth, and the otherworldly things that emerged from it, before the satellite crashed. Either into one of the teeth, tendons, or possibly the opening itself.

And then a new, broader view.

Banners indicated that it was live footage from the International Space Station. Visual proof that the Earth's rotation was still active, which made sense. If the giant "teeth" were really locked into the Earth's crust, and the gaping hole was somehow a fixed object, then the planet and its people would face cataclysm.

This wasn't the case.

The tear in space moved with the planet. But it was not attached like a harmless remora to the bottom of a shark. Nor necessarily a parasite. It didn't appear to be taking anything from the planet, only the opposite.

Uninvited generosity.

Before the video feeds changed, Eddie batted his eyes rapidly. He had a splitting headache and couldn't begin to fathom what was happening or how it had come about. Nothing made sense, really, not in the logical world he was familiar with.

Luke had become separated from him in his own spell-bound journey closer to the screen.

And then somebody bumped into Eddie, a familiar face. Two of them, on his flanks. Hands and arms over his shoulders. Comforting. Voices came through and he gradually regained full awareness, snapping out of his daze.

He was 5'10" but built like a linebacker. In the moments preceding his reclamation of self, he felt small, he felt puny and lost.

Then…

His Clan. His team of other Mech pilots.

Some of them.

"Eddie, Eddie, stay with us," Nomi Mwangi repeated, giving him a firm shake.

As he reoriented, he waved his hands and nodded repeatedly.

"I'm here, I'm here." He sighed and kneaded his temples. "Fuckin' hell."

He shook his head, trying to dispel the dizziness.

"Don't bail just yet."

"Mal?" Eddie said, looking away from Nomi to see Mallory Capurro standing to his left. She wasn't even looking at him. Her eyes were fixated on the screen, but her right hand was on his shoulder.

"Where's Luke?" Nomi asked.

Eddie hated to see Mal so shaken. He deduced that she and Nomi had entered the mess hall and located him before they really ingested what they saw on the screen. Now it was hitting Mal and he feared she would react the way he did, if not worse.

But Nomi helped him gather his bearings.

She had that capability, no matter the circumstance. During the War, her commanding voice alone, often complemented by her fierce eyes, could shake a man free from the distress of battle. Or witnessing the loss of another pilot.

"Eddie, where's Luke?" Nomi asked.

"I...I don't know, we got split up. Shouldn't...he shouldn't be far. F-Fuckin' Fox is on a table somewhere."

Nomi rolled her eyes. She looked around, and tiptoed. She was 5'11" with strong shoulders and a lean frame. Capable enough to be a Mech pilot for fifteen years, two of which were spent in the Great War.

All of them as an Ember Wolf.

Her eyes scanned the crowd before them, not yet really focusing on the screen.

"I *fucking* knew it!" Someone shouted, swinging at the air.

Nomi spotted Fox on one of the tables, close to the screen. Some people looked at him and shook their heads. Others just didn't even look.

Nomi shook hers, for sure.

She was the same age as Fox but, she believed, older in a fashion. She felt as if she was more tenured in combat, but like herself, Fox had joined the Ember Clan as a cadet, twenty years old, in the midst of war. They weren't waiting around for graduates in those times.

Fox was a flight pilot, though, and although Hawks were considered aerial Mechs by some, most Clanners would argue.

Still, they were on the same team.

She looked at him like a little brother of sorts—but

19

adopted.

"See him?" Eddie asked.

"No," Nomi said. "Just Fox's dumb ass."

Eddie scoffed. He then sighed and kneaded his fore-head.

"He *was* right, gotta give it to 'im."

"As often as he preached about UFO's," a strong fem-inine voice from behind them, "it was only a matter of time."

Eddie spun to face Charly Fallon.

Tears matted her cheeks, but aside from that she was as naturally beautiful and kempt as the situation would al-low. She wore battle fatigues, unlike most of their crew. Mal and Nomi were both in their homogenous sleepwear.

"Can you believe this shit, Charly?" Eddie asked, rhe-torically at this point.

"Hardly have the stomach for it. Seen Brick around?"

Mal turned, facing them but burying her head in her hands. She sobbed quietly.

Charly's brow furrowed and she went to comfort her. Then she looked up, over Mal's shoulder, and observed the screen. A new graphic appeared, something that was nei-ther a photograph nor video. It was a rendition of North America, and all areas affected.

Large, pulsing red circles indicated where the massive "teeth" had touched down. San Francisco, Vancouver, Denver, Austin, Winnipeg, Chicago, Mexico City, Mem-phis, Havana, New York City…

Next to each of these red circles were casualty num-bers, rapidly scrolling.

Charly clamped her eyes shut and wept with Mal, embracing her. Eddie's face was streaming tears before he even realized it.

He knew that Mal's parents lived in Austin, and Charly's entire family in Vancouver.

Eddie's brother, his only surviving family, lived in London. Nomi's older brother died during the War, and her father passed from cancer in 2062. The Ember Clan was her only family.

The same could be said for H and Brick, wherever they were.

Most people with healthy families didn't enlist. Despite twelve years of peace, being a pilot was still a dangerous career. Stressful, to say the least, especially for those not cut out for the physical demands.

Eddie reached for Mal. For Charly.

Nomi had already started moving through the crowd, likely to locate Luke and probably yank Fox off a table.

Eddie's hand found Mal's shoulder, and squeezed it. She touched it and Charly began to hug him, too. He melted in their embrace, his teary eyes nonetheless searching the screen.

Its view of North America scaled back. Shifted across the globe. A view of England, Europe, Africa, Asia, and Australia filled the screen. More pulsing red circles. More numbers.

More nausea.

Cities like Istanbul, Moscow, London, and Madrid were essentially epicenters.

Eddie's legs felt weak. He imagined his brother struggling to make sense of the catastrophe as it happened, the fear and panic setting in like a virus.

Supposing he even had the chance to.

What if he was in one of those buildings?

The image on the screen panned to India, Japan, and Australia. Surrounding islands, including Hawaii, had not been spared. It seemed that high population centers were targeted, but spaced apart.

"Answer the phone, answer the phone," somebody said, behind Eddie and the others. They were at the back of where the crowd was thickest. Behind them, in the latter half of the mess hall, people were scattered. Some sat in chairs with heads in their hands, some on their phones, and others scurrying out the doors, bumping into people who were just making their way inside.

One man stood out in particular.

At least to Eddie, who immediately made his way toward him.

He began yelling at his cell.

"Answer, answer the *fucking phone*!"

"Wally, Wally!" Eddie wanted to call out but Brixton Knight got to him first. He had just entered the mess hall, trailed by Helena Hendricks, who immediately sat in a chair and watched the screen with a nauseated expression.

Brick was aptly nicknamed, at 6'2" and over two-ten. Despite his imposing build and the sheer sternness of his carriage, he was one of AMF's smoothest Hawk pilots this side of the country.

He put gentle-giant hands on Walid Meskin as the man crumpled around his phone. He ultimately dropped it to the floor and clutched his teammate, somebody to confide in. There was nothing to be said in the moment, nothing that could be uttered, by anybody.

Wally sobbed against Brick's chest.

They were both wearing T-shirts and sweats.

Soldiers and pilots woken from their slumber, after a previous night's rigorous combat drills. Shaken, stirred, chewed up and spat out.

All in the span of minutes.

"He could be okay," Eddie lied through his teeth, as he joined Brick in clutching Wally. "The whole cities aren't—"

"She's not answering, either," Wally wept.

They had met Farooq and his fiancé on a couple of occasions. The gravity crushing Wally's heart in that moment, however, was something they couldn't—

A fight broke out farther into the crowd, close to the screen. It created waves, people pushed back like an aftershock. Someone bumped into Mal and Charly, knocking them back.

Mal immediately reached for someone to hit, in a blind rage.

Charly tried pulling her back, but as athletic as she was built, Mal had a fighter's physique, and a short fuse.

H stood from her chair and marched toward them, blinking rapidly to clear tears. She reached Mal before anyone was hit, and helped Charly restrain her. Mal turned and hugged H, dispensing her emotions through more lamentation.

H was a tall, buxom woman who had seen the Great War from beginning to end, and was among the founding members of Ember Clan. Training to be an instructor at the Mech Academy in Fresno, circa 2048, where Eddie,

23

Charly, and Brick met and became friends. H repeatedly failed instructor class due to authority problems, but eventually became a mentor to the other three, and after the War formed the Ember Wolves. Their experience with the others in 2051 served as the foundation to what would later become known as a Clan.

A team of eight to ten pilots, or just five if only Mechs. Otherwise, these "Wolves" were joined by VTOL combat jets, known as "Hawks."

H was often seen as the "Clan mother" of Ember, and not just to her teammates.

Mal felt that analogy now more than ever, as she embraced the forty-eight-year-old woman, and was in return held.

Charly put her hands on their shoulders and struggled to get a grip on her own tears.

Eddie moved away from Wally and Brick, eventually tapping Charly on the shoulder. She turned to face him, and over his shoulder spotted the unmistakable figure that was Brick.

Eddie simply nodded, to which Charly returned the gesture, and then proceeded to meet up with Brick and Wally.

Wally was the third oldest on the team, with Brick at forty-seven. Still, as the second oldest *Mech* pilot, Wally served as a sort of father figure to most of them, even Eddie at forty-two and Charly at forty. Age was irrelevant when it came to camaraderie.

Mal was the third youngest, at thirty-seven. She was only twenty-two when she met Eddie and the others during the War. That conflict alone aged all of them several years, a measurement that couldn't be given a specific number.

Their growth as a team—as a Clan—over the last fifteen years made them an inseparable unit of fortitude and capability.

There were three Clans to every major population center. The Bay Area had the Ember, Onyx, and Mako Clans. They were never positioned within a city, though, as the spaciousness for a Mech base called for a more rural setting.

They were a ten-minute helo ride outside of Sacramento.

"Turn it up! Turn it *up*!" Voices shouted toward the front of the crowd.

Possibly the source of the fight minutes ago.

The screen volume was cranked, and a reporter's voice boomed into the mess hall.

"...not the only things coming from the Tear," she said, speaking of the massive fissure as a tear in the fabric of space. *"As you can see, the tendon-like tentacles are acting as a, uh...as a sort of carrier system for these, uh...these anomalies. And I'm getting word of...of larger anomalies coming from the, uh, the giant teeth-like structures, they...oh my God, they..."*

The voice broke up in a burst of static.

Volume was no longer needed. The reporter had heralded the video feed now on the screen, well enough. Everybody watched in awe, filling the mess hall with gasps and some people even screamed.

An aerial view from a broadcast helicopter showed live footage above Denver, Colorado.

Emerging from the giant tendon-tentacles were creatures the size of cars, grotesque in appearance and malevolent in nature. They made their descent to the ground, and immediately caused havoc. Some were traditionally limbed, others slithered and crawled, up and down buildings, or leaping from one to the next.

Meanwhile, the giant teeth-like structures began to crack in places. Breaking free were enormous creatures the size of six-story parking garages. Each "Tooth" seemed to house two of these behemoths.

Video footage alternated to other cities around the world, from South America to Europe and Australia. Soon the screen became so densely populated with various feeds from various cities that it was a thousand-piece puzzle of mayhem.

"Touch-down," Eddie muttered.

Mal looked up at him, through a wall of tears. H started to look at him, but then saw Nomi come through the crowd toward them. Luke was at her heels, followed and soon passed by Fox.

"What?" Mal asked.

Eddie shook his head, brow furrowed. His gaze wandered, and he looked at the ground. At people's feet. Seldom was a boot spotted. Laces untied, when he did. Everyone here had been roused from their bunks by alarms.

Good-fucking-morning.

Suddenly his gaze shot up and he locked eyes with Wally. The man's grizzled-black beard was moistened with tears. His eyes, pink from crying. Brick had a hand on Wally, and didn't look very good himself; they were all either trying or failing to hold it together.

26

Wally nodded at Eddie, from twelve feet away.

Eddie returned the gesture, and then looked back at the others—Mal, H, Nomi, and Luke. Fox had passed them to greet Brick and Charly.

Without warning, Eddie put two fingers in his mouth and whistled. It was strident enough to not only make everyone stop talking but actually warrant a few annoyed reactions.

He figured this was a step in the right direction.

He turned and found a chair next to one of the long, rectangular tables. He used it as a step and rose onto the table, in socks no less. Like half of them here.

Waving burly arms above his head, Eddie gathered a good hundred's attention. He realized he didn't need to whistle again.

With no more audio coming from the screen, he wouldn't have any competition.

"Look, I know everyone is terrified and confused, and a lot of you are mourning," he said, realizing suddenly that he was speaking through his own lamentations. He sniffled and batted his eyes, looking up briefly.

When Eddie looked back down, his gaze sweeping the personnel, he resumed. His voice, with a London-born inflection but still coherent, and booming.

"We're all mourning, one way or another. But we aren't *here* to mourn. We don't wear the AMF letters to *mourn*. We are *fighters*! We carry burdens nobody else can bear. So I don't care if you're a Clanner, a wingnut, a tank jockey, or a guy who fetches coffee for an officer—you all have places to be! Purposes to serve. Whatever's *out there* is being *way* too generous; let's buckle up and rudely refuse anything that isn't human."

Scattered, boisterous cheering.

Most of those who didn't cheer or applaud Eddie's speech were already moving, acting on his words.

Brick walked up to the edge of the table and offered Eddie a hand. Eddie smirked and knocked it away, hopping down himself.

Brick grinned briefly and shook his head.

"You Clanners sure do love a good speech."

Eddie shrugged. "We can't all have our heads in the clouds."

Brick chuckled and sniffled.

"And they call *me* the leader," H said, smirking through a tear-stained face.

Ember Clan gathered in a cluster, while others moved around them, as a creek would a rock.

Some of those who walked by clapped or patted their shoulders.

"A little incentive goes a long way," Eddie shrugged.

"What're we waiting for?" Wally said, gruffly. He was already breaking away from them, toward the doors.

Eddie motioned for them to go. As he followed, Brick lagged behind. He, too, had a strong, British voice. It was even more thunderous than Eddie's, though.

"Hey!" He shouted, to the last few dozen people who loitered by the screen. "Somebody shut that shit off! You can say "hi" in person—right to their ugly faces!"

3

An exodus of AMF personnel flooded the corridors, from the mess hall to the east wing of the base. Mech bays and Hawk hangars were cordoned off, though. Tank crew and other vehicle personnel were able to reach the tarmac outside.

Clan teams were being guided to briefing rooms, en masse. No segregation based on Clan or vehicle type. Mech and flight pilots alike.

Ember, Onyx, and Mako Clans meshed as they migrated into the largest briefing room in the base. It was essentially a small auditorium.

They flocked to their seats, bumping into different Clan pilots along the way. Nods and handshakes, shoulder pats and brief hugs. Nobody was as familiar with each other as they were within their own Clans, naturally, but they were all San Francisco family.

Ember was the most tenured, with the Onyx and Mako Clans settling years later. Mako, composed of five pilots, moved down from Seattle, and Onyx, originally eight, transferred from Carson City; one of their three Hawk pilots died during an exercise, after experiencing a malfunction. Months later, the other two were transferred to Albuquerque, as it was deemed that Ember's three renowned Hawks were sufficient for the region.

It didn't take long for Clanners to comingle with each other. They usually mixed well with their own; it was only when introduced to "wingnuts," or Hawk pilots, that some tensions arose. But it seldom went beyond juvenile competition and fun-natured jokes.

Afterall, "wingnut" began as a derogatory term for Hawk pilots, *by* Clanners. Hawk pilots proved their good sportsmanship by adopting it as their own.

Most of them, anyway.

Given the right—or wrong, in this case—inflection, it could still be used disparagingly.

There was a woman at the foot of the auditorium seating, standing beside a podium. She seemed to have no interest, nor need for it. Behind her, an archaic pull-down map of the Bay Area, including Sacramento.

She abruptly cleared her throat, which was a louder gesture than anyone could have expected. Those chatting amongst themselves, and those still finding their seats, quickly gave her their attention.

She wore full battledress, with the exception of a hat. Her black hair was trimmed short, an inch or two shy of a buzz-cut.

"You'll have to excuse the paper for now," she announced, pointing at the map. Her name-badge read 'Bonheur,' beneath Captain insignia. There was a vague French accent, but the sternness of her voice was undeniably American-raised. "The base's power, down to the last ion, is being routed to focus on vehicle preparation. Particularly, your Mechs."

The congregation of pilots stirred a commotion of ambivalence.

Ember was mostly quiet.

Fox nudged Brick, trying to stir something.

Wally muttered to nobody but himself.

"Attention!" Captain Bonheur snapped. Everyone stopped talking and looked forward, down, and heeded her every word. "Now, as you may already know, the situation is no less than *fucked*. We have zero Intel about the enemy, except for what the footage has shown us. Right now our directive is to defend the homefront against this bizarre enemy, and make deductions after. Or, as the old idiom goes…"

She paused for effect.

"Shoot first, ask questions later!" A pilot from Mako Clan shouted.

Some hooting, hollering, and high-fives followed. Immature as some of it was, Bonheur didn't object. She raised her eyebrows and shrugged, nodding simultaneously.

The commotion died down in respect for their CO and what she had to say.

Most of Ember recognized her. She had instructed them before, on two previous exercises in the last three months. A few members from Onyx remembered her from a debriefing weeks ago.

"Absolutely," she eventually responded. And then raised her voice. She smacked fist to palm. "Which is why we should not delay another second! Unfortunately, our strategy is limited. But luck is on our side, because *firepower* is on our side. The enemy seems primitive and devoid of technology. We'll take advantage of this, and utilize what the AMF has granted us." She paused, reading the room, and then snapped: "Listen up!"

31

They were all already on the edge of their seats; Captain Bonheur had her audience by the eardrums, throats, and hearts.

Now they *really* leaned in.

Readier than before.

"San Fran is getting hit the hardest," she said, a dire tone not lacking untapped emotion underlining every syllable. She wielded a small laser-pointer and indicated Sacramento on the map. "*But*—there has already been activity reported in Sac."

A mild commotion.

Somebody spoke up. It was Fox. He half-stood from his chair, his voice, though younger than he was, rising the rest of the way.

"I thought the anomalies were only making landfall in bigger cities," he said. Everybody in the room pivoted to stare at him. Bonheur crossed her arms. He looked around and stammered, shrugging. "I, uh, that's, that's just what the news said. They had a, uh, map…"

"That would be correct," Bonheur blurted. "Unfortunately, though, they have *legs*. As for the structures, or *Teeth*, well, they gradually decompose. Once the behemoths climb out, the Teeth collapse. This alone causes vast destruction. Same goes for the *Tendons*, and the creatures that crawl out of them."

"S-So they're numerable," Wally thought out loud. Eyes now pivoted toward him. He reluctantly stood up, and gestured at Bonheur. "Uh, apologies, Captain. I just…that means…their numbers are limited. And whatever's coming down, wherever their source is, they aren't omnipotent."

"Precisely, Meskin. Which means, what?"

"They can be defeated," Eddie shouted from where he sat, broad arms crossed rigidly. He didn't budge. Inside, he was a maelstrom.

"Correct!" Bonheur said, loudly. Unable to fully suppress a grin. She then utilized the laser-pointer again. "Which is why we'll be dividing our resources to focus on getting help to San Fran, without abandoning the surrounding areas.

"Hawks are to head to San Fran *immediately*. Mechs will stick to the ground, and follow a tank-convoy en route, clearing immediate cities in their…"

Bonheur paused and stared at them wide-eyed. She suddenly clapped her hands together, frantically.

"Hawks, let's *go, go, go!*" She shouted. "I've kept you all long enough! Your VTOLs are waiting."

The three flight pilots in the room stood up, Charly more gracefully than Brick and Fox. All of them exchanged hasty farewells and wishes of good luck with not only their own Clan, but Mako and Onyx as well.

"Fly safe," Eddie double-gripped one of Brick's hands, from where he remained sitting.

"Walk safe, eh?" Brick replied, smirking and saluting.

Eddie shook his head. He touched Charly's hand as she walked by.

"Make sure Fox doesn't do anything stupid."

"That'll be a challenge," she smirked.

"Can't tell a shark to stop swimming, boss," Fox said, nodding at Eddie.

Once their blood got to pumping again, the three pilots moved with great urgency. Still, Fox tripped over seats and legs on his way to the door.

"Don't get any bright ideas while you're up there, mister!" Nomi called out to Fox.

He just saluted, casually, and blew her a theatrical kiss from the door. She exchanged sarcastically worried looks with H.

"Victory declares swift wings, pilots!" Bonheur proclaimed, as the wingnuts bustled out of the auditorium. She took a deep breath and then said: "Now that the sky-jockeys are out of the room…"

The Mech pilots collectively laughed.

"In all seriousness," she said, "they'll be making first contact with the enemy, likely an hour before any of you. San Fran is…a mess."

"Will we have comms with them?" H asked.

"Absolutely." Your Mechs are presently charging and loading. Ought to be ready any minute. So let's wrap up."

"What about us?" An Onyx Clanner asked from her seat.

Bonheur raised her eyebrows.

"Will we receive updates from Ember's Hawks, on the status of S-F?" The pilot followed.

Bonheur nodded. "HQ will regularly update all Clans in the Bay Area while you're in the field. We're all in this together, folks."

The Onyx pilot nodded, satisfied.

Bonheur resumed the use of her laser-pointer on the pull-down map.

"Onyx and Mako are to take the southbound route, which will include passing through Stockton. A tank convoy will travel with you, and branch off to sweep Berkeley and Oakland *after* Stockton. Modesto, Fremont, and San

Jose will be the focus of tanks and helos. Clanners, you are *not* to pursue any hostiles that deviate from your path through the aforementioned cities, or away from San Fran. Free to engage any threat that crosses your reticle, but no pursuit. That is the ROE of this mission. Understood?"

Everybody nodded, without a single hint of uncertainty.

"Reports indicate that the anomalies are favoring cities with higher population," she continued. "We believe the enemy uses biological infrared sensors, like pit vipers. Little else is known about the enemy right now, but new Intel will be fed to you as we receive it. Your Hawks won't be left out, of course, and will be briefed during their boarding shortly."

She took a deep breath.

She could tell, easily, at this point, that all of the Mech pilots present were itching to leave. To fight.

"Ember Wolves," she said, the solemnity in her voice palpable, "your primary directive is sweeping Sacramento. Once Sac is clear, you'll be air-lifted and taken to San Fran immediately. Tank battalions and other aircraft will sweep Davis, Woodland, and Santa Rosa. The same rules of engagement for Onyx and Mako apply to you, Ember. Stay on path. After Sac is clear, radio for air-lift. Do not stray from your waypoint. Clear?"

Nods and mutterings of "copy."

Bonheur pocketed her laser-pointer, stooped, and snapped the map. It rolled up, loudly.

"That's all I've got for you, Clanners," she said, sounding defeated, but not entirely bereft of hope. "Fresher Intel, hopefully, awaits you in your Mechs. Field reports

35

will be coming in like artillery, HQ will do their best to rectify errors, clarify Intel, and feed you the need-to-know details."

Eddie stood up. H followed, and then the other Clanners eventually rose to their feet. H saluted the Captain, mutely, and then headed for the exit.

Onyx and Mako filtered through the doors, exchanging farewells and wishes of luck. Most of Ember were included, but Eddie, Nomi, and Luke lingered by the entrance, held open by a few of the other Clanners.

"Captain," Eddie asked, from where he stood, about thirty feet up from the stage.

"Yes, Locke?"

"Got any inspirational quotes for *us*?" He asked, in reference to what she had told the Hawk pilots during their exit.

She smirked and shook her head.

"You're Clanners. *Mech* pilots. You don't need any of that horseshit."

Eddie and Nomi exchanged grins. The few holding doors open chuckled.

"Give 'em hell, Wolves," Bonheur said, saluting.

"And then some, Captain," Eddie said, returning the salute.

Nomi followed him out. Into the corridor the Mech pilots found themselves kindled with new vigor. The oddest thing was that most of them were still in their sleepwear, or wore only half of their uniforms. They knew that whatever they needed awaited them in their Mech bays, as was SOP in case of emergencies.

This was unlike any drill they had ever performed before, though.

Unprecedented.

But not completely off-guard.

Twelve years of peace lent a lot of room for preparation.

The pilots' sojourn from the briefing room to the Mech hangar was mostly quiet. And fast. Now that they had been given a specific mission, rules of engagement, and a little more to go on than what the mess hall screen gave them, there was rejuvenation.

Incentive and haste.

They no longer mourned, at least not in the traditional sense. Not the way civilians lamented the tragic deaths of loved ones, let alone the impending apocalypse, it seemed.

As Eddie said earlier, they were men and women with capabilities that exceeded those of common folk. They had a collective purpose to serve, roles to fulfill, and oaths to uphold.

Knowing that the fiercest machines of combat ever invented awaited them down a series of corridors was added motivation.

Nonetheless, in the back of their minds, always, was the thought and concern for their relatives. None of them seriously contemplated trying to contact anyone at the moment, not just because of the urgency of their mission, but rationale.

The airwaves would be so congested from military transmissions, that it any attempt would be a waste of time. And where the power had not been killed from the enemy's presence, there was no doubt too much interference.

SAT phones would prove worthless, too, given the current debacle in the planet's exosphere.

Accepting these notions in stride was a mental and emotional challenge that every pilot worked through with each step.

It got easier once they arrived at the Mech hangar, however.

That much closer to their true purpose…

The pilots were granted access with very little security. Just nods and glances. The emergency of the situation dissipated certain protocols, discarding most of them as unnecessary.

Someone could impersonate a Mech pilot only so far. Even if they were experienced, each Mech was locked via retinal scanners outside the cockpit hatch, and voice recognition once within. This was a failsafe to prevent Mech-hijacking, although attempts were made during the War, and succeeded in earlier years, before certain models were given the upgrade.

Entering the Mech hangar cued a cacophony of sounds that overwhelmed the pilots. For them, though, it was a familiar discordance. The blowtorches, flying sparks, and smoldering of repairs. Wrenches clanking and cranking, high-tonnage jacks clicking, fusion engines humming as they charged, or whirring to life.

Outside the massive hangar, other sounds could be intermittently heard.

The rumble of tank battalions, their tracks crawling across tarmac en masse. And louder yet, the roar of Hawk VTOLs taking off. A steady hover levitated them into the air, and then their tilt-thruster wings angled for high-speed propulsion.

Rotor-based VTOLs, attack helicopters, and fighter jets were also in commission, but their capabilities paled in comparison to the Hawks. In addition to their superior propulsion, which utilized Bell-Boeing engines complemented by small fusion reactors—compact versions of what Mechs used—these VTOLs had multi-terrain skids capable of magnetically attaching to buildings, jointed armaments, and energy-based weapons, or EBWs.

The only other place EBWs—commonly Lasers and PPCs—were utilized, were on Mechs.

Hawks were, naturally, louder during takeoff than regular VTOLs and other aircraft.

The Clanners currently rushing through the hangar could distinguish these sounds outside of the building. It offered more hope for the battle that awaited them, knowing that their winged comrades were out ahead of them.

It also amplified their impatience to exfil.

"Saddle up!"

"Take care of yourselves!"

The Clans divided at the center of the hangar, each group headed to their respective bays, labeled in case they got lost. After so many years, it was all muscle memory.

Striding into their 'corner' of the hangar, the Ember Wolves were met by two personnel driving a UTV. It hauled a small wagon stacked with folded navy uniforms and black boots.

"Get 'em while they're hot, Clanners," the driver said, thumbing over his shoulder.

The other man just watched, speechless.

"Seen a ghost or something?" Luke asked as he jogged past.

"Oh, that's Irwin," the driver said. "Dummy stood too close to a reactor undergoing repairs. Fresh outta class, didn't know any better, at least not given the news. Everyone's running on fumes."

"No excuse to abandon common sense," H said, stern as ever.

"Deaf and blind, huh?" Luke asked the driver, grimacing. He pulled on a pair of battledress pants and then shirt, but didn't button it up. None of them did.

"Poor bastard," the driver said. He patted the passenger's leg. The young man flinched, jerking his head in that direction. The driver sighed.

"At least he can't see or hear what's happening," Wally said.

"No, he knows," the driver assured, sadly. "Thing is, seeing y'all come in just now, fuckin' *the* Ember Wolves…" He clicked his tongue. "Would've cheered him up. Hope's low, y'all."

H felt bad for what she had said.

She walked over to the UTV and cupped the young man's cleft chin. She planted a kiss on his temple. As she pulled away, she donned her uniform shirt, leaving it unbuttoned like the rest. They had good reason.

This didn't register for the driver, however. Unlike the doe-eyed, smitten passenger, he found it difficult not to ogle her H's prominent chest.

She cleared her throat.

The driver shook his head and apologized.

"Just tell your friend," she said, "that Helena Hendricks appreciates his service. And that hope will never leave the menu."

"You bet, ma'am!"

H nodded and turned toward the others.

Wally smirked, an expression the others tried to hide. Except for Luke. His scars paled in comparison to his big grin, especially with his distinctly sharp canines.

"Cool your fuckin' jets," H said, shaking her head.

"Uh-uh," Wally said, waving a finger at her. "You big softy."

H let a smirk escape before they turned around to face their row of Mechs. Each one stood in individual stalls, or bays, fifty feet high. The Mechs themselves were generally shorter than that, though some taller than others.

A few scattered maintenance personnel, or Mech-techs, waited near the feet of each machine. They wore navy jumpsuits with AMF badges, gloves, and hard-hats. They either paced back and forth, or lingered, waiting for the pilots.

"Saddle up!" Eddie shouted.

The Ember Wolves exchanged fist-pumps all around.

Nomi hugged Luke, who had saved her life back in '52. During out-of-Mech infantry work, in an all-too-intimate firefight with the enemy. Their bond became closer after that day.

There was nothing romantic there. If anything, their respective homosexuality was something else they could bond over.

Meanwhile, Eddie exchanged a lateral hug with Mal. Back pats and gentle forehead-bumps.

"Ruthless, toothless," Eddie said.

Mal growled dramatically. They shared smirks before parting ways.

A year after the AMF formed, Mal's Mech license was suspended due to reckless behavior during an exercise. Two nights later, Eddie and Brick bumped into her at a bar in Sacramento. They didn't even know she was there until the fight broke out. Someone had put a hand on her. She nearly killed the man, and gave his wingman a concussion, along with knocking out most of his teeth.

Eventually the fight in her was quelled, mostly by the alcohol, and with the help of her two comrades, she was restrained from the bar. They weren't immune to the law, however, and she served a few months.

After three years of sobriety, she only drank on occasion, and her issues were under wrap.

Eddie was about as terrified of Mal, as he was in love with her.

Whether or not she knew that, he could tell she felt something. Even if it was just a striking reverence, and an inseparable camaraderie.

At any rate, since that night, Eddie never stopped underestimating her. He and Mal formed a secret "ruthless, toothless" motto before certain exercises.

This was no drill.

So the words carried even greater weight.

"Shaw, your vest is on the *Rhino*," the Mech-tech said, jogging to match Luke's pace. He raised his hand to keep his hard-hat from falling off. "Loaded with fresh coolant, ready to go. Cockpit's all set, small arms and ammo in the back. Optimal prep."

"Appreciate it," Luke said, nodding.

"Go get 'em!" The Mech-tech dropped back.

Luke made a saluting gesture into the air, over his shoulder.

The other pilots were greeted similarly, their respective Mech-techs sharing the same information.

Boarding any Mech was, more or less, a pain in the ass. No better method had yet been invented, unfortunately. Despite all of the superior technology in the world today, the pilots still had to climb up legs and an occasional mounted rung to reach the entrance hatch. Which was typically located on the top of the Mech's torso, or sometimes from the side.

Never directly in front, nor behind.

The front of every Mech was their primary carapace of Tungsteel armor. A compound tungsten-steel alloy trademarked by DARPA in 2044, three years after its first successful testing. Lightweight enough not to terribly burden a Mech's movement, depending on the Class, and easily the most resilient and heat-resistant metal composition to date.

Backsides of Mechs, on the other hand, were traditionally least-armored, in favor of hop-jet thrusters and heat ventilators. Although some heavier models had thrusters in their legs instead.

At least in climbing a Mech of any height, the mounted rungs were easy to distinguish—protocol yellow. The body coloration of most Mechs was a standard gunmetal gray, but aesthetic modifications as per the pilot were allowed, within regulations. Some Clanners even favored vintage jaws painted onto their cockpits, a la World War II planes, most commonly seen on the *Fenrir*.

Most Clans had, at the very least, a custom emblem durably painted onto their Mechs, somewhere visible. Usually a shoulder, cheek, and or shin.

The Ember Wolves each wore theirs on a shoulder and opposing shin. Their emblem consisted of a black wolf's outline within a red teardrop.

They were most visible on Mechs that had the basic gunmetal coloration. Which, for the Ember Wolves, were: Eddie, Mal, and Wally. Although Wally's *Mastodon* had knee joints and shoulder panels featuring yellow-and-black caution stripes, the rest of the giant Mech was gunmetal.

Even still, H's *Fenrir* was the only Mech that had a strikingly different coloration. It was a navy and olive-green camouflage, which blended into the night beautifully, but in daylight was unmistakable. Especially the stark red-gum white-teeth jaws painted onto the lower half of the protruding cockpit.

H was a classy woman.

Nomi's *Rottweiler* on the other hand, had a dull brown palette with a square black snout, inarguably an homage to its namesake. The Mech's ballistic barrel-arms were always a polished black steel that added to this dichotomic motif.

Luke's *Rhino* was very similar, aesthetically, except with a sandier tone to the armor. Although they were located in the greener regions of California, the deserts weren't very far, and over the last decade they had performed many an exercise against that harsh ochre backdrop.

44

This was his reasoning for the desert-camo.

Fox had joked that it was merely his bland taste in fashion.

Of course, Luke's retort was the obvious—that Fox was, like the other Hawk pilots, jealous. For they lacked the freedom of customization with their aircraft, which were all the same model of assault VTOL, albeit exclusive to Clan pilots.

Eddie looked up, and wondered where his winged comrades were at this point. Even once their Mechs were powered on, they wouldn't be within communication range of the Hawks until they reached Sacramento.

His gaze fell from the rafters of the hangar to the fifty-foot Mech towering over him.

Before making that climb, each pilot had to do something they loathed more.

Coolant vests were a necessary evil, to endure the extreme heat generation within a Mech cockpit. Certain models produced less heat than others, especially Light Class Mechs, but a coolant vest of some kind was required for everyone.

Technically, it could fit over a pilot's uniform, but nobody liked to do that. The vests were bulky enough as it was. So they shed their uniform shirts, tying the arms around their waists, and donned the coolant vests.

They were constructed of breathable material interwoven with thousands of tiny, flexible cooling lines. A compact coolant pump strapped to the waist would connect to the cockpit seat once the pilot was situated. It would then draw power from the Mech in order to circulate the coolant and protect the pilot from heat build-up in the cockpit.

Certain vests were bulkier according to the Mechs operated, as lighter classes produced less heat than heavier ones.

Same with the uniforms and boots supplied by the UTV driver, the coolant vests were essentially tailored. Their Mechs weren't recycled from pilot to pilot, and weren't kept in random bays. They were specific, their location in the hangar always the same, and the Mechs themselves, as intimate to their respective pilots as the underwear they wore.

If not more so.

And the retinal scans kept it that way.

The only personnel capable of overriding access to the hatch were Mech-techs, in order to supply freshly loaded small arms, coolant pump replacements, rations, medical kits, and to confirm the safety and maintenance of the cockpit itself.

Overriding the voice recognition to start up the Mech, however, was not permitted to anyone.

After donning his vest, the arms of his uniform top tied around his waist, Eddie began climbing his Mech. It was an average-sized beast of Tungsteel, for its class, standing forty-nine feet from toe to shoulder cannons. He had to ascend about forty, which was a little more than a lot of pilots whose Mechs had lower cockpits.

Eddie's *Adversary*, first introduced in 2062, was an imposing revision of the *Avarice*, combined with design elements of the AMF-iconic *Fenrir*. He had quickly fallen in love with the *Adversary*, which wasn't surprising considering its impressive payload, speed, and heat management.

The biggest downside was a significant lack of torso armor, in exchange for heat ventilation. Due to this design, the *Adversary* required less heat-sinks that would other-wise make it bulkier, giving it the agility that most Assault Class Mechs didn't have.

Eddie was a skilled enough pilot to make everything count, and take advantage of the Mech's maneuverability to avoid perilous damage.

He knew, though, that this particular enemy they would soon face didn't have projectile weapons. At least, not to their understanding. Which made combating them a whole different ballgame than the battles they had so much experience in.

Once he reached the side-hatch into his cockpit, which on the *Adversary* was a sort of small snout set between bowl-like shoulders, overlooking a rack of eight short-range missiles, Eddie paused. He hung there briefly, catch-ing his breath and sweating already. The Mech hangar was hot, but ventilated enough to keep the giant war machines from collecting heat before they even powered on.

The towering bay doors toward the front of the hangar had yet opened.

Hanging outside of his hatch, some forty feet off the ground, Eddie tucked his lower lip and whistled. He caught the attention of his Mech-tech, who was not his usual guy. Eddie imagined that with everything going on, they were cycling shifts like crazy.

"When are we getting those doors open?" He called down to the young man.

The Mech-tech stepped out of the bay and gazed down the wide aisle to the end of the hangar, about three-hundred feet away.

"Soon—oughtta be any minute!" He replied.

"Now, get 'em open now! Call whoever you gotta. Or we're gonna make our own exit!"

"You got it!" The Mech-tech shouted back, slapping his hard-hat. "Give 'em hell!"

"Nothing less!" Eddie thrust a thumbs-up into the air. He then heard a shrill yet soft sound, like a high-pitched wind, from the other side of the hangar. He glimpsed pilots from Mako Clan ascending their Mechs, a couple whistling and waving. Eddie waved back, and saluted. They were little figures at this range, clinging onto their Mechs like toy soldiers.

He then leaned toward the hatch. The integrated retinal scanner read his green eyes, and the security decoded. The hatch locks hissed and he pulled it open, swinging inside. He shut it behind him, secured the bolts, and strode toward the pilot seat.

His cockpit was fairly small, less spacious than most on Mechs of this class. He didn't mind. There was still two feet of head clearance standing, and canopy to the back of the cockpit, side to side, it was roughly the dimensions of a small bedroom. He trusted his Mech-tech had in fact supplied freshly loaded small arms—usually an AMF-standard pistol and compact shotgun, with some spare ammunition—rations, med-kits, and coolant pumps.

He untied his uniform shirt and draped it over the back of the large seat's headrest, then sat in it as if it was a throne.

For any Mech pilot, it basically was.

Eddie couldn't help but pause, again, and let the weight of this whole debacle pass through him, much like the coolant would soon surge through his vest. He imagined Mal, and all of his other teammates, going through the same thing as they got situated in their Mechs. And then he broadened his mind. He pictured every homefront in every country across the globe, Clanners of various races and backgrounds climbing into their Mechs, some more dated models than others, some pilots less experienced but no less zealous to get out there and defend their home.

Their species.

"Let's do it," Eddie said out loud, and pulled his game face on.

He secured his harness belts, which added to the discomfort of piloting a Mech, as if the vest wasn't enough. He, like the rest of his team, though, was already so accustomed to these "necessary evils" that it barely fazed him.

Securing the coolant pump affixed to the side of the vest to the line that protruded from the left side of his seat was as easy as 1-2-3. He then slid the seat forward, on its rails, bringing him closer to the control panel beneath the reinforced three-pane canopy that gave him his view.

Suspended from the ceiling, to his left, was a water supply tube for drinking. SOP required that it be as fresh as the ammunition in the Mech, and would be cooled to a crisp level once the engine came online.

After a meditative deep breath, Eddie resumed his start-up routine.

It was the same for every Mech.

The primary joystick was on his right, complete with weapon controls, from grouping selections to triggers. A thumb analogue stick, attached to a rotating ball on the inside left of the joystick, was used for precise aiming. The arms of a Mech could pivot at the elbows, but were otherwise stationary, although some models had fixed arms, especially for heavier weapons such as the Railgun, and any higher-caliber Autocannon, or ACX.

Shifting the joystick itself moved only the Mech's torso, pivoting it at a maximum 180 degrees. A skilled pilot could engage a mobile enemy Mech without ever taking a step himself, if he or she had torso and arm maneuvers mastered.

A throttle handle, shaped like a curved teardrop, was on his left. Pushing forward accelerated the Mech, and backward was reverse. It required the depression of a thumb-button to use, so as to avoid accidentally bumping it during combat.

Pedals perforated at an angle, for traction against a pilot's boots, were integrated into the cockpit floor below the control panel. These were used for turning the Mech's feet, and activating its hop-jets. Depressing the left pedal pivoted the Mech left, and so on. Applying pressure to both, simultaneously, activated the hop-jets, which burned hydrogen from the fusion engine to propel the Mech airborne. This process was still a very touch-and-go system, as AMF had yet perfected the technology for such heavy machines.

Joint actuators in a Mech's legs could easily be destroyed or damaged if the it landed too abruptly, which called for a pilot's steady feet and a keen eye on hydrogen supply, heat levels, and of course terrain, when using hop-jets. Lighter Mechs, naturally, could sustain longer air-borne time and thus used less hydrogen, producing minimal heat. Heavier Mechs were the opposite.

Hop-jets were only used to traverse certain obstacles on the battlefield that couldn't necessarily be navigated otherwise, or to avoid lengthy circumvention. Also, at the hands and feet of a skilled pilot, hop-jets could be used eva-sively when engaging an enemy Mech, just as well offensively.

It was a lot to control all at once, for any Clanner. For the Ember Wolves, their cockpit was a home away from home.

For many of them, it was their one true home.

"Enough chitchat, shall we?" He said out loud, and reached for the ignition switch, a red knob to the right of the joystick. He turned it to the right, and closed his eyes. Loudly, he spoke his name: "Eddie Locke."

"Welcome back," an automatic female voice an-nounced, through the cockpit's systems.

Pilot confirmed.

The *Adversary*'s GM-375 fusion engine rumbled awake. It began as a low growl, until it built into a higher-pitched whir. This filled the Mech with power, breathing life into the *Adversary*'s actuators, cockpit oxygen supply, coolant systems, heat-sinks, radar, communications array, and heads-up display.

The HUD was projected onto the canopy before Eddie via a semi-opaque hologram. The primary color scheme was green and yellow, and red in places while systems self-checked and powered on. Once everything was primed, most of the HUD was green.

Additionally, an assortment of small monitors lined the bottom of the canopy's forward panel, and a few along the top, above Eddie's head.

"All systems optimal."

Eddie opened his eyes and double-checked the screens before cuing the communications channel. It was already defaulted to the Ember Clan's personal frequency, which could be interrupted at any time by Headquarters, as Captain Bonheur mentioned earlier.

Just the same, any AMF personnel in the field, whether a Mech pilot or a tank driver, could contact HQ directly, themselves.

Or try to, dependent on range.

Once the *Adversary*'s fusion engine calmed to an idling hum, he could hear the others whirring from their slumber. Wally's was easily the loudest, as his *Mastodon* was the only Support Class Mech in the Clan.

All of a sudden a Mech walked out in front of the *Adversary*.

Eddie's comms crackled to life.

A familiar voice.

A strong, eager voice. Tinged with anger, sadness, and bloodthirst.

"You coming or what? War doesn't wait for those not ready."

"Quoting Snow, now, are we, Mal? That's gotta be a first for you."

Henrik Snow, the chairman and founder of AMF.

"He knew what he was doing. Do you?" Mal snapped back, smoothly. Her *Bandit* turned on its four-toed feet, and started walking away. It had a T-shaped torso, its "arms" lacking the elbows that most Mechs had, ballistic weapons hanging from the shoulders and protruding forward. They were still pivotal, though, providing the Light Class *Bandit* with agile combat capabilities. Needed for such a nimble Mech, engaging targets on the run.

No wonder she was already out of her stall. The *Bandit* was a sixty-ton, thirty-foot-tall Mech with a Ford 300 engine and only eight heat-sinks.

Supposing Mal, with all of her eagerness to fight, didn't take the pauses that Eddie did, it was reasonable that she was ready to go before any of them. Even if she did double-check her systems, which, despite her current mindset, Eddie was sure she would have.

"Is it just me," Luke's voice sputtered into Eddie's comms. "Or does she wait 'til she's in a sixty-ton war machine to go at you like that, Eddie?"

"I'll pop out this hatch right here and now," Mal retorted without hesitation. "And we can settle it toe-to-toe, Cyclops."

"Girl, I know you didn't just—"

"Enough!" H's robust yet distinctly feminine voice was unmistakable. "We're a *Clan*, for fuck's sake. Whatever the hell our enemy is, they aren't human. But we *are*, so start acting the part."

Eddie blew air out of his lips, shook his head once, and let a little smirk loose. The plus side to talking to anyone in a Mech was, they couldn't see you.

"Happy to have you with us, H," Eddie said. "Everyone optimal? Crazy as Mal is, she's right. And so was Snow. War don't wait. And there are people in need."

He walked his *Adversary* out of the stall and spotted Mal's *Bandit* already halfway to the open hangar doors. Sunlight flowed into the building, which was previously only artificially lit.

"I for one wouldn't want to be anywhere else," H said, and her *Fenrir* stepped out of its stall. An iconic Mech, one of the very first AMF designs, and still an intimidating threat, with twin shoulder-mounted missile racks, a rounded snout housing a capacious cockpit, and curved elbows. The arms were usually twin PPCs or an array of Lasers, sometimes both.

"Nor I," Nomi chimed, and her *Rottweiler* stepped into view. A stocky Mech that met Light Class criteria, but was a ballistic nightmare to come face-to-face with.

"Nor I," Mal said, a touch of acquiescence in her voice.

Eddie glanced at his communications display on the HUD. Surnames of his teammates flashed when they spoke. He recognized their voices, so it wasn't necessary. But confirmation was nice to have, especially under duress.

Luke's *Rhino* stepped out of its stall, joining the column of Ember Wolves down the main aisle of the hangar. It was a Heavy Class Mech despite being the same height as Nomi's *Rottweiler*, and a few feet shorter than Mal's *Bandit*. Despite its squat build, it had more armor than most models its height, not to mention an intimidating left-arm Railgun.

Eddie pivoted his *Adversary*'s torso, looking around. He glanced at his HUD, bottom center. The active radar, currently focused on a hundred-foot radius. It could be zoomed in or out, in fifty-foot increments, no less. Friendly

Mechs, and other vehicles, would appear as green arrows against a black and blue infrared screen. Enemies, once marked, would show up as red arrows. When a Mech used any of its weapons, its icon would flash. Any Mech, vehicle, or enemy not immediately visible would appear at the edges of the screen, which was outlined with a compass.

Wally was the only one currently not visible through his field of vision.

"Wally, how you doing?" Eddie asked.

A moment.

And then a gruff breath carried over the comms. Eddie glanced at the top left corner of his HUD and saw "Meskin" flash.

"Hot as fuck in here," he finally said.

Eddie smirked and imagined most of them doing the same. They could just as well speak without it passing through comms.

Transmission required a button, located on the movement joystick for ergonomic accessibility. One could also toggle a switch on the control panel to leave it always open, or indefinitely closed.

Most pilots toggled it open once they were actively moving. And it was SOP to keep it open the moment a target was highlighted.

Eddie felt both excited and terrified for whenever that moment presented itself.

"But, uh," Wally continued, his voice cracking.

Eddie could have sworn he felt the vibrations in the ground, up through the *Adversary*'s legs, as the *Mastodon* took its first steps since yesterday. It emerged from its stall, lumbering into view. An appropriate representation of Wally's strength and rage, even in its most inert state.

His tone was husky and filled with the rawest emotion. Nobody pressured Wally to speak.

"I swear I can...I can *feel* him in here," he ultimately said. "I know he didn't...I know he didn't design the damn thing with his own hands, but..."

"I'd not be shocked if he was, Wally. In there with you. With all of us. And all our loved ones, they..." Eddie took a deep breath and released the transmission button. He got choked up for a second, unexpectedly. He pressed it again, his voice firmer now. "Alive or otherwise, they're with us in spirit, even those whose names we don't know. They need us."

A pause followed, transient.

The silence was interrupted by a heavy marching sound, which to Clanners was like sweet music. They pivoted their Mechs to watch Mako and Onyx stride toward the hangar doors.

Mal took advantage of her pivotal rotary-cannon and nodded it in a waving fashion. A passing *Pluto* mimicked this gesture with one of its own Laser-mounted arms. Another Mech, a blue and white striped *Fenrir*, physically nodded its entire torso, spun to face the Ember Wolves to its left, while its legs remained facing forward.

It was enough to make Eddie chuckle.

He then glimpsed H do the same with her own *Fenrir*, albeit standing still.

One of Mako Clans' Mechs paused to stand before the Ember Wolves. It was a Support Class model, the most humanoid Mech in the AMF roster. A *Tyrant*, whose awe-inspiring sight was softened a little by the cobalt coloration and seafoam-green waves painted on the upper torso.

Nonetheless a nightmare to duel in battle.

Eddie sure was glad their enemy wasn't composed of other Mechs. Not that he was necessarily relieved their opponents were otherworldly beasts, either.

"Carmine Hollander here," a husky voice came over Eddie's comms. It was the local frequency, which could be piggybacked by anyone within a fifty-foot radius, so long as their comms had AMF credentials. "Mako Clan. Just wanted to say…we're all big fans. Ember has a powerful reputation, inimitable some might say…"

"So, no pressure, huh?" H said, the smirk she wore magically audible.

Carmine chuckled deeply. "No pressure, on any of you. Just wanted to give y'all my condolences, my well wishes, and a nod of respect. We've done exercises in the past, but it's been months since we've worked together on something."

"Looking forward to crushing the enemy by your flank, Hollander," Eddie said. "I hope to see those waves splashed with the blood of our foes, next time we cross paths."

"Whatever color they bleed, I'll wear it proudly, brother."

The sixty-foot, ninety-ton Mech dipped its torso forward, in a bowing gesture.

Eddie performed the same with his *Adversary*.

Carmine slowly turned the *Tyrant* to walk away, trailing his teammates, including the Onyx Wolves.

Ember watched the two other Clans exit the hangar and bank right, due southeast. If Captain Bonheur was correct, they would be convening with a tank convoy and begin their urgent trek toward Stockton. Ultimately, San Francisco awaited them.

Eddie hated to even acknowledge the thought, but he feared that there wouldn't be much left of the city by the time they got there.

They had to sweep Sacramento first, supposing any of their extraterrestrial enemies had ventured this far inland.

Part of Eddie, a big part, hoped not.

A smaller fraction bittersweetly hoped they had…

He now ached with bloodthirst.

"You think the convoy's ready?" Mal asked, and Eddie could hear the impatience tickling through.

"Ready or not," Eddie said, shy of a growl. "Here we fucking come."

4

Fusion propulsion scorched the dry air like a barbecue two-hundred feet off the ground. The Hawk assault VTOLs cut through the sky with their tilt-thruster wings angled back like a fighter jet's. The urgency of the mission left little room for dillydallying.

It was only when the Ember Hawks flew over Sacramento that they doubled-back for a scrupulous hover. Tilt-thrusters adjusted, pointing down, and the aircrafts idled a hundred feet above the tallest buildings. Belly-mounted cameras fed the pilots' HUDs with crisp video footage.

"Well that ain't good," Charly muttered over their team channel.

The three Hawks hovered above the city's southwest district. Mostly local shops and small businesses. They had not detected any signs of distress farther north, where the city was densest.

"Fox, wanna earn an extra buck?" Brick asked.

"Boy, do I."

Brick rolled his eyes. He knew he or Charly could just as well perform the task, but Fox had the zeal—and brazenness—for it.

Besides, he was the smallest of the three. Arguably leaner than Charly, even, but a scientific three inches shorter. None of that had anything to do with a pilot's skills, but Brick would debate to the day he died that Hawk cockpits were far too cramped.

On that note alone, he was covetous of Mech pilots; not that he would ever announce it.

Hawk cockpits were narrow and borderline claustrophobic, especially for a man built as he was. While still not nearly as cramped as other fighter craft, it certainly offered no room to stand up and walk around.

He would, however, argue that the controls were easier, simpler, and smoother than any Mech's.

"Brick," Charly said. "You thinking a low-fly photoshoot?"

"Copy. Relay the feed to HQ, before we break range."

Brick referred to the point-of-no-return for transmitting video recordings; there was no PNR for audio communications, not in a Hawk. They had four times the effective radio range of any Mech.

"Give our boys something to go on," he added, with a lick of confidence.

Charly manually slid open the left-side protective metal panel from her canopy and leaned her shoulder against it. She peered through the reinforced glass, tilting her hovering Hawk to look below. She wanted to see it with her own eyes.

Even from up this high, without magnification, Charly could spot movement.

And then some.

She pulled away, shaking her head and securing the panel again. Unlike Mech cockpits, Hawks' were entirely shielded. The canopy was reinforced, but for the sake of aerodynamics and added protection, the shield panels were used. This of course meant that, unless the pilot retracted the panels, they would have to fly using only external cameras, and HUD targeting.

An experienced pilot saw no issue with this.

"They're gonna need all the help they can get," she eventually said.

"So I'm green?" Fox asked, itching to disengage the VTOL's hover thrusters.

"You're greenlit," Brick said. "Just don't get—"

Fox killed his thrusters and the aircraft dropped like a brick. He hooted the whole way down, making his teammates wince from the crackling comms.

"Cocky," Brick finished, sighing.

Seconds before his VTOL fell between a water tower and fire station on opposite sides of the road, Fox reengaged his thrusters. The Hawk bounced up with a jolt, rattling him in his seat. Grateful for his harness, and even more grateful for the AMH technology that made flying such a machine possible, Fox howled with excitement.

It was his way of detaching from the solemnity of the situation.

Up above, Charly shook her head.

She understood Fox's mindset, but didn't entirely condone it. Mentally alienating to alleviate one's stress levels was one thing, but to escape the weight of battle was inexcusable. Craven, even.

She knew Fox was no coward, but if he continued like this into San Francisco, they were going to have problems.

Charly was already dealing with the burdensome thought that her whole family was dead. Or moments from a terrifying end.

It took a lot of might and fortitude not to abandon her Clan and make a mad dash for Vancouver. Even if she did, she wouldn't make it without having to refuel, and although there were AMF bases between here and there, she'd be alone. Further afflicted with the guilt of leaving behind her *other* family.

Ember.

Leaving them to God knows what fate, and without her help. Her loyalty.

Today would take from all of them a whole lot, and everybody in the world would be tested in extraordinary ways.

So Charly fortified herself from within, and focused on the mission. On how to help those she could, here.

Brick, meanwhile, did a great job at not letting his mind wander. At all. He was in the zone, almost robotically, but never without spirit.

He toggled something on his control panel, and switched to a private channel with Charly.

"He's nuts, but he's good," Brick said, observing Fox's low-altitude reconnaissance over the city, from his belly camera. "Can't deny him that."

"I'll turn a blind eye if I must, should he carry on so recklessly." Charly's piercing green eyes darkened as they narrowed on her video feed. "This isn't a drill. People's lives are…"

She trailed off, gnawing on the inside of her cheek.

"He knows," Brick said, reassuringly. He almost sounded unfazed. Almost. It was merely his trained poise. "Mistakable as a cadet in ways, but he knows. Trust me, first sign of how real this is, and everything will fall into place up there."

Brick tapped his temple.

Not that Charly could see him, but she deduced as much.

She didn't reply. She just watched, impatiently.

Meanwhile, Fox was weaving between buildings, keeping an eye on his speed. He didn't want to go too fast, and compromise the quality of the video he was recording.

It didn't take long for him to see the first of what he hoped would be the last.

Although intrigued and bewildered beyond reason at the existence of such organisms, much less on Earth as they now were, their feral malevolence was nauseating. Mindless, they seemed, and indiscriminately violent.

As if the creatures served no purpose other than destroying and devouring.

Fox recalled the giant Teeth-structures that descended into the planet from a tear in outer space. And then the serpentine tendons. He imagined that Earth was being slowly consumed by some other realm. First, infected with flesh-eating bacteria, to weaken the planet's immune system. And then, less surgically, ingested.

His stomach turned.

Then his wings.

He evaded the towering steel chimney of a factory and rolled the VTOL through the air, ascending simultaneously.

He left Sacramento behind and below, the aircraft trailing thin streams of scorched air from the angled thrusters.

"I tell y'all what," Fox said, upon returning to a stable

hover with his teammates. Once the thrusters were locked, his hands turned dials and fingertips typed at keyboards, allocating the footage he just recorded.

"Well?" Charly pressed, waiting.

Brick had since closed his private channel with her, and listened to the team frequency.

"I, uh, don't think they're here for peace-talks."

"What gave you that idea?" Charly said, her sarcasm as dry as Fox's mouth.

He dragged a swig of cool water from his drinking tube and took a breath.

His forefinger tapped a button that transmitted a segment of the footage he just recorded, across their HUDs.

They were all grateful for superior AMF technology, but in that moment they hated how crisp and clear the full-color video was.

Creatures as large as cars ran amok through the city, one every hundred feet or so. They trampled vehicles in their wake, or slammed through them like battering rams. Amalgamations of disarrayed teeth, tongues, and claws yielded no mercy. Monsters of flesh, bone, and zero conscience laid waste.

The only plus side was that there didn't seem to be a whole lot of civilians running around in a panic. The majority were likely locked away inside, or had taken to bomb shelters. Sound advice, which was probably—hopefully— issued by the President whenever the first *Tooth* made landfall.

Hours ago?

More, less?

The pilots' concept of time was already beginning to

warp amid the debacle.

"Can we do nothing?" Brick suddenly exclaimed, sickened.

"Yes and no," Charly said, no less nauseous. She raked in a deep breath. "We have to get to San Fran. I don't see any of the bigger hostiles on Fox's footage, like we did at base. We'll be the city's first-responders, AMF wise, and we're already late as fuck."

"Lead the way, Fallon," Brick said.

Usage of her last name, or any of theirs for that matter, was typically restricted to times of grave seriousness, or a sarcastic expression.

Basically, polar-opposite moments.

This was obviously the prior.

"Only if you can follow," she said, disengaging hover thrusters.

"Try me, Clanner," Brick smirked.

Charly's VTOL boomed through the air, westbound. Brick followed suit.

They didn't even say anything else to Fox, who stayed back, hovering above Sacramento. He was itched with the urge to descend and open fire, but knew it would be too risky to engage such agile hostiles that were also warm-blooded, which complicated infrared targeting.

This enemy was so vastly different than battling other Mechs or engaging aircraft in the sky.

Fox would trade that for this, any day.

The only plus side was that at least it meant their twelve years of peace wasn't for nothing. That the enemies they would be fighting weren't men and women, but some-thing else altogether.

Something far worse.

So Fox transmitted the video footage to HQ, and toggled his hover thrusters. As the VTOL's wingtips tilted, he muted comms, while looking at the sky before him, and the propulsion trails left behind by his teammates.

"Fucking lovebirds," he smirked.

* * *

The M1AX battle tank growled as its steel-linked synthetic rubber tracks drove it across the asphalt. Fifty tons of ceramic-plated reactive Tungsteel, a Honeywell hybrid-electric diesel turbine engine, steel tension bar suspension and rotary shock absorbers cruised at a steady thirty miles-per-hour.

The tank's maximum speed, on pavement, was fifty. Impressive, considering that the lightest Mech in the AMF arsenal topped out at fifty-five, but most Assault Class models couldn't exceed forty.

For a tracked vehicle, the M1AX was a dangerously effective pawn on any battlefield. In the company of Mechs, they made for a great escort. Capable of accelerating ahead of even the antsiest Clanners, either to draw fire and reveal enemy locations or to simply run a recon route.

All the more reason why the Ember Wolves' convoy consisted solely of M1AX tanks. No Humvees, APC's, or any other vehicles.

Apparently the base had already dispatched their whole Apache squadron at the first sign of conflict in San Francisco. Most of what Captain Bonheur told them earlier was taken from pilot reports. Unfortunately they could do very little from the air, given the population of the city, and widespread panic.

A ground assault team was called for, hence the Clanners. The Hawks would serve a purpose, too, as they were more capable of precision attacks from the air than any other fighter craft.

The rest of base's forces had been scattered to surrounding cities for additional support, particularly Fresno, which was the nearest place they could refuel.

"It's a shit-show out here," H remarked, as their team of Mechs followed a column of three tanks.

"I think the word you're looking for is "clusterfuck," darling," Luke said.

H could tolerate casual sass from Luke but anyone else and she'd bite their head off.

"Both are applicable," she replied.

Nobody objected.

Eddie was at least glad they were talking again. Since debarking from base, there was a pressing radio silence as everyone just sat in their own melancholy. Or tension. Or a combination of both, and then some.

The only things that could be heard during that time were the sounds of machines advancing. From six Mechs marching in line to the steady rhythm of four tanks cruising across pavement on their tracks, engines humming and growling.

Every time a Mech's torso pivoted, a harsh mechanical sound added to the mix. Grinding gears and droning actuators.

An extremely experienced Clanner with a meditative mind could even pinpoint the sound of coolant and water supplies sloshing inside their Mech. The only people capable of this here were Wally and H, but Wally was past the point of meditation.

H dabbled in it sporadically, just to keep her wits aligned.

Upon contracting the four-tank escort that completed their convoy, and leaving base behind, the Ember Wolves familiarized themselves with the M1AX crew on a very basic level.

Due to urgency, the pilots had not gotten the names of every personnel aboard the tanks. The commander of each M1AX had given their callsign, not to keep anonymity—their enemies clearly were not radio users—but to facilitate operations.

"Simplicity is often the key to winning the most complex battles," Henrik Snow once said.

It was a quote that the commander of the lead tank tossed into the air, when Eddie asked his name.

"Lead Ax, speaking, is Alpha," the tank commander said. Ax was a colloquial term for the M1AX.

"Second in line, Bravo," the next commander said, his voice sleeker than the heavy gruff of Alpha.

Eddie smirked and shook his head. He wondered if the others had the same reaction. Part of him wanted to familiarize himself with the Ax crews on a more personal level, as it helped him humanize battle. But he wouldn't argue, given the circumstances.

Besides, he alone recognized Bravo commander's voice. He had only glimpsed the commanders poke their heads through their hatches when the tanks first fell in line off the tarmac to lead the convoy. Bravo commander was

Casey Schaub, one of the youngest to seize his role, and perform it with flying colors, this side of the country.

He was an inspiration to tank cadets across the nation, and had the respect of many older commanders.

Unfortunately, Eddie didn't recognize the other voices, or glimpsed faces, of the rest of their convoy. This of course did not diminish his trust and faith in them and their abilities.

Behind Bravo would have been callsign Charlie, but instead they chose Chapman, to avoid confusion with Ember's own, Charly Fallon. She had a reputation that carried to even tank ranks. Even more so to the commander whose callsign was Chapman, as she, too, was a woman.

Female Ax commanders were rarer than Mech or Hawk pilots, but commoner than any of the other crew in a tank.

Three personnel per M1AX.

One driver and two gunners.

The main armament, a 120mm smoothbore cannon, was self-loading. Additionally, each M1AX featured a .50-caliber armor-piercing machinegun emplacement, both remotely operable from within the tank, and accessible via the secondary hatch. Mounted to the commander's hatch was a 7.62mm belt-fed machinegun, hybridized with a 44mm grenade launcher.

Whoever operated the 7.62 was the commander, a role responsible for directing the driver and the gunner, who also operated the main cannon, sans reloading.

The AMF was currently working with DARPA and the Israeli government to perfect a tank system capable of handling both the ACX and Railgun seen on Mechs, but the amount of recoil and ammunition storage was proving to be a challenge.

Also, it just didn't seem that necessary, what with the diverse roster of Mechs available.

The first three tanks led the convoy, their commanders keeping an open eye for potential threats at all times, in addition to their primary gunners, whose viewports focused on the vehicle's left periphery.

The single tank that trailed the Mech column lagged behind a couple hundred feet to deter or counter ambushes.

Its commander, whose voice sounded about as young as Bravo's, had a mousy tone that wasn't too comforting.

"I know what you're thinking," Delta said, his voice carrying over the Ember Wolves' team channel, which they currently shared with the tanks. "I don't sound fit to be an Ax CO. But that just makes me more excited to prove my worth."

"Nothing to prove, Delta," H said. A pause. "But I wouldn't mind seeing some fireworks, if it saves our ass."

A few seconds passed, and then a chuckle carried over the comms from Delta's end, but it wasn't the commander. Anyone listening could distinguish a voice in the background with ease.

"Apologies," Delta finally replied, a peculiar confidence to his mousy inflection. "My driver's had very little sleep, and doesn't know when to bite his tongue."

H sighed into the frequency.

"Alright, let's hear it," she gave in. "We're all running on fumes, anyway. Won't be room to shoot the shit anytime soon."

Delta grunted into his mic. And then cleared his throat.

"Well, uh, my driver just said, if it came to *your ass*, there'd definitely be some, uh, some fireworks."

Luke laughed into the frequency. Theatrically. Some chuckles from Bravo.

"How charming," Mal said.

"I'm flattered," H said, blandly. "Just be sure your driver knows one thing."

"What's that, ma'am?" Delta asked.

"The Ember Wolves are a *Clan*. So, my ass is their ass. That's three women and three men, one of whom might get down on *his* knees, if you were to beg."

Luke scoffed. "I would *never*."

"Well played, ma'am," Delta said.

"Hendricks is right, Delta," Alpha said. "So zip it. As long as we're a convoy, *their* ass is *our* ass, too. We travel as one, we fight as one."

"Lest we run into something that requires division," Bravo said.

"Ember will have the say on that," Alpha said, "when the time comes, as I imagine it will."

"Thank you, Alpha," Eddie said. "We appreciate the deference."

"Always." The Alpha commander grunted. Last Eddie recalled, the man looked like he would have been better fitted in the Viking era. "I might be an old sum'bitch, lost some fingers in the Great War, but I didn't lose my common sense and battle-manners. You Clanners, I'll admit, are a shifty bunch, but the Ember Wolves oughtta be on Cali's flag, I tell you that much."

It was a lot to ingest, especially from such a gravelly voice, but Eddie cherished the candor.

"We're beyond humbled, commander," H said.

"And we look forward to defending our country with you in our ranks," Nomi said.

She just wished she could see the forward tank column, but at least she had eyes on Delta. She could either swivel her *Rottweiler*'s torso while crabbing down the road, and face the tank herself, or simply glance at her spinal camera.

The tank was the only one in the convoy that had traditional desert camouflage, a splash of light and dark browns, stitched together with white and black lines.

She had seen the tanks come off the tarmac earlier, in an agile column, before disseminating into the Mech's own linear formation. Alpha, Bravo, and Chapman were all a dark jungle coloration, with no patterns or emblems, except for standard AMF badges.

Eddie was, for all intents and purposes, the Clan's leader. There were no specific ranks within a Mech Clan, but leadership roles were typically designated once a team had enough experience together. While Wally and H had more tenure as pilots, Eddie had proven the most reliable and effective "captain."

Sometimes when he issued an order, though never despotically, he was met with "you got it, boss" and the like. Seldom "sir," unless someone wanted to be sarcastic. Clans were indeed families in essence, and didn't communicate with the same rigidity of most military commands.

This of course didn't undermine the efficacy of a Clan. Most Mech squads were more effective because of their flexible leadership.

Nonetheless, the second that the tanks came off the tarmac to join the Ember Wolves, already briefed on their mission, Eddie didn't hesitate. He told his pilots where to be in their column, according to subtle strategies. Naturally, Eddie was at the front, his *Adversary* trailing a safe and steady fifty feet behind the Chapman tank.

Nomi, meanwhile, was directed to the rear, due to her long-range ballistic capabilities, which could easily shoot over Delta without fear of any energy splashing. Her Railgun used caseless ammunition, and the Vulcan rotary-cannon powerfully ejected brass that wouldn't torrent the tank.

In front of Nomi was H, her *Fenrir* supplying the rear of their formation some diverse firepower, should the tank and *Rottweiler* not suffice if flanked. And in front of H was Luke, his stocky *Rhino* a hillock compared to the *Mastodon* in front of him. Fortunately the sun was to his right, otherwise he'd be cast in its shadow, indefinitely.

Mal wasn't thrilled to have the *Mastodon* lumbering behind her, for a few reasons. One, she could feel its every step on the pavement through the lean legs of her *Bandit*. Two, it gave her flashbacks to the Great War, having it always on her spinal camera; not that the *Mastodon* existed back then, but other Support Class giants did.

Lastly, it made her feel insignificant.

Why Eddie had chosen to sandwich her *Bandit* between his *Adversary* and Wally's *Mastodon* was beyond her.

Although she didn't complain, she did have to bite her tongue about the formation itself. Mechs seldom marched in columns. Their payloads made this a dangerous strategy, as did their sheer size. Mechs bumping into each other was always more than a moot fender-bender.

At least they weren't packed into a sardine march. Their column was lenient in spacing, more so with the Mechs than the tanks. Each M1AX trailed the other by a single tank's width, no more and no less. The Mechs never strode closer than thirty feet apart, although their pilots favored fifty.

The route they were taking felt like it lasted forever. First they simply had to walk—or in the tanks' case, roll—off the military property. Redlining, this would only take them two to three minutes, tops. After they passed the gates, they were home-free—and officially in the "civilian world." This simply meant they needed to be keener to their surroundings than before, especially the closer they got to civilization, naturally.

After transitioning from unmarked pavement to the painted routes of a four-lane highway outside of Sacramento, they knew things were going to complicate real fast. It was a tacit understanding, and within seconds they realized they had underestimated the panic.

With what was happening in San Francisco plastered on the news, where broadcasts were still active, and likely the internet as well, the common city slicker wasn't going to wait around and see for themselves.

Eddie liked to believe these were the smarter people—to an extent. Collectively, one person acting on a whim became a horde of thoughtless, selfish creatures. Where the panic mentality thrived, dangerously.

The column of Mechs and tanks were hugging the shoulder of the highway leading into Sacramento for

maybe ten seconds of quiet before they witnessed pande-
monium in action.

Droves of cars were pouring down the interstate, honking and speeding and veering. Tires screeched and, to the
pilots' dismay, some drivers even took the oncoming lanes.
They seized advantage of the thin traffic, as opposed to any
other time, given what was happening in every major city.

Vehicles fitted with four-wheel-drive abandoned the
asphalt in favor of the even, grassy terrain off the shoulder.
Some never made it, though, miscalculating and nose-div-
ing into a ditch off the edge of the shoulder. Several cars
honked madly as they passed the column of military vehicles, and an occasional middle finger was thrust out of a
window.

"What did *we* do?" Delta scoffed.

"Nothing, yet, and that's why," Mal said, embittered.

Eddie could tell that the spite in her voice was not directed at the angry drivers, but inwards. Whether at herself
solely or at all of them as a whole, he couldn't be sure.

Before anybody could say anything, Eddie took initia-
tive. Not just to relieve Mal's impatience, but to prevent it
from exacerbating in himself. And his other teammates.

"Alpha," Eddie said. "Mow some grass and punch it.
We'll keep up."

"You got it, Ember," Alpha replied.

Eddie watched the lead tank veer right, its tracks
bouncing fifty tons over the ditch and plowing through soft,
grassy earth. Chunks of dirt and turf flew through the air in
its wake, and the other two tanks behind it followed suit.
Within seconds all three battle tanks were peeling across
the field to the right side of the highway. They pushed their

maximum off-road speed, which topped off around thirty-six miles-per-hour.

"Let's go, Wolves," Eddie said, and followed the adjusted formation.

Unlike tracked vehicles, Mechs did not have a diminished top speed on terrain when it wasn't paved. The large Tungsteel feet were indiscriminate when it came to propelling a Mech. Of course, the design of a Mech's feet varied per model; Mal's *Bandit* had a four-toe configuration, in a plus-sign arrangement. Eddie's *Adversary*, while four-toed as well, had star-shaped feet, each digit more triangular than the rectangles of the *Bandit*.

The variations in design were for supporting different weight distributions and even load-outs.

For example, all Support Class Mechs had blocky elephant-like feet, to bolster not only so much weight but also the recoil of their heavier weapons.

The feet of H's *Fenrir* was similar in design to the *Adversary*, save for one toe. The three digits were sizable enough to support the Assault Class Mech, not needing an additional toe due to its less mobile capabilities compared to the *Adversary*.

Luke's *Rhino* was unique in that the feet were similar to Support Class Mechs, but had small toes, too, for articulation on uneven terrain. Even more unique were the feet of Nomi's *Rottweiler*, which were hybrid tank tracks; when walking, the Mech had digitigrade feet, more nimble than they might seem at first glance. If desired, or under the circumstance of a damaged knee actuator, the Mech could lower itself onto its tracked soles, and travel like a tank.

At any rate, all of the Mechs made good time off-road,

on top of their inherent preference. Most Clanners would choose a battle on unpaved terrain if given the option, due to the less rattling strides, not to mention quieter.

Of course, once the guns started to rip, none of that really mattered.

Presently, they were just hauling ass the fastest possible way, to reach Sacramento sooner rather than later. The only downside to Eddie's decision was that the lead three tanks would enter Sacramento's outer limits well before the Mechs, but he had already taken this into consideration.

"Once you see that welcome sign, Alpha," Eddie said, "pull onto the road. Trust me, cars will get the picture. If they're too dog-headed, hug the shoulder; but as soon as we reach our first exit, we've got no choice."

"Copy. Permission to use the megaphone?"

Eddie smirked. "Sure, but let Bravo handle it. His voice is…well, no offense, Alpha."

"Ha! I've heard it all before."

Eddie was beginning to really like this guy. He wished he knew his name.

"You know the drill, Bravo. Sweet-talk 'em into submission."

Bravo snickered softly onto the channel. "Copy."

Moments later, they reached a side road that crossed a bridge, streaming over the interstate.

"Look both ways, hold hands," Wally muttered.

Completely upright, when the *Mastodon* was not hunched over during battle, its cockpit was at a superior height than most Mechs. The fact that it could easily in that position see over the top of his *Adversary*, let alone its dual shoulder armaments, unnerved Eddie a little.

Or maybe it was just jealousy.

The Alpha tank crossed the two-lane road after a brief pause, letting a pair of vehicles pass in a hurry. Bravo followed curtly, not waiting. An SUV slammed into its horn, and brakes.

"Drive safe, do not panic," the commander said nonchalantly into the megaphone below deck. "The Ember Wolves are here."

Vehicles still honked their horns and even shouted out of their windows.

"Gotta love Cali," Chapman said, shaking her head. She advanced the tank across the road after waving the SUV forward. Only to cut off another vehicle behind it.

"Can't win 'em all," Eddie sighed over the frequency.

"At least y'all have a better vantage point up there," Chapman said. "Any Ax CO would be lying if they said they weren't envious."

"In all honesty," Luke said. "I can't think of one thing I prefer about a tank."

Some chuckles over the channel.

"Luke, you ass," H said, exhaling lightheartedly.

"Honesty is the true victor," Luke said, high-and-mightily.

"Shit, is that another Snow quote?" Eddie asked.

"Nah, I just made that shit up right now."

Some more candid laughter.

"Act alive, folks," Alpha blurted. "I got movement ahead. Coming down the exit ramp."

"*Our* exit ramp?" Delta asked.

"Affirmative."

"Is it a car? A person?" Delta asked.

Poor Delta, caught behind the Mechs, and essentially blind. He wasn't sure whether or not he was permitted to cruise out ahead of the Ember Wolves, after Eddie gave that order to Alpha.

"Negative," Eddie said, his jaw dropping. Seeing those creatures on the aerial footage back at base was one thing. Seeing it now, in the flesh, albeit from a Mech cockpit, was a whole other ballgame. How it moved, like a cross between a boar and a lion, was very unsettling. Its physique was closer to that of a boar, except that it was as big as an SUV; a little larger than the convertible Porsche it now chased.

The exposure of raw flesh and muscle, contrasting with the bone carapace along its pitted snout, six rising tusks, and rocky limbs, reminded Eddie of the "Teeth" and tentacles that were ravishing San Francisco.

Eddie gulped, scrutinizing it through his magnified reticle.

"Hard negative," he finally said, his joystick hand sweaty already. He toggled his weapons.

"Good Christ," Alpha muttered in awe.

The column of Mechs essentially zig-zagged as they continued striding forward. Each one stepped out of formation, just enough to witness what Alpha and Eddie were reporting so vaguely.

Swerving down their impending exit ramp, which curved up around a greenbelt, and out of view, but into Sacramento, was a silver convertible Porsche. It dodged the occasional car going with the natural flow of traffic, honking its puny sounding horn incessantly.

In a heads-up manner, Eddie imagined.

The pursuer juked on all fours, galloping down the curved exit ramp, intent on catching this particular car for some reason. Its front hood was missing and both headlights were smashed. It had clearly been in some kind of accident already, or perhaps it had collided with the creature that now chased it.

"I, uh, I don't have a clear shot," Alpha said, regrettably, although evidently he was still processing what he witnessed.

"Stand-by," Eddie said, arming his Mech's chin-mounted twin Lasers.

Their column had decelerated significantly, to calibrate how they were going to engage this threat. The amount of civilian presence in the immediate area complicated things, but it was a factor they knew to expect.

Worst of all, they weren't even *in* Sacramento yet.

Not technically.

Eddie had stepped out of formation to stand still, training his HUD-magnified aim.

"Anytime, champ," Alpha said. His tank column continued forward, albeit at half their original speed.

The Porsche had reached the interstate and now tried cutting across into oncoming traffic.

"For fuck's sake," Eddie muttered.

As it turned out, though, this maneuver by the terrified driver drew the creature into the open for a split-second. Eddie took the shot, squeezing the joystick trigger. The twin Lasers punched out perfect red beams of high-energy light, concentrating heat on their target for a standard duration of three seconds. It took half that to cross a distance of one-hundred feet.

Eddie didn't have to hold the trigger. The Laser armament was designed to produce a three-second beam, no more so as to limit heat generation and no less for effective damage. Cool-down time was three to six seconds, depending on the Mech, its heat-sinks, and how many Lasers were being used. For Eddie's *Adversary* configuration, the two Lasers couldn't be fired independently; this had its pros and cons, naturally.

The sight of the twin red beams cutting through their target was more satisfying than he expected. The creature might have seemed like its shoulders and back were armored, but the Lasers were designed to melt external layers of Tungsteel.

Apparently, extraterrestrial carapaces were no match for such concentrated heat.

The beams caught the creature midstride, in its left shoulder, and swept right, to its tapered hindquarters. As soon as the three-second beam dissipated, Eddie witnessed the result.

"Direct hit!" Bravo exclaimed.

The creature had been cut in two, from the side. The wounds were mostly cauterized, but not seamlessly. Some of its vivid orange innards oozed onto the road, steam rising from the puddle.

"Put that sum'bitch outta commission," Alpha said with satisfaction.

"Flesh is flesh," Eddie said, scowling.

He had seen Lasers cut through infantry before, but was never at the controls for it. Most Clanners—even before they were called such—used their Mechs' machineguns to engage infantry. The caliber of Lasers had the probability of killing a person without any chance of survival, but there were cases of things and people catching fire if they were nearby, but not close enough to be cut through. Or melt.

And Eddie liked to avoid that cruel possibility, even in the throes of war.

"Ember, do you read?"

A voice sputtered through their comms channel. For most of the Wolves, it was awash in static.

Wally's *Mastodon* had the best communications array present, and its height enhanced reception.

"Loud and clear, HQ," he replied. "What have you got for us?"

"Received aerial footage from the Ember Hawks minutes ago, in downtown Sac. Large package. Had to assess. They should be in S-F by now."

"Copy, anything we should know?"

"Be prepared for heavy enemy contact, small but high in numbers. Uh…"

A pause. Headquarters' radio personnel seldom broke away from rigid, succinct transmissions. Whatever the man had seen in that footage had shaken him, even now.

"It…It's a slaughter, Ember," the voice finally returned, empathetic. And then another pause, followed by a sterner tone. *"Shoot to kill. Check your fire."*

"Solid copy, HQ," Wally said. "Give our best to the Hawks. Ember out."

The transmission ended.

"You get all that?" Wally asked the rest of the team. Everybody copied.

"Too bad we're out of range to actually *see* the footage," Nomi said.

"I have a feeling we won't need to, shortly," Eddie said, proceeding to stride forward. His Mech's four-toed feet lifted chunks of grass and soil in his wake.

"Taking the ramp," Alpha announced.

"Following," Bravo said.

The two lead tanks transitioned from grass to pavement, leaving dirt trails from their tracks. The exit ramp was wide enough for a tank and a small car side-by-side, with mere inches between them. It was a path intended for one vehicle at a time, with some cushion between it and the barriers.

Fortunately, drivers were keen enough to pull off to the side. Some of them lost side-view mirrors, and a few even honked as if it made a difference.

"Alpha, permission to submit a request," Eddie said, watching Chapman proceed to the exit ramp.

"Tracking."

"Have Chapman and Delta hold back, in case any enemy activity occurs on the interstate, that bridge, or slips by us, onto the exit."

"Copy. Logical. Chapman, Delta."

"Affirmative," Chapman said, no objections. She directed her tank to peel left, just before reaching the exit. The M1AX plowed through some cones and occupied, thus blocking, the far right lane, its main cannon facing forward, toward Sacramento.

"Will hang back and cover the bridge," Delta said, and his tank spun around to sit in the field about a hundred feet from this side of the bridge, facing it.

"Restrict your comms to each other, radio us if anything pops up," Alpha said, his tank out of sight now, continuing up the exit ramp. "Sit tight and good luck."

"Happy shooting," Chapman said.

"Appreciate it," Eddie said, and strode closer to the ramp's base.

Cars were still pulled off to the side, some not moving. Others hurriedly exited the ramp, hauling ass onto the interstate, away from Sacramento.

Eddie sighed. "I don't think these people realize just how big we are. Mal? Could you rally some common sense?"

"On it," she said, knowing the drill. She had done so fifteen years ago, back when her voice was younger and thinner. Even then, she had a robust tone. Now, it was tenured in battle, age, and various other experiences.

She jogged her *Bandit* to the base of the exit ramp and spoke into her external mic. Through speakers, her voice boomed into the air.

"Please clear the ramp, drive safely," she said. It took an aggressive repeat for drivers to start reacting accordingly. Then she calmed her voice a touch, while sustaining an urgent tone. "Thank you for your cooperation. Drive safely. Avoid big cities. Thank you."

Some courtesy taps on horns sounded as cars drove by. Even some friendly waves out of windows.

"Love to see it," Eddie said.

"Thank you," Mal said again into her external mic, actually smiling inside her Mech.

It both filled her heart with hope and broke it simultaneously, to witness the kindness in normal people.

84

Knowing what was coming down to them, unwarranted, from above. From…who knew where?

"Now imagine if that was Alpha on the horn," Luke joked.

"Ha-ha," Alpha said sardonically.

"Let's *move*," Eddie demanded, and proceeded onto the exit ramp.

Mal followed, and their column strode up the ramp.

"Enemy contact," Alpha said, his voice calm at first. Then a sputter of gunfire, not through the comms but up the ramp, on the other side of the greenbelt, out of sight. It was a mounted 7.62 hosing out rounds, and an occasional burst from the .50-cal. And then he was back on comms. "F-Fucking hell. Lot of 'em."

Eddie's adrenaline pumped.

"Tracking multiple hostiles," Bravo said. The intensity in his voice picked up, fast. "Seven…eight on the ground. Check that roof!"

His comms cut out.

A tank round discharged, thunderously. Eddie glimpsed the tops of trees flutter from the shockwave. An explosive sound followed.

"Mobile or stationary?" Eddie asked. "Are you guys mobile or—"

"Stationary. Forked. Come through." Alpha replied, almost robotically.

He muted his comms sporadically, to avoid crashing the channel with gunfire. The Wolves were different, since they weren't exposed to their Mechs' weapons, although they were still radically loud.

Eddie glanced at his radar. Alpha was 130 feet and

closing. Stationary, as he said. Bravo was about 180 feet, and closing, but slower; he was far left of Alpha. Also sitting still.

But Eddie imagined there was nothing inert about their engagement.

Machinegun fire, from 7.62 to .50-cal, was almost constant. They restrained from using their main cannons for a reason, save for that one shot earlier.

As soon as Eddie reached the top of the ramp, he realized why.

The two tanks were sitting fifty feet apart, angled away from the exit ramp and facing the crossroads ahead. A high bridge to their left, whose pillar-supported underpass was being covered by Bravo. A large gas station across the street, straight ahead, about three-hundred feet away. The intersection was maybe a hundred. Alpha was engaging hostiles darting across the road which led down their right. Both routes curved into town, the outer limits of Sacramento.

Civilians were scattered, mostly in their vehicles. Driving madly, trying to escape those chasing them. There were more creatures than cars, though.

Eddie assessed all of this in seconds.

And then he tracked targets, and marked them on his HUD, highlighting their mobile positions for the rest of his Wolves.

"Clanners, engage," he said. "Watch your fire."

"Copy," H said, speaking for everyone. And then: "Fan out. Nomi, Mal, assist Bravo. Wally, on me. Bank right. We got you, Alpha."

Everybody complied.

"Luke, snipe what you can," Eddie added, knowing he was a sharpshooter with the Railgun.

"Copy." Luke sat back, between the two tanks, concentrating on the gas station across the street. There was one car struggling to drive away, while two creatures played cat-and-mouse with it.

The poor driver was essentially cornered.

As for the enemy, they weren't all the same. The boar-like creature from earlier constituted two or three of the eight creatures present. The others were roughly the same size, possibly a little smaller, that of a small sports car.

'Small,' of course, was relative. Their ferocity was uninhibited, and their feral nature made them seem bigger than they were.

Eddie noticed the canopy above the gas station was destroyed at one corner, rubble on the asphalt below. He remembered hearing a tank round discharge earlier.

Yet saw no sign of a slain creature, suggesting that the shot had missed.

He started to aim, focusing on one by the gas station. His observation of the creature was swift, but the disturbing effect slowed his reaction time.

It was dark blue on top, everywhere except its lower jaw, throat area, and chest, which was all a glistening red, like exposed flesh and tendons.

Not unlike the Boar, these features reminded Eddie of the tentacled things that slithered through buildings in San Francisco. From which eventually crept foul organisms.

He wondered if this was one of them.

There seemed to be no doubt anymore.

Sharp barbs protruded from its carapace of a face,

head, and shoulders. The teeth looked alarmingly sharp and jutted outward from the jaws to form what had to be a devastating bite, not necessarily made for chewing but for puncturing and ripping.

No eyes, from what Eddie could tell.

Horns honked and drew his attention to the top of the bridge to his left. He glimpsed white-hot tracers from machineguns streak the shadows of the underpass, punching into concrete columns and ripping through an evasive Boar.

Eyeless as both creatures appeared to be, they were far from aimless.

He recalled what Captain Bonheur had said about the possibility of their enemy possessing heat vision.

Hence the targeting of high-population areas.

Luke's Railgun discharged a round, thirty feet to Eddie's left. The surrounding air made a sound akin to an eardrum popping, tenfold. Eddie watched one of the creatures at the gas station explode like a flesh balloon. Chunks of its blue carapace littered the asphalt.

A vapor trail from the magnetically-charged tungsten projectile faded from the air in hardly a second.

The driver that Luke had essentially saved, finally fishtailed out from under the canopy. The car veered around a pile of rubble, down the road, and—

Toward them.

Luke and Eddie stepped aside, as the car peeled off down the exit ramp. The no-bullshit sense of urgency was something that Eddie could applaud.

He nodded, more to himself than anyone else, as an idea traveled through him.

"Mal, hop back on the horn and spare no bark. Escort civvies to the exit ramp."

"Copy," she said. Her *Bandit* broke away from Bravo's tank and Nomi's *Rottweiler*, paired up on engaging hostiles darting back and forth under the bridge. There were some homeless there that could not escape, and a semi that had flipped, its driver's fate unclear.

Mal's voice returned to her external mic, but was far less clam than before. As Eddie had said, spare no bark. And when Mal barked, she had bite, too.

"Exit ramp, everyone take the exit ramp," she all but shouted, while striding from car to car. She was hot on her .50-cal, too, burst-firing at any creatures that came near the drivers she addressed, or her own Mech for that matter. "Follow me!"

Cars fell in line, honking. Perhaps to alert other vehicles in the area, too. There were gradually more than at first, as they funneled out of the city and into the intersection.

"Bridge, bridge, bridge!" Wally shouted. "Nomi, fall back!"

Eyes up.

A semi was being pursued by a creature—a *beast*—twice as big as those below. The semi was fishtailing, taking its trailer with it. And then the beast slammed into it, knocking the trailer over. Toward the concrete barrier. A steel railing bent, but sustained against the pressure of the trailer.

It was no matter.

The beast shoulder-checked the trailer again, this time closer to the cab.

"I don't have a clear shot!" Wally griped.

Nomi had withdrawn safely, and Bravo's tank reversed, too.

Mal was busy leading a string of cars to the exit ramp. She stepped aside to witness the eighteen-wheeler roll over the railing of the bridge fifty feet up.

The cars didn't wait around. They beelined to the ramp, careening down it.

The semi rolled, its trailer pulling it down with a jerk. Gravity be damned. The cab hit the pavement in a fireball, which engulfed it and was close enough to trigger the *Rottweiler*'s heat sensors.

"Motherfucker," Wally growled.

The beast stood at the edge of the bridge, looking down at them. Wally's cockpit was nearly even with the height of the bridge. It growled directly at his Mech, fearless of what appeared to be a giant, armored version of the people it was used to terrorizing.

The beast was about half the length of a tanker rig, nose to tail. Vaguely crocodilian, but stockier and more muscular limbs to carry its ungainly form at a pace fast enough to keep up with a semi. The coloration and anatomy was almost identical to the "smaller" creatures they were used to seeing.

It bellowed at Wally as he placed his HUD's aiming reticle over its eyeless, salivating snout.

Range was about 120 feet.

"Die, scum," Wally said, and his finger stroked the trigger.

The beast lurched back, in preparation of leaping off the bridge.

Wally's right shoulder-mounted Autocannon roared like dragon's breath. The report was thunderous, five times that of Luke's Railgun. The 180mm ACX slung a cluster of three high-explosive anti-tank rounds, one after the other, in the blink of an eye. It seared through the air in a bright, white-hot streak. The large creature exploded, snout to rump, spraying the bridge with its flesh and innards. Left behind was a plume of smoke and a few feet of intact tail.

As much as they wanted to celebrate the spectacular hit, the death of the truck driver and others around them kept their mood grim.

"Tracking another, my two o'clock," Bravo announced, and his tank started to pivot. The commander himself longed to use his 44mm grenade launcher, but unfortunately the civilian presence made this a no-go.

Down the road, coming from Sacramento, two vehicles sped. One was a Suzuki motorcycle and the other a sports car. The motorcycle sped out in front of the car, weaving around an abandoned vehicle. The driver glanced over his shoulder, and didn't account for a dead body in the middle of the road. The front tire struck it at the wrong angle and hurled him off his seat. The motorcycle cartwheeled forward, missing him on the road.

Behind, the car continued, weaving in a panic.

The pursuer was another Gator, like the one from the bridge.

"Got it," H said, and hit the large creature with twin Autocannons. They were a much smaller caliber than the *Mastodon*'s; cheek-mounted on her *Fenrir*, their recoil still rattled her cockpit. Her teeth chattered and she barely noticed, reveling in the sight of the beast being knocked

91

asunder by the four-round cluster. The 60mm HEAT rounds were made to puncture tank armor, which meant they did a gory number on flesh.

The beast's left arm blew off at the shoulder, and two of the rounds had bored through its torso, exploding in their wake. Its back half lied on the road behind a thick trail of gore, but its front half continued to crawl forward.

H grimaced and switched to her Lasers.

Wally took two big steps forward and crushed the beast's oblong skull with a heavy foot. Nearly a hundred tons' worth of weight pancaked cranium and brains into the pavement.

"That works, too," H shrugged.

"Fucking wretches," Wally grumbled. He wanted to spit on its corpse but had no way to.

The Mechs and tanks looked around. Their enemies had been slain, the ones in the area at least.

The car that had been evading the creature found its way to the exit ramp, courtesy honking en route. The motorcycle driver got to his feet, waving and returning to his bike. He drove off seconds later, following the car's path.

Eddie thought it was funny how straightforward the fight-or-flight mechanism was in people, sometimes. How robotic it made their actions. Yet at least there remained a pinch of humanity left in them, enough to acknowledge those who were here to help.

Even if they were running late.

"Good shooting, everyone," Eddie said. He walked his *Adversary* closer to Alpha's tank. Bravo assembled. "We should split up, cover both routes into the city. But retain tank and Mech presence for both."

"Can't argue," Alpha said, with a deep, haggard breath. The commander emerged from his hatch, peering up at the *Adversary*.

Eddie pitched his cockpit down enough to see the Nordic-bearded man, with a weathered face and dark blue eyes.

"No offense, commander, but I'm gonna tag along with Bravo. Taking Mal and H with me; attaching Luke, Nomi, and big ol' Wally to you."

"None taken. Happy to have *any* Mech company. Especially the Ember Wolves."

"Cheers to that," Eddie said. "Been a pleasure already. Excited to kill more of these bastards while sharing your ranks."

"Amen, brother."

"One favor, though, since they're your team."

"Shoot."

"Radio Chapman and Delta, tell 'em to keep up the good work, but do their best to prohibit any cars from taking that exit," Eddie said, centering the *Adversary*'s torso only to swing it in the direction of the exit ramp. A Mech way of pointing. "If we can, as we go, we'll keep directing cars that way; best case, they'll do it on their own volition, versus looping around for the proper exit. Sooner the better that they get the fuck outta dodge."

"I hear that."

"Excellent. Oh, and let 'em know…to keep an eye out for, uh, *bigger* hostiles."

"Shit yeah," Alpha said, and patted a gloved hand on the tank armor beside his open hatch. "I'll tell 'em not to shy from the big guns."

"Exactly."

"What's your ammo count on those things?" Mal asked. "Forty rounds?"

"Forty-six," Alpha replied. "Bravo's down to forty-five, now. Blasted the hell outta one of those *things* on top of the gas station earlier. Well, tried to."

"Couldn't resist," Bravo said, matter-of-factly. "My gunner's one hell of a shot, though. Or so he insists."

Eddie smirked, glancing at the destroyed corner of the gas station canopy. And the corpses of their enemies littering the crossroads.

"Will be excited to witness that myself," he added, with no sarcasm.

Already, as per Eddie's mention of splitting up, and who he wanted to go with either tank, the Ember Wolves had divided their ranks. H and Mal stood at Eddie's four and eight o'clock, respectively, while the others were huddled to the right of the intersection, awaiting Alpha to take that route into the city.

"We better get to it, then," Alpha's commander said, ducking back into the tank, and saluting Eddie on his way down.

"Looking forward to convening with you downtown," Eddie said, and started to stride away, toward the bridge. "Wolves, pick a local channel for the three of you, and Alpha. We'll do the same, and radio each other if needed."

"Copy," Wally said.

Just as Eddie was going to instruct Mal and H which channel to hop onto, their team frequency crackled with a long-range transmission. It was Headquarters again. The static dispersed quickly, for every Mech, not just Wally this time.

"Ember, do you read? Urgent."

"We got you, HQ," H said.

Eddie immediately went to work on the small keyboard below his comms monitor to permit Alpha and Bravo's access to his team frequency, albeit listen-only.

Whether or not HQ intended their tank convoy to hear what they had to say.

"What's your position? Transponders are reading your team at the northeast side of Sacramento."

"Correct," Eddie said, withdrawing from the control panel. He took a drag on his water tube.

"What is your status?"

"We had enemy contact, nine or ten hostiles. All neutralized. No damage sustained. Some civilian casualties."

"Understood. The good and the bad."

"Copy."

A pause.

"What's this about, HQ?" Eddie pressed.

"We received a report from your Hawks," the male voice from Headquarters said. There was a hint of despair in his tone, slowly building. It unnerved Eddie. *"They've reached S-F and have assessed the damage. It's not good. The city is compromised. Civilian casualties are immense. Structural damage is even worse."*

A deep sigh.

"They've been ordered to maintain medium altitude, and engage hostiles at a safe range. Their reports align with previous reports on the enemy. Small, large, and extreme. The largest move very slow and none have been reported outside of any high-population centers."

"So that's...good," Mal said.

"Another point of good news," the HQ transmitter said. *"Despite the massive loss of civilian life, according to aerial infrared scans, thousands are clustered in subterranean bunkers throughout the city."*

Sighs of relief blew into the comms channel from various pilots.

Eddie thought to himself, that something good came from the Great War. Given, the AMF was the main thing, secondary of course to the unity. Government-funded, citywide bunkers now served a purpose beyond their expectancy.

"Excellent news," Eddie said. "Any update on Sac?"

"The main reason we wanted to reach you before you moved in."

Eddie waited, his anticipation bubbling.

"Much of the city's residents have done the same thing. However, there are far less bunkers in Sacramento than S-F. Fortunately, infrared picked up less than forty-percent the enemy count than in S-F. Still, they are highly aggressive and active."

Eddie nodded. "We're eager to roll in and kick ass, HQ. I hate to be that guy, but get to the point so we can do our job."

"Copy, Ember. You might be happy to hear, then, that you've been cleared to SAK."

Eddie's eyes widened.

"No shit—we get to SAK Sac?" Luke chuckled. "Fuckin' A."

Sweep And Kill was a mission type similar to S&D, with open rules of engagement and typically reserved for environments clear of civilian presence. Unlike search and destroy, however, SAK was specifically for Mech teams, turning any Clan into a kill-squad.

Their sole objective was to eliminate the enemy until aerial infrared deemed the site clear of targets, and then immediately withdraw. What followed was an insertion of infantry to "mop up," and secure any civilian survivors.

"Copy. Be mindful of civilians, but according to satellite footage, their above-ground presence will be minimal. You're clear to engage all enemies. SAK Sacramento, radio for exfil, and await airlift. Will update your HUDs with a waypoint."

Eddie's widened eyes finally shrunk and he nodded repeatedly.

He was partially crushed by the news that San Francisco had been practically wasted by the enemy, but relieved that his Hawks were doing good. The order to SAK Sacramento was surprising, but only for the first few seconds. And then it sunk in and the true magnitude of this catastrophe struck him hard.

SAK missions typically weren't arranged until weeks or even months into any major conflict. Theoretically, of course; in the Great War, it wasn't until the third month that a SAK mission, upon its conception, was executed. And that had been in another country.

Conducting a SAK mission on the homefront felt wrong, but also so right. Again, he reminded himself, and knew that his fellow pilots had to feel the same way—that it was an indication of just how dire the situation had become.

No more pussyfooting.

Eddie's HUD blinked before him and he spotted the

blue waypoint, a caret on the far left side of the display.

"Happy hunting, Ember," the HQ transmitter said. It had become a standard message before a SAK mission, started as a trend during the War.

In this situation, something about it felt off.

Then again, maybe Eddie was overthinking it.

There was a lot askew about this whole conflict. How and when it started, without any warning or attempt at communication. An unexpected, unwarranted attack. Indiscriminate slaughter. Bizarre, inhuman enemies.

Eddie was still reeling from it, subconsciously.

He had to assume that most of them were, even the most battle-hardened.

As soon as the transmission from Headquarters cut out, a lot of the pilots exhaled deep, haggard breaths into their mics.

"I appreciate the access," Alpha said. "Would've been bummed to have been deaf to that whole conversation."

"Of course," Eddie said. "Besides, I'm not a big fan of relaying orders."

"Asshole didn't even *mention* us."

Eddie shook his head. "No, he didn't. But I hate to say it, commander; it was for a reason."

"Run that by me again."

Eddie didn't like it, but he understood it.

"SAK is a Mech-specific mission type. I assume you've heard of it by now."

The Alpha tank commander sighed gutturally. There was defeat in his tone. An admittance not only to what Eddie was asking, but what he already alluded.

"Yeah, you bet," Alpha ultimately said.

"And although Mechs aren't our enemy this time around," Eddie explained, "the criteria still stand."

"We gotta hang back," Alpha said, not much of a question, but an open-ended statement.

Eddie sighed, audibly. "I hate it as much as you do, commander, but I have to admit, I understand the strategy. No offense to what you and your crew are capable of, in those Axes, but with this enemy…their agility, and the size of the bigger ones…it'd be safer for your team if you didn't engage in the close quarters that await us."

A few seconds.

"We copy, Ember," Alpha said, disappointedly but there was understanding in his voice. "Don't we, Bravo?"

"Sadly, yes, sir," Bravo said.

"SAK is an urgent, high-priority order, gentlemen," Eddie said. "I hate to rush any farewell, but a lot is at stake. And every *second* that those *monsters* breathe Earth air is a crime punishable by death."

"Amen, brother," Alpha said, sounding minutely rejuvenated. "You give 'em hell and remind 'em whose home this is."

"You got it." Eddie started to stride his *Adversary* toward the bridge. "Give Chapman and Delta our regards. I'd advise you keep to the interstate, and patrol the exits around the city. Radio us if anything calls for it. We'll keep your Axes painted on our systems."

"Copy, Ember. Happy hunting."

"Likewise."

The Mechs watched the two tanks take the exit ramp. The commander of Bravo popped his torso out of the hatch and waved back at the Ember Wolves.

"Was that Schaub?" Mal asked, raising an eyebrow.

Eddie smirked. "Yeah. I recognized him earlier."

"I'll be damned," H said. "I thought I recognized that handsome bastard."

"I never had a doubt," Luke said.

The team shared some chuckles. Eddie was lightheartedly relieved that he had not been the only one who recognized Casey Schaub.

In hindsight, he wished he had gotten the names of the other crew, before conducting this SAK mission. The Alpha commander, at the very least.

Retaining hope, he accepted that he would get their names upon exfil.

"We still splitting up?" Mal asked.

"Affirmative," Eddie said. "We'll be more effective, and better avoid crossfire."

"Copy that."

"Wally, Nomi, Luke—focus on the west side. We'll take east, and move inward. If we don't cross paths near the Capitol, convene at the Tungsteel factory, northwest Sac. Setting a waypoint now."

Eddie used his finger on the touchscreen radar monitor, and within seconds set a yellow caret waypoint that would reflect on everyone's HUD. It was about two miles from HQ's exfil waypoint.

"Solid copy," H said.

"Happy hunting, Wolves," Luke said.

Their divided teams marched down their respective routes. The Mechs did not follow a linear formation anymore. They trampled street signs, strode through small plotted trees, and leveled curbs, all in their casual stride.

100

Fortunately, most of the country used underground powerlines these days. It had become standard in all cities with populations of 100,000 or more. As of 2065, Sacramento had a little over 612,000, albeit paling in comparison to San Francisco's near-million.

To know that possibly half of the city's 989,000-some citizens were already decimated by this morning's attacks, nauseated Eddie.

Knowing that at least half of them were safely secured in their bunkers, not including others hiding in homes and buildings, did assuage Eddie some. And knowing that his own Hawks were keeping a vengeful eye on the city from above certainly gave him hope.

San Francisco had not been outright taken *yet*, but it was clear that even the AMF wasn't prepared for such a widespread, immense attack.

It was mind-boggling to even grasp that an unarmored, essentially primitive enemy was capable of such destruction, not to mention so quickly.

For every action, however, there was a reaction.

And an AMF reaction...

Eddie's right hand, although clammy already, firmly gripped his joystick. And his left, on the throttle, kept it forward. Cruising at sixty-percent speed, his *Adversary* led Mal and H through an underpass, around debris and corpses, human and otherwise, and up a road that approached a slew of businesses.

They were just at the cusp of Sacramento's outer limits. What awaited them, they hoped was truly a tiny scale version of what San Francisco suffered.

That way, they could blow through this SAK real fast

101

and be on their warpath into San Francisco. Every one of the pilots ached to bring their firepower to their enemy; to show the creatures the same ruthlessness that they had shown defenseless civilians, tenfold.

"Remember," Eddie said. "SAK protocol entails the infil of infantry to mop up and secure civvy survivors. So focus on the enemy. Watch your feet, watch your fire, but if you're boxed in, take the shot. Building damage is an inevitable collateral; let's keep it to a minimum, but don't overthink it."

It was all information that Mal and H knew going into any battle, SAK or not. It was drilled into their brains since day one of the Great War, and every exercise since.

They had training operations in abandoned towns, and environments staged for urban warfare.

Still, Eddie had to say it.

"Copy," H said, easily the most experienced among the three of them. Still, she followed Eddie's leadership, and would cover his six into hell itself if she needed to.

They were all in this fight together.

Not just this particular conflict, but any fight that called for Mechs. Because any such fight meant that a Mech's level of firepower was required, which said a lot about that conflict from the get-go.

And if it took place on American soil, all the more reason to give their all.

Every heartbeat. Every bullet.

Eddie glared at his HUD, through his Mech's canopy. Both hands surgically focused on the controls.

"Weapons hot."

5

Charly hated this. Not just what had become of San Francisco, but having to maintain a certain altitude, and only engage hostiles at a limited range. Which meant that she and her team could only focus on the largest enemies, which they had already dubbed Titans. These were gargantuan, and ranged from elephant-sized to the height and breadth of a six-story parking garage.

She could not object to opening fire at any of these wretched creatures, but only engaging Titans felt like a waste of their time.

While the massive creatures were undeniably destructive, she feared that it was the smallest ones, and their slightly larger kind, that posed the greatest threat to hiding civilians.

For once, she agreed with Fox.

It obviously wasn't the first time ever, but she couldn't have expected to back his opinion so soon in the battle.

After receiving the order from HQ, following their field report of San Francisco's status, Fox gave his teammates a piece of his mind. And didn't care to hold back, like usual, but then he had been most expressive.

Fact was, Charly agreed.

Brick did, too, but was less bent out of shape about it. He happily engaged the Titans, and even argued that they posed just as much threat as the smaller ones, especially if people were hiding in buildings.

The Titans seemed intent on demolishing every structure throughout the city, from libraries to office complexes. Their targets met no specific criteria, and clearly their might wasn't to be underestimated.

So, Brick enthusiastically targeted them.

He enjoyed it on another level, too.

Arrogance, one might say.

He wasn't shy about admitting it, either.

"We're way up here, and big as they are, they're way down there," Brick said, while intermittently Lasing a Titan, and burst-firing his rotary Vulcan. He even smirked, shrugging. "Fuck 'em, ya know? Light 'em up, and at the very least, distract 'em from playing wrecking-ball while people try to find better places to hole up."

Charly tried to see the logic in that.

It wasn't difficult. Brick made great points.

Perhaps she was being too headstrong about what her anger and grief wanted from her. Which was to swoop down like a bird-of-prey mounted with an absurd amount of firepower and mow down the smaller creatures like helpless ants.

To save, to protect, but mostly, to avenge.

She was human enough to give in to that emotion, but soldier enough to recognize its fault.

"Fucking hell, Brick. You're right." She finally caved to the sounder logic. She nodded repeatedly and brought her VTOL around to rejoin Brick's airspace. "And if all three of us concentrate fire on a Titan, one at a time, we can bring it down like bloody Jenga. Quicker than if we diver-sify targets."

"Y'all are bonkers," Fox shook his head rapidly. "I can't believe this. HQ, low-IQ. They don't know shit. Just a small roll of film and our by-the-numbers report. They don't actually *see*—"

"Goddammit, Fox, fall in!" Charly snapped. Spittle sprayed her control panel.

"Jeez, say it don't spray it, lady," Fox mumbled, as if he was in her cockpit.

She sighed, rolled her eyes, and wiped her console. Then she initiated a hover, forty feet above the tallest build-ing in their sector. It was a standing office complex. Fifty feet below, at about half the building's height, lumbered a Titan wounded by Brick's weapons.

He now engaged his own hover thrusters, an aircraft's length away from Charly.

Fox banked high, spiraling over and circling the two of them before hovering to her left.

"Sorry," he formally apologized. "I just wanna...fuck-ing *kill* these things, ya know?"

"Don't I," she said firmly, but not aggressively. She knew the importance of promoting teamwork. "So *help* us. We take down the Titans, then descend the ladder, and pick off the next biggest threats."

"Solid copy," Fox said. "We should strategize, though. Target areas."

"Right, I was thinking that," Brick said. "See, they might not be Mechs, but we can still target arms and legs."

"Too bad they're all fucking eyeless," Fox said dis-gruntledly.

"But I think we can still blind 'em," Brick said.

"How's that?" Charly asked.

"Remember what Bonheur said? Infrared sensors. I think they've got some kind of pit-viper shit in their heads, for sensing concentrations of heat. They might even be focusing on buildings where there are *for sure* a lot of people inside."

"No shit," Fox said, taken aback.

"Any idea where exactly these sensors might be?" Charly asked. "'Cause they have pretty fat heads."

"Well, while y'all have been bitching about our orders," Brick said, "I've been placing my shots and testing weaknesses. Examining 'em, too. I tell you what, our Mech buddies might have better firepower but *we've* got better eyes."

"Fuckin' A," Fox said.

"So what have you found, smart guy?"

Brick ignored the sarcasm, and appreciated her intrigue. It was definitely there, under the many layers of sass. He knew how to read Charly at this point.

And he enjoyed it every time.

"Look at the one below us," he said, pointing at his own belly-camera video feed. "See the lumps on its back and forehead?"

Charly grimaced. "Yeah. They look like huge cysts."

"My bet is it's those. I've blown out a few on its back. Shots to the rest of it seem to barely faze the thing. Those pop, though, and it lashes out. Can't risk getting too close with those feelers, though."

Tentacled feelers protruded from the Titan's dark, fleshy body and moved about it, in the air, as if sentient

106

themselves. Each one was a dirty red color, slightly brighter than the giant's ruddy-gray body. They were about as thick as a station wagon, some forty to fifty feet long, and thickest at the base but tapering to a tip that had smaller tendrils coming out of them, like crimson eyelashes. Feelers on feelers. There were six or seven of them snaking from its upper to lower back and shoulders.

Brick assumed the term "feelers" instead of "tentacles" because, unlike the serpentine, barbed tendons coiling around and worming through buildings, these didn't seem malevolent. Not in their own right, anyway. They simply floated in the air, possibly tasting it, and whenever the beast lumbered past a building—one that it didn't outright swing at or walk into—the feelers would probe it with intrigue.

Even if his infrared-sensors theory was wrong, it was clear that the Titan wasn't entirely blind.

"Is it possible, Brick, that, oh, I don't know," Charly said, such attitude in her voice, the thing goes ape-shit because you're *pimple-popping* it with a Gatling cannon?"

Brick grinned and shook his head. He half-wished she could see his reaction.

And then it faded and the gravity of the situation returned to him full-force.

"Don't be a bitch, Charly, and think about it. At the very least—humor me. Could you do that? Before it saunters right through another goddamn building?"

"Speak of the devil," Fox said, and disengaged his hover. Below, the Titan approached a shopping center, and didn't seem like it had any intention of avoiding it.

Fox zipped around, and engaged the Titan from behind. Instead of using his 20mm Vulcan, Fox utilized the dual Lasers integrated into the VTOL's nose. They were the same design as those mounted on Mechs, and operated the same. He squeezed his joystick's trigger and dragged his aim up the giant's back. Below the highest lumps were curved barbs protruding from its spine. After Lasing through one of the huge lumps and popping it in a spray of slime, the two red beams cut into its thick hide on either side of these spikes.

The Titan reacted as Brick had said.

Fox pulled up immediately, evading the monster's lashing tail. It otherwise dragged behind it, like a massive slug, and the fact that the creature could lift that thing sixty feet off the ground was alarming in itself. The Titan was roughly eighty feet at its highest point, which would be its grotesque head, mounted on a thick neck. The jaws were a mess of jagged teeth and bony mandibles that dripped dense ropes of saliva.

It let out a guttural yet piercing roar as it flung its tail, which ended up demolishing a two-level parking garage.

"Partial success," Fox said, rounding his Hawk back around to hover with the others. "Lased a cyst, pissed it off. What next?"

Brick shook his head. "Fuck it. Y'all focus on the little ones, satiate your impatience. I'll bring this fucker down myself.

Charly started to say something, and then heard a pinch in the audio. She glanced at her HUD, top left corner, where it listed the people on their frequency. Brick's surname grayed out.

108

She scoffed. "He fucking muted us."

A laugh blurted out from Fox. "Sorry, but that's classic. Alright. I'll bite."

Before Charly could address Fox, his thrusters disengaged and he literally dropped from her starboard camera's view.

He jetted toward the buildings below, maintaining a lower altitude than advised. He zipped in front of the lumbering beast, which dragged itself along on its forelimbs, giant knuckled claws of fleshy bone. It bellowed and snapped its jaws at him, futilely.

Ferocious and intimidating as it was, its sluggishness was no match for the assault VTOLs.

Hovering behind it, and about sixty feet above the nearest building, Brick armed his SRMs. A rack of six short-range missiles protruded from an underbelly bay on the aircraft.

Via his HUD, left hand on the touchscreen targeting monitor before him, he painted precise targets. Red triangles lit up around them—two large, pulsing white cysts on the Titan's back.

"Two away," he squeezed the trigger and said, to nobody in particular, since he had wisely muted Charly and Fox.

Two of the four seventy-pound missiles streamed through the air, self-propelled and trailing smoke toward their target. The high-explosive, armor-piercing warheads detonated on impact, finding their targets with pinpoint accuracy.

The Titan had been unaware of the attack, mostly thanks to Fox's distracting sweeps in front of it. The twin explosions ruptured both lumps on its back, and the blasts shattered nearby windows.

It howled a terrible sound of pain and teetered as if it was going to fall.

Sputtering screams erupted far below, not that any of the pilots could hear them so far up and in their sound-dampened cockpits. What poor civilians were in fact on the streets below now scurried in a panic to safety.

Each heavy footfall from the atrocious giant rattled steel and glass on taller buildings, while shattering those at ground level, including car windows.

"Direct hits," Brick said, and elevated higher.

He glanced at his lateral camera feeds and saw no sign of Charly. According to his radar, she was a few miles away. Her icon was not flashing, so she wasn't in an engagement.

Brick would be lying if he said he didn't prefer this kind of combat over what he and everybody else had been accustomed to.

Being shot at was something he certainly didn't miss. On the other hand, there was the undeniable, guilty thrill of engaging an enemy, no matter what kind. It was a drug he had not experienced for twelve years.

Fox was obviously in the same boat.

He whipped his Hawk around, strafing the Titan's left side with his Lasers. Red beams sliced off one of the monster's feelers, spewing thick globules of blood. It stopped teetering and roared thunderously at Fox as he flew by.

Hot, wet breath slammed into his Hawk. Its heat sensors rose into the low yellows, nothing to be alarmed about, just sickened by. Simultaneously droplets of slimy moisture spattered the external canopy and camera lenses.

Fox grimaced and started to bank left for another pass, but something else caught his eye. Through the beads of saliva, or mucus, on his underbelly camera, Fox glimpsed movement below. To the extent that he could not ignore.

He squinted for a brevity before magnifying the camera.

Two boar-like beasts on the streets below, pursuing a pick-up truck struggling to evade. The roads were littered with abandoned vehicles, wrecks, debris, and corpses. Plowing through these obstacles, able to dodge only a few, the large pick-up was losing speed—and its pursuers were gaining faster.

One of the Boars leapt onto an overturned bus and bounded across it, magically not falling through any of the windows its bony, cloven feet shattered. When it reached the end, it leapt off of the bus and missed the truck by mere feet.

Fox descended, tilting his wings to squeeze between neighboring buildings and soaring over the mouth of an alleyway. Thrusters spewed burnt hydrogen and air, an upper-level window shattering in the process, but nobody there to scream about it.

Ahead, in Fox's trajectory, a low bridge complicated his flight path. Street lamps all but overlapped above the road beyond it, making evasive maneuvers pointless in a few seconds.

He risked the shot and opened up with the VTOL's chin-mounted gun. The three-barreled M63 Vulcan rotary cannon spun, spitting out 20mm HEAT rounds at four-thousand feet-per-second. A torrent of five-inch-long ejected casings fell below the craft, clinking off buildings and cars. Every eighth round was a tracer, so to a spectator it would almost look like a streak of white fire hosing the street.

Of course, he only held the trigger for two seconds. And then he pulled up, in the nick of time. The pressure from his VTOL soaring overhead rattled a street lamp and shattered its bulb.

Once clear, he swiftly circled around and decelerated to observe the street through his underbelly camera. A deep sigh of relief channeled through Fox's lips when he saw the truck careen through an intersection and vanish into a tunnel.

Fox eventually spotted the two Boars he successfully mowed down, their once bulky bodies now splattered roadkill.

Meanwhile, Brick circled the Titan to engage it from the front. It had been looking around, confusedly he would describe, despite its eyeless face. Blood and slime dripped down its back, and Brick, strategically hovering, aimed to bleed it from another place.

"Two away," he growled, and fired two more SRMs. They converged on their radar-marked target two seconds after leaving the missile rack. Twin fireballs merged into one, engulfing the Titan's grotesque head.

It teetered back, and the weight of its giant body on its tail was too much.

Watching it fall was bittersweet for Brick. In hindsight, he wished he had strategized it better, and taken it down in a parking lot or courtyard. As it were, it crashed into a Target, leveling the entire structure. At least the building came down on top of it, too, a mess of heavy debris exacerbating its damage.

And shame.

Brick couldn't help but savor the irony that his target fell into a Target.

He ended up smirking, and as dry as the humor seemed, it was genuine, and as brief as it was, it helped.

Helped remind Brick that he was a human.

"Boom, baby," Fox's voice startled him in his cockpit. He forgot that he had unmuted Fox and Charly before circling the Titan.

Mostly because he had started to worry about Charly, and regretted muting her.

"Thanks for the assist," Brick said.

"Anytime, wingnut," Fox said, with exaggerated smugness. "Say, where's your girlfriend?"

Brick scoffed. "You're an ass."

In his cockpit, Fox looked around and shrugged, wide-eyed.

He didn't say anything at first.

"Could use some help, if it's not too much trouble," Charly said, through a soft burst of static.

It was only because of her range.

Brick glanced at his radar. She was three miles northeast. And mobile. And firing her weapons.

"En route," Brick said, and punched his thrusters.

Fox followed.

"What have you got?" Brick asked.

"Decided to heed your advice. You can spare me the "I told you so" line and just revel in silence."

Brick smirked. "A Titan?"

"Copy. One of those Hammerheads we saw during our flyby."

"Christ, they're huge."

"You can say that again. Agiler than Lumpy, too."

Brick smirked again, this time audibly. He shook his head, and in his mind knew he would have to come up with a more befitting name than that.

"Should be fun taking it down with you," Fox said. "Not that I didn't enjoy giving Brick the assist."

"So I heard," Charly said, and grunted before cursing under her breath. The rattling of her cockpit as she fired her Vulcan could be heard, faintly, in the background of her transmission. Then, a sigh. "So, y'all put it down?"

"Should be dead," Brick said, "but who knows."

"Down for the count, for now at least," Fox said. "Also, I killed two of those Boar things chasing some poor guy in a truck."

"Nice," Brick said.

"Want a medal?" Charly sounded so nonchalant.

Brick really did love her.

As soon as his and Fox's Hawks arrived at the scene, what they witnessed troubled them on various levels.

Charly was actively engaging another Titan, but in a much more open space than the other had been. It was stomping around in a circle, swinging a long, swift tail that ended in an arrow-shaped chunk of bone. Below it were two opposing two-lane roads, with a grassy median between them. Hundred-foot buildings on one side, much shorter structures on the other. Banks, parking garages, and office towers.

114

A quarter mile away was a giant Tooth-structure, whose tapered point was buried in the ground. It had cratered the edge of a Costco, and drilled into the parking lot. From where the pilots hovered, its visibility was striking and its sheer enormity was something to both marvel and fear. Even the dark fissures demarcating where the Titans had originally emerged, were massive.

Not just the immensity of the structure was awe-inspiring, though. The fact that, from where they hovered, which was hardly 120 feet off the ground, a horde of them could be seen. Maybe six throughout the entire city; and those they couldn't see clearly from their position were just vague outlines in the distance. Their pale, bone-like coloration made them almost blend into the midday horizon, and surrounding skyscrapers.

Buildings coiled by those barbed, vibrant red tendons were what really shook the pilots' minds.

They weren't here to simply spectate, though.

That time had passed.

What Charly referenced as a Hammerhead, their impulsive callsign for it, was about twenty feet taller than the other Titan, quadrupedal, and more navy bone carapace than soft flesh.

Which made injuring it quite the challenge.

Before now, they had only observed it in passing.

Charly was quickly learning more about the giant creature, but was too busy evading its swinging tail to converse with her teammates about it.

"Pull up, we need to strategize," Brick said, him and Fox hovering a couple hundred feet away. Watching in disbelief.

"Hell I will," Charly retorted, "I got it in the open. Less obstacles for me."

"And for it," Fox said.

"Plus," she growled, "when I bring it down—with or without your help—there'll be no collateral."

Brick nodded. "I learned that the hard way."

"Of course you did." She grunted, juking her Hawk and burst-firing at the Titan's hammerhead shark-shaped, eyeless skull with her Vulcan. She periodically cycled between the rotary cannon and her dual Lasers. "Well, y'all gonna watch and Dutch-Rudder each other or you gonna help?"

Fox laughed and Brick shook his head.

They both adjusted their thrusters and flew into action at the same time.

"This thing is all bone, where am I shooting?" Fox asked two seconds later.

"Center face," Charly replied. "That alcove between its skull protrusions. The sweet spot. Lost three SRMs trying to hit it, but the one that landed pissed it off something fierce. Dizzied it, too, almost fell."

"The sweet spot," Fox repeated.

"Infrared organ, you think?" Brick mused.

"Likely. There's something fleshy in there, hard to tell. A nice, challenging target, though."

"Yeah, like a Mech's armpit," Fox said.

Between the enormous lateral protrusions of its skull, which constantly moved on a thick yet agile neck—above sharply jagged shoulders—was a small alcove. About the size of a minivan, which might seem large, especially to the forty-foot VTOLs and their accurate pilots, but comparably it was quite small. The Titan was gigantic, nimble, and the swinging of its perilous tail made it even more elusive.

Additionally, this alcove sat directly above horizontally crescent-shaped jaws. It kept snapping them, even when not lunging for Charly, making that proverbial sweet spot even harder to hit.

With any weapon.

The Hammerhead's forelimbs were of burly flesh between shoulders and elbows, a rare exposure of what made it an organism and not a sculpture of bone. The only other parts of its gargantuan body that were exposed like this were its thighs and undersides.

Everything else was jagged, dark blue bone. The Titan was eighty-percent carapace, making it a tank of a creature.

Almost the exact opposite, composition wise, of the Titan that Brick and Fox just took down.

Fox swooped low, always the more daring of the three, at least when it seemed unnecessary. The open space between buildings, however, made his maneuvers less risky than usual.

He Lased one of the Hammerhead's exposed arms, but missed. The red beam cut a trough in the asphalt below. As he circled, a mere forty feet off the ground, he spun his chin-mounted Vulcan and hosed out a dozen bullets in a nanosecond. The 20mm explosive rounds found their mark and chewed through the burly musculature of the Titan's left bicep.

It uttered a thunderous cry and swung its tail in Charly's direction, as she circled it up high, still trying to shoot that alcove. She crossed paths with Brick's VTOL and they wove around each other, narrowly evading the massive tail-rock. Its pointed tip grazed a nearby office tower, about eight stories up, shattering glass and severing steel beams as if they were paper.

The eleven-story building lolled to that side, half of one level taken out in an instant.

Nobody noticed.

Fox pulled up, climbing his Hawk through the air, and rising above that same building.

"I think I found a weakness," he said. "Upper arms. Red between the blue. Maybe we can cripple it forward, then swing around and hole-in-one a missile between the eyes."

"It doesn't have eyes, but I get you," Charly said.

"Righty-o."

The three pilots assembled into a collective hover eighty feet above the Titan's head, while it reoriented itself.

They didn't give it long.

Without actually mulling over their whimsical plan, Brick and Charly acted on Fox's proposition with aggressive devotion. It both surprised and delighted Fox; this made him hesitate only briefly. And then, before the massive creature could compute, all three aircraft were circling it, sporadically firing at its exposed upper arms. A scolding, penetrative combination of dual Lasers and rotary cannon volleys chewed through the Titan's fleshy biceps in a matter of seconds.

In its frenzy of pain and disorientation, the Hammerhead abomination snapped its jaws futilely, thrashed its tail ineffectively, and howled in pain. Its deep, gravelly vocalizations were for once alarmingly shrill, all the more evidence that the pilots were achieving their goal.

In the back of Charly's mind, she feared that its cries might attract others to its aid.

For the time being, she focused on this one and this one alone.

Less than thirty seconds after the trio swooped in on Fox's impulsive plan, and worked together as they were destined to, the Titan plunged forward. Its arms were a bloody mess, and perhaps exacerbated by fatigue, it could no longer support its massive torso and skull.

"Shit, that worked better than expected," Brick admitted.

"Don't go kissing Fox's ass so soon," Charly said, determined as ever. She would be damned if she admitted how exhilarated she was from this one little victory.

At least, not until it was confirmed.

Her Hawk circled around, while her teammates hovered far above the Titan's fallen head. It started to lift its skull, while its bloody arms lied on the streets below. Before it could lift its flat chin to peer up at the VTOLs, however, Charly appeared before it, a distraction from the distraction.

No, not quite—she *wanted* it to see this coming.

"Open wide," she growled, her Hawk's SRM rack lowered. Her right finger squeezed the red trigger.

Half a breath after the first missile left its pod, a second followed in its smoke trail. She had already marked the target on her HUD, a red triangle framing that minivan-sized alcove betwixt its skull protrusions.

119

One after the other, before the Hammerhead could register the decision to act, the two missiles struck their mark. They entered that pocket of bone, wherein lied a hidden infrared organ.

Or so Charly, Brick, and Fox imagined.

They could see it clear as day in their minds—

And then, in an instant, it exploded. Beautifully. Vibrant flesh-confetti of pink and red and orange, birthed by a dark plume of fire.

The Titan recoiled, howling a terrible sound, its head whipping back. Swirling with black smoke, twin fireballs rose from the alcove.

All three pilots cheered over their comms at the sight alone. Only once the smoke cleared and the Titan's head lulled forward did they glimpse a sight for sore eyes.

Gelatinous, copious orange blood poured down the center of its curved face. Additionally, the bony protrusion from the left side of its skull had cracked all the way down to its leathery gumline.

The Ember Wolves' excitement was unchecked when they witnessed that half of the Titan's head split open. Chunks of fuchsia brain matter fell out in a vivid mudslide. Its head, what remained of it, dropped to the street below.

A tremor shook nearby cars and building frames.

"You *know* I can't resist saying it, *now*," Fox said, his whole face a sweat-beaded grin.

Charly's VTOL levitated in front of Fox and Brick, the latter of whom deeply cachinnated over the channel.

Fox knew he couldn't get a word in until Brick stopped laughing.

And then he heard Charly snicker in the background,

before he saw on his comms monitor that he had just been muted.

By both of them.

The violent dissonance of atmosphere ripping apart caught their attention. A split of lightning punctuated the structure's descent, in sound alone.

The Ember Hawks scattered not from panic but an aerial shockwave. The Tooth-structure had made landfall six-hundred feet from where they were hovering. A St. Regis hotel burst like a glass beneath a mammoth's foot. The towering Tooth, whose topmost section could not be seen from below, nor anyone on Earth for that matter, was finally at rest.

It only now groaned quietly, or as quietly as such an organic structure could.

Nothing survived within a block of its impact.

The three pilots reoriented themselves, grateful for their Hawks' thrusters and balance. Not to say that alarms didn't ring out for ten seconds. Now that their VTOLs were soundly hovering again, and damage reports found nothing, the pilots themselves could catch their breath.

Despite the healthy camera feeds, Charly manually yanked open her canopy shields. The panels clanged one by one, until her cockpit was engulfed in sunlight. And, given an obvious lack of clouds in the immediate area, it was a lot.

Unusually beautiful weather, on humanity's ugliest day yet.

It wasn't their fault, though.

They couldn't even begin to fathom what would have warranted this.

"Are you guys seeing this?" She asked, squinting and letting her jaw drop.

Fox had miraculously opened his shields barely two seconds after Charly. His small frame shuddered in the aftermath of an adrenaline storm, its residual debris still affecting him.

Brick was not terribly keen to follow in their steps, but ultimately he surrendered to the intrigue and awe. As soon as he did, he gulped and nodded, eyes wide.

"Oh, yeah," he said slowly.

Seeing the structures impaling the earth like monolithic Teeth—well after they had fallen, on a screen no less—could not compare to this. Not even flying by them when they first reached the city.

Firsthand experience of one crashing down from its unfathomable jaws was a whole other; especially that they could look out their canopies and see it six-hundred feet away...

Despite having felt it first, like some kind of fleeting virus, Charly was not last to snap out of it.

She shook her head as if manually dispelling the shock, and then accelerated her thrusters. Not away, but forward. *Toward* it.

She did not close her canopy shields, though. No, she embraced seeing her enemies as they were, and as they would die.

Minus blindfold, Charly cut through the air, ready for battle.

As if reading her mind, the gargantuan Tooth began to crack. Jagged fissures started to open, and enormous, vicious shapes crawled out.

Fox was quicker to follow her than his fear would like to admit, but he didn't relent.

Meanwhile, from around several wrecked buildings, earth and pavement alike split open. Fleshy, toothed tendons snaked out, thick and twisted, muscled and dripping.

"Aw, hell."

Brick sighed and gunned his thrusters.

6

Taking the city by storm was essentially what they were doing, and some Clanners would argue it literally. For their teams of Mechs were war-sculpted families capable of bringing hell to their enemy. Even if their enemy seemed to be hell itself, from above and below, and far outweighed their own violence.

Even still, any Clanner would vow to fight to their dying breath to protect their loved ones.

And in this case, their species.

"Gator's pulling away, tag it!" Eddie exclaimed.

Mal strode around the corner before Eddie's *Adversary* could angle a good shot. Its right arm had been adjusted to blow a leaping creature out of the sky.

Her *Bandit* torso-spun just in time to catch the Gator from slithering into the shadows of a parking garage. A mass grave of fencing lied around her Mech's careless feet. As long as they didn't step on people, the pilots didn't fret about it.

Their focus was slaughter.

As opposed to combating other Mechs, this left the Ember Wolves feeling unnaturally superior. The ineffectively armored soft-bodies of their enemies were no match for AMF firepower, especially alternated between Mechs.

Unfortunately, the Clanners could not sustain their

124

power-trip.

The agility of their enemies, and a hunch that even *they* worked together, too, quickly frustrated the pilots. Mal's *Bandit* was the only one of them capable enough to maneuver obstacles and pursue most of their targets. Especially the ungainly Gators and some of the Boars. Hounds, as they had come to call the vaguely-canine quadrupedal creatures, were far too agile to be caught by any pursuing Mech.

Hunted by one, however, was different.

That seldom happened here, though.

Most of the creatures were either foolish or adamant enough to attack the Mechs themselves. Some tried overtly, without a mote of strategy or thought, captives of their feral nature. Others plotted and hunted, only in packs of their own kind.

This suggested to Eddie's curious subconscious that whatever these abominations were, they *belonged* somewhere. Perhaps some kind of animalistic, biological caste.

His brow furrowed but it never really loosened as engagements seemed unrelenting.

If they really had come from an environment above, and not in a random or fabricated way, then that meant their numbers weren't infinite.

This gave Eddie just the right amount of motivation to not give up. He hadn't quite reached a hopeless moment, but it seemed to lurk in the shadows before that thought.

Fortunately, his *Adversary*'s main innovation was giving agile legs to a powerhouse of war.

Although not adeptly keeping up with Mal, whose *Bandit* was lighter than the *Adversary*, Eddie and her did a good job of dealing with the Hounds and Boars.

Meanwhile H prided herself with stalking the elusive Gators, when she wasn't cutting down anything else for attacking her *Fenrir*.

Regardless, the trio never strayed too far from each other. Even if they exited another's line of sight, as long as they remained within a two-block radius. That way they would appear on everyone's radar, but also not be a vacation to reach.

Only now did a Gator slip by H, after she swung her torso to sling a Hound off her left shoulder. The creature had slammed into a bank's front window, shattering more than just glass.

Now Mal sprinted around a corner just in time to glimpse the Gator's orange-bellied, dark blue tail trail into a parking garage. Stocky legs lowered, it skulked its way under the clearance bar. At ground level, its angle from Mal was inopportune, despite the close range.

Thirty feet from its tail to her *Bandit*'s foot.

She cursed under her breath.

"I don't have a clear shot!"

Her ballistic weapons could not slice through the parking garage at that angle without devastation.

And against the fear that people could be hiding in a packed parking garage of all places, she stayed her trigger finger.

"I do, on your nine," H said, and Mal looked to the left. Eddie was two buildings away, the top half of his Mech visible over the shorter structures.

H's *Fenrir* had approached close enough to time a low-crouch. The Mech was one of two AMF models that could squat its hocked legs the lowest. This maneuver required a locked standing position, no foot movement, and no torso pivoting until after the crouch was achieved. Used primarily for instances like this—acquiring the lowest possible shot.

Additionally performed before a pilot exited his or her cockpit, in order to facilitate dismounting. For ease of cleaning and repairs, AMF protocol prohibited Mechs from being in a crouched state while in their bays.

Presently, H took advantage of her *Fenrir*'s impressive squat. Peering into the sunny-dampened shadows of the parking garage, she adjusted her aim. Before firing the Mech's chin-mounted, integrally belt-fed, .50-caliber machineguns, she glimpsed movement in the structure. Movement that didn't belong to the Gator, nor another creature.

Civilian.

Human.

She briskly lifted her hand from the joystick entirely, not just lifting her trigger finger.

"Advised, advised," she blurted onto the team channel, "I've got civvies in the parking garage. Ground level."

She paused, raking in a dry breath, and raised her reticle.

Crouching people with hands over their mouths darted back and forth, between parked cars. H's heartbeat fluttered and her sinuses tickled with despair. The faces of children hiding in cars with their families could be seen on the second level.

H muted her teammates and a quivering breath of mixed emotions sputtered out. Her brow furrowed and her teeth gritted.

She returned her hand to the joystick and using her left, disengaged the Mech's crouch.

Speaking over Eddie's response, H's voice was fierce and unwavering.

"More civilians on the second level, including children in cars. Here's the deal."

Her spinal cameras picked up movement and she glanced at the monitors. Hounds were moving in, a wave of three pairs, at a distance but closing. Juking around obstacles or leaping over them.

Her deep, surly green eyes stared forward.

"You two, pursue on foot," she said. "I'll hold 'em off up here."

"H, we can't—"

"If you don't, Eddie, *I* fucking will," H said, turning her back to the two other Mechs, and to the parking garage. "But we need at least one powerhouse out here to defend the site."

Eddie grunted through a scoff. "This is insane."

"Are you not an Ember Wolf?" H asked, her implication matter-of-fact. It might have been amusing on a fun night with the crew, but here and now, it was a fervent reminder.

Eddie bit, and H never had a doubt.

"Copy. En route, Mal."

"Feet on the ground in ten," she said, crouching her Mech at the front corner of the parking garage. She urgently engaged standby procedures one second later.

"The hell you are," Eddie said, pushing his Mech to circumvent the buildings as swiftly, but safely, as possible.

The roads were too narrow and buildings not quite short enough to use his hop-jets in the area.

Screams overlapped and echoed out of the parking garage. They were loud enough to seep through H and Mal's cockpits, so Eddie caught the sound in the background of their comms.

"Mal, goddammit," Eddie insisted, "just wait ten fucking seconds and we'll—"

"Eddie, relax!" She shouted, silencing but not halting him. And then her Mech was squatting, its fusion engine not shut down but on standby. She shrugged, a dubious smirk fluttering on her face. "I already did."

Eddie heard the click of her harness release and five seconds later saw a hiss of pneumatic air discharge from her cockpit hatch. She emerged from the squatting *Bandit* moments later, descending to the pavement quicker than he would have liked.

He glimpsed her from his canopy forty feet above, seeing that she was carrying two weapons. A carbine in her hands, attached to a sling she wore, and a pistol…

Tucked into the back of her uniform khakis.

She was really in a rush.

She had, of course, removed her coolant vest but did not bother with her uniform top for obvious reasons.

The three h's. Haste, heat, and heft.

Eddie was so clammy he could hypothetically *streak* through the city, so he of course neglected his long-sleeved uniform top as well.

Arriving two seconds after Mal's boots touched down, Eddie cursed under his breath and hurried to repeat her actions. Crouching the *Adversary* and putting its engine and systems into standby mode.

As a larger Mech, this would take about six or seven seconds longer than Mal's.

He went from standing to crossing the cockpit in one breath, and opened the small arms hatch in the bulkhead. He snatched up a radio earpiece and configured it in three seconds. Then he slung a Daughtry shotgun, the strap featuring several loops that held eighteen extra shells. It was a compact semi-auto shotgun that operated around a six-round cylinder system, utilizing double-ought buckshot, hence its name.

A semi-auto .327 Magnum Corvin pistol got tucked into the tail of his pants, too. He stuffed two extra twelve-round magazines into his side pockets, and reached the cockpit hatch.

"Standby...in effect," the Mech's system voice announced.

"Finally," he sighed, and punched the open button on the wall beside the hatch.

Air hissed and the door opened. He ducked through and descended the squatting Mech, having to relinquish the shotgun briefly. It dangled close to his torso, but as soon as his boots were on pavement, he shouldered the compact Daughtry and rushed into the parking garage.

After Mal.

After the Gator...and anything else that was not human.

"Mal!" He snapped, albeit quietly, and his earpiece picked it up.

Already on the other side of the parking garage's lower level, Mal paused and touched her earpiece. She received

Eddie's transmission, but had to adjust the volume.

The devices were defaulted to the Ember Wolves' specific team frequency, but had limited range.

"I think it went up the ramp," she said, not whispering. She turned on her heels and started walking back.

"H, do you read?" Eddie asked, his voice still hushed. He moved toward the center ramp that ascended to the second level. He passed parked vehicles and cleared every space between them, as well as the cars themselves.

It was only when he reached the base of the ramp that he spotted movement. He shouldered his shotgun and aimed at a car, but slowly, a small boy's head peeked up from the backseat. His mother held a hand over his mouth, her teary eyes implicitly pleading for help.

Eddie's brow furrowed and he lowered his weapon, only to lift a hand, palm facing out.

Slowly, he put a single finger to his lips.

A universal gesture.

She nodded and the two of them slunk back down, out of sight.

A figure appearing to his far right startled him. He swung his shotgun around and a little gasp escaped Mal's lips.

Eddie exhaled deeply and shook his head.

"Almost cut you in half, Mal, Jesus," Eddie exclaimed under his breath.

"I'd have gotten off a shot," she smirked on her approach.

A corner of his mouth curled up but still he just shook his head repeatedly.

"H was right. There are people in some of these cars,"

Mal said. Then she gestured at the ramp. "And this is just the first level. Two more up."

"I'm always right," H's voice summoned in their earpieces.

"Never a doubt," Mal said.

The raucous sputter of .50-caliber gunfire echoed outside. It didn't necessarily startle the two pilots, but it did alarm them.

"Hell's hounds either want in there," H said, through her teeth. "Or in here."

"Give us five," Eddie said, newly determined. He nodded at Mal, whose face was now nothing shy of solemn. She joined him up the broad concrete ramp, six feet to his right.

They passed vehicles, spotting an occasional person or even family hiding inside.

Eddie was relieved they had found a reliable spot, but knew that in larger cities this would not be safe. Nothing seemed to be in places like San Francisco, where titanic monsters could walk straight through buildings like this.

He still eagerly awaited an update from his Hawks, and already regretted not contacting the other Wolves before he exited his Mech.

The adrenaline was flowing more than twice as vigorously as any other time he had exited his Mech during combat. War with men was atrocious in its own way; but these enemies presented an unprecedented predicament. Unparalleled anxiety.

Mal was holding it together a little better than he was, it seemed.

As they ascended to level two, H defended the parking

garage—and herself—from a small horde of Hounds. Six of them attacked in pairs, alternating. She reduced them to four in seconds, her .50-cal cutting through one and its companion in a single sweep.

And then two bounded at her, one missing but the other hanging from her Mech's right arm. Its legs kicked under it, trying to haul itself up onto the horizontal armament.

She swung the *Fenrir*'s torso, hard, and the Hound miraculously held on. Snarling and drooling over Tungsteel as it pulled itself up and tried climbing onto the *Fenrir*'s right shoulder. A large square rack of long-range missiles occupied both shoulders, so it wouldn't be going anywhere—

H looked to her right and saw the creature growling through its disturbing pair of jaws, on the other side of her canopy.

Her reticle floated over another pair of Hounds that were coming at her again, this time on a lower building's rooftop. They had actually strategized to attack her higher up.

She shook her head, amused at their futility.

Her right hand toggled the *Fenrir*'s cheek-mounted Autocannons, hoping that the Hound was in fact standing on one of the barrels. Regardless, when she fired, the ACX recoil was enough to imbalance the Hound, and it fell to the street below.

The other two sprinting across the roof in front of her were sundered by the ACX burst. Explosive-tipped rounds made one erupt in a plume of gore, staggering the other. It rolled off the roof and flattened a hedge bush below.

Another Hound escaped her sights and she glimpsed it run past her, into the parking garage.

"One got past me, coming in hot," H briskly announced, a little disappointed in herself.

Inside, Eddie and Mal spun around to aim down the ramp. A snarling Hound bounded up, juking and dodging their gunfire. Eddie held his after the first impulsive shot, while Mal struggled to track her target. The Condor carbine was a powerful short to medium-range weapon, albeit with advanced blowback compensation to reduce recoil when firing the high-caliber 7.62mm ammunition. Nonetheless, even in Mal's capable hands, it wasn't keeping up with her target.

The Hound didn't just juke to avoid gunfire, it leapt on top of cars and bounded between them, across the whole width of the ramp.

Which made targeting the creature harder, for fear of missing their shots.

Fortunately the creature didn't hurt any of the civilians hiding inside the vehicles as it leapt, given its near-car-like dimensions. Windows did shatter and people did scream, however. If it wasn't for the sporadic gunfire, and the exposed "prey" of Eddie and Mal, the Hound would have turned toward those hiding in cars.

Finally it reached the top of the ramp and pounced toward them, Mal having since backed up to use a pillar on the second level for aiming support. Eddie fully retreated behind one on his side of the ramp's peak, opposite Mal, just as the creature leapt.

It probably assumed that its prey was running.

Eddie hoped for this, and as the Hound turned the corner he knelt, Daughtry shouldered and aiming up. He squeezed the trigger before the creature could realize what had happened, supposing it even had that capacity. Without traditional eyes, Eddie doubted it could see details.

Regardless of its mystifying anatomy, Eddie was certain of one thing—these nightmares *bled*. Easily, too, given the right angle and firepower.

This one took a 12-gauge load of double-ought buckshot to its exposed, fleshy chest. The Hound was knocked back and released a whimpering sound as it hit the concrete. Red and orange blood misted the ground, and Eddie's boots. As its legs kicked and it started to hoist itself up, viscously salivating, Mal stepped forward. She put a three-round burst into its spiked carapace of a head, making its skull bounce on the pavement. Bone or whatever composed its natural body armor had cracked, and from the navy fractures oozed orange gore.

The clawed feet stopped kicking.

Outside, Eddie and Mal heard the sizzling resonance of Lasers discharging.

They exchanged nods and hastened their steps, dividing to cover more ground. They swept the second level on quick feet, aim sweeping and trigger fingers extended, but ready. They didn't want to risk being startled by movement or sound and accidentally shoot a civilian, or a car with them in it.

"Coast is clear," H said, spotting nothing on her motion sensors. Things as small as people didn't show up; it was made for tanks, vehicles, and Mechs. These creatures, even the "smaller" Hounds, fell into the vehicle category, mass and momentum wise.

H took a drag of her water supply. She exhaled and rolled her shoulders. The coolant vest, although burdensome in its own way, was something she felt grateful for. The *Fenrir* cockpit was hot, despite being so capacious. Having twin Autocannons mounted on either side, and machineguns embedded in the chin, definitely didn't help.

Although their heat generation paled in comparison to energy-based weapons, or a cluster of LRMs.

She then surveyed the seven Hounds she had just slaughtered, including one crushed beneath her Mech's right three-toed foot. It was now one with pavement, and the edge of grass.

Two others had come at her after that one crept by and entered the parking garage. She had handled them appropriately.

There was an invigorating relief that fighting these enemies saved her and the others from worrying about armor damage. Ammunition consumption was not a different variable, though…

"Copy," Eddie said. "Still searching for that Gator. It's possible it crawled right on through."

"Possible but unlikely, especially if there are people in there," H said.

"And there are. A lot, in fact. More than expected."

"Good," she nodded. Some relief flowed through her, not unlike the coolant in her vest. "Will make it an easy evac for the SAR team."

"Go ahead and contact HQ."

"Who's Q?" H replied, smirking.

Eddie smiled briefly and shook his head. "Never gets

old, does it?"

"Not yet, Eddie," she replied.

Mal, on the other side of the parking garage, smirked but it didn't last.

She glimpsed a thick, dark blue, barbed tail drag across the concrete, bumping into the rear tire of an SUV, about fifteen feet away. She dropped to a knee and aimed, firing one shot. It missed, popping the tire instead. The vehicle's alarm went off.

The others had not, suggesting to Mal that the SUV was empty. In sudden hindsight, she wished she would have opened fire.

She couldn't have known, though.

"Contact, coming your way," Mal said.

"Copy," Eddie replied, and stared down the iron sights of his Daughtry. He then heard the car alarm cut off, and assumed that Mal disabled it from under the hood. Meanwhile he hurriedly trotted toward the end of his side's row of cars, ready to turn the corner and face the Gator, with Mal far behind it.

As he made that turn, though, he only saw Mal.

"Where did it—" Eddie started to say, and their gazes tracked irrefutable movement.

Center of the back aisle of parked cars, above and behind the lower ramp, were wire railings. They were coiled, making them extremely secure. Apparently just enough to sustain the weight of a truck-sized crocodilian monster as it climbed from the second to fourth level. The next ramp leading to the third level was on the opposite side of the garage, giving the ramps a zig-zag cross-section.

Which meant that in order to reach the fourth from the

137

second, one would have to be about ten feet tall, with a fourteen-foot reach. Stocky as the fifteen-foot Gator creature was, it managed to use its tail as support to help it reach the next landing.

In this case, the inside edge of the top level.

Mal jerked her carbine to aim, and put two rounds into the creature's thick tail before it could pull it up all the way. It snarled out loud, a croaking sound, and then crawled its body out of view. The wire railing along the edge of concrete was practically crushed.

"Roof, H, it's on the—"

"Top floor," Mal said.

"What? How'd it reach the..." H stopped mid-sentence, and her motion sensors picked up something. She spun her entire Mech to face the parking garage. She didn't even need to magnify her reticle. The Gator was five feet at the shoulder, and about sixteen snout to tip of tail. It lumbered across the top level, bumping into cars.

Alarms went off left and right.

"Do you have a clear shot?" Eddie asked, motioning for Mal to follow her.

They ran around to the next ramp.

"Negative. Too many cars. I've glimpsed a few people hiding. Most are...staying hid."

"Smart folk," Eddie panted.

"Why's it running in the first place?" H asked. Then, sarcastically: "Scared of *you* two?"

"Ha-ha," Eddie said.

"It's *gonna be*," Mal's response was much more acrimonious.

She gained speed out ahead of Eddie. Although in

great shape, Eddie was stouter than Mal, and debatably had worse cardio.

"Dammit, Mal," Eddie panted, picking up the pace. The Daughtry didn't help. While not necessarily heavier than her fully-loaded Condor, it definitely wasn't lighter.

"I've got HQ on the line," H said. "Patching you two through."

Neither Eddie nor Mal acknowledged; they were in the zone.

Mal circled a pillar at the top of the parking garage and a pair of jaws lashed out at her. She gasped, her own breath condensing between misshapen teeth as the jaws snapped. The sound itself was startling, and she reeled back. The carbine fell from her hands, but remained slung. She impulsively drew her pistol as she fell back.

Eddie saw her stagger into view again, top of the ramp. He was a few feet away when she fired her pistol. It had two over-under barrels, shrouded by the slide, to increase rate-of-fire. Or, to be fired simultaneously. The recoil of triggering two .327 Magnum rounds at the same time, however, was a struggle for most to handle.

As she fell, one of the barrels flashed and the report was thunderous, but less so now that they were in the open. On a lower level it would have reverberated their eardrums.

The Gator roared and crawled toward her, jaws snapping again. This time more than just gelatinous saliva slung from its mouth, but blood, too.

She had hit it.

Unfortunately, it wasn't hindered.

Only angered.

Eddie, below, shouldered his shotgun and fired twice,

successively, his aim fairly low. He wanted to anticipate the recoil, and handle it preemptively. The first shot was lost mostly to the ground, but some pellets did catch the creature in the lower right stomach. Orange-colored and soft, far more vulnerable than its upper layer.

The Gator growled and whipped its snout to the right. No eyes to glare down at Eddie, but somewhere in its skull, something indicated to the creature that its enemy was nigh.

Eddie wondered if the heat-vision pits were located in its pebbly snout.

It reacted accordingly, spreading its imposing jaws and hissing more than snarling. It turned toward him, and immediately he backpedaled. Down an incline.

Its thick, bleeding tail swung toward Mal. She rolled to dodge it, just as it lifted off the ground to balance its hefty body during an intimidation technique.

Although neither a crocodile nor an alligator of any sort, the otherworldly creature was vaguely similar enough to confuse them even more.

Eddie stopped backpedaling and aimed low, slightly to the left—trying to avoid potential friendly fire, should any pellets stray right. He fired, and the heat splash alone from the short-barreled shotgun wafted into his face; but the buckshot was far worse for the Gator. It walloped the beast in its jowls, and blood dripped out, stippling the concrete.

It stopped walking and shook its head, groaning.

Above and behind it, Mal had stood, wielding her pistol. She fired three rounds into its upper back, around a cluster of protruding spines. She didn't spot any blood until the third shot. She fired a fourth time, into the wound from

140

the third round, and the Gator's head fell forward.

It slumped onto the ramp, potentially crashing into Eddie had he not sidestepped in time. In the same motion, he fired his Daughtry again, hitting it in the left cheek. Where dark blue turned to a fiery orange coloration, which they had established by now was the softer section of these creatures' bodies. Even on the Boars, too. Another trait they all had in common.

Eddie cycled the Daughtry's cylinder and loaded individual shells from his strap.

"Thanks," Mal said, nodding down at him.

"Likewise," he replied, and then hiked the rest of the way to the top of the parking garage.

Their earpiece radios were quiet.

"H, you there?" Eddie asked, touching his earpiece to confirm that it still worked.

"Copy," she said, with a heavy sigh. "Sorry, I chose to mute y'all so we wouldn't distract you. I imagine engaging these things on the ground is much more nerve-wracking than any firefight."

"Affirmative," Eddie said. He exchanged surefire looks with Mal. They then looked out and saw the *Fenrir* standing fifty feet away, its cockpit about eight feet above where they stood.

"Are they still on the horn?" Mal asked, waving over her head.

H pivoted her Mech's torso in a head-shaking gesture. Her voice was confirmation.

"Negative. They, uh, didn't have much to say. But I gave coordinates for a SAR evac."

"ETA?" Eddie asked.

"Forty minutes."

Eddie and Mal exchanged shocked, irascible expressions.

"They're sending a helo as soon as they can. They've been swamped. Turns out Mako and Onyx have hit some major opposition in Stockton. Lost half their convoy already. Possibly a Mako casualty."

"In their *Mechs*?" Eddie exclaimed.

Mal just ran a hand through her hairline, but not her ponytail.

"She had exited," H explained. "To help a civilian. Her death is unconfirmed, and they didn't give a name."

"These fucking *things*," Eddie growled, shaking his head and pacing.

"There *was* word from San Fran, though," H said, her voice heavy.

Mal perked up.

Eddie did, too, in a way—but he detected the somberness in H's tone.

"And?" Mal said.

H sighed. "No word from our Hawks, just reports from scattered news copters, and medevacs, about another structure making landfall."

"They're in the fucking *air*, how have they not—" Eddie cut himself off. He stopped pacing and grabbed Mal's arm. He wasn't hurting her; she was nearly as far from glass as a Mech was from plastic. He didn't hold onto her for long, for he knew she would get the gist of it quickly. And she did, following him right at his heels as he descended the ramp, and spoke assertively. "We're returning to our Mechs. What's the status out there?"

H paused and observed her monitors.

"All clear," she said. "In fact, I've noticed less and less are showing up. Might be a hint that we have 'em beat, and the other Wolves have been kicking ass."

"Might be," Eddie said, his voice gruff.

"Wait," Mal said, tapping Eddie on the shoulder. He paused and faced where Mal had walked off to. Away from their direct route down the ramps, as they wanted to avoid using the stairs.

She had been waved over by a couple between two vehicles. Both people were in their upper twenties and looked like they had seen better days, by their faces alone. Distress had roughed them up something fierce, but comparably Eddie deduced that they held it together well enough.

"Where are you going!?" The young woman exclaimed quietly, clinging to her boyfriend, who clung in return.

"We've radioed for SAR—search and rescue—who will come via helicopter, big enough to evac half of you, if not all of you, in a single trip."

They stared at Mal.

Eddie snapped his fingers, and like cats their eyes jerked over to him.

"It'll be here in half an hour," he said, lying a little. He paused. "Forty minutes max. But they'll be right *here*, and they won't be unarmed. You just have to wait it out. We've cleared this area, we're taking back the city—"

"Thank you, thank you so much!" The woman practically shrieked, but kept her voice hushed. She looked from Eddie to Mal, and released her boyfriend to hug her. "Thank you for your service!"

The boyfriend exchanged nods with Eddie. He was trying his hardest to stay composed under the situation, but it was evident that he had the same gratitude for the pilots as his girlfriend. It was just less emphatic.

"We're very grateful for everything you Clanners do," the young man said. His eyes drifted down to Eddie's chest. He wasn't wearing his uniform, so no Clan insignia. Just a white tanktop clinging to his sweaty, robust torso. The boyfriend then looked at Mal, after his partner detached from her. Above her navy khakis, she wore a black tanktop, over a black sports bra. Although not as outright as Eddie, the fabric did stick to her sweaty skin.

The coolant vests in their Mechs helped while inside, but were not flawless. And out here, beneath the early afternoon, April California sun, doing what they've done, profuse sweat was normal.

If anything today could be called normal...

So, no insignia on their garments.

"Are you two...Ember or—"

Eddie and Mal nodded.

"Our third Wolf is outside, see her legs?" Mal said, pointing at the gap between levels two and three. They were currently on two, by the ramp descending to the bottom.

The couple looked, and saw the *Fenrir*'s hocked legs outside.

"We have three others," Eddie said, "hunting in west Sacramento."

"Hunting?" the girl asked Eddie.

He nodded. "We're here to take the city back. And we won't relent until our Intel says it's safe to."

"The people are grateful," the young man said.

Eddie nodded heavily. "We sure hope so. We're doing our best."

"No, no, I mean," the guy said, waving at the other cars nearby. "These people *are* grateful. We trust you pilots; America owes you a lot. Before you were even called the AMF."

He and his girlfriend, who clung to each other once more, nodded briskly. There was hope shimmering in their kind eyes.

Eddie bowed his head. "We are grateful, too, for your faith and support."

"You'll be safe," Mal insisted, Eddie already on the move. She started to leave. "Stay in your cars. Wait for search and rescue. Don't leave at the sound of rotors or thrusters. *They* will find *you*."

"Thank you!" The couple called out after them.

Mal turned to look at Eddie as they trotted down the ramp.

"You think most of 'em are like that?"

Eddie nodded. Once. "A lot sure are. And the rest? I'll give 'em the benefit of the doubt. Because it helps *me* keep going."

She smiled small, at him. He didn't notice.

He tried not to, anyway.

"It's nice hearing this side of you," she admitted. "The speeches to the team are one thing, but that…that was raw."

"I'm always sincere with my team," he said stiffly.

"Not insinuating you aren't. But it's different, talking to seasoned pilots, and talking to twenty-something civvies under stress. Especially in the face of some alien enemy."

145

Eddie paused, about twenty feet from the sunny mouth of the garage's bottom level. The ankles of H's *Fenrir* could be seen. He looked over at Mal, an inch shorter than him. He seldom could tell.

"You're right," he said. "It *is* different. And I don't expect any of us to act a certain way under these circumstances."

"Meaning what?" She asked, brow furrowed.

He found himself lost in her brown eyes. The sweat on her brow darkened the umber hair above her eyes. The absence of electricity in the parking garage added to the shadows on her face. He could discern nothing shy of beauty in every angle.

Eddie started to raise his hand. To touch her face, or hair. To pull a stray strand from its matted spot on her forehead. To lift her chin. To kiss her.

Some gesture.

A rumbling snarl pulled their attention toward it. An oblong figure emerged from between the hedge bushes just outside and the exterior barrier of concrete. They saw a Gator's jaws lift above the short wall, painted in sunlight. It hastily crawled around the corner of a pillar, entering the parking garage.

"Fucker was lying in wait this whole time," H said, fumbling with her controls.

"Big as they are," Eddie said, shouldering his shotgun. "They sure can hide."

He and Mal began firing. It shook its head at them, jaws swinging and snapping at the same time. Buckshot and bullets alike pattered its snout, shoulders, and some even entered its mouth. It was much tougher than the one earlier on the ramp, and possibly even bigger.

Outside, an unconquerable shadow fell over the tail end of the Gator, which protruded from the garage. Above, H angled her Mech's arms, and fired both Lasers. Two red beams crossed paths, cutting the Gator in half, above its hindquarters.

Inside the building, Eddie and Mal witnessed a flash of red and a splash of warmth. They were substantially startled, and leapt back.

In three seconds the Lasers were gone, and the remains of the Gator painfully crawled forward, using only its forelimbs. Its wound did not gape, instead it had partially cauterized. Where it wasn't, orange entrails oozed out from behind it. The creature became a slug with a slimy trail of its own viscera. Whether stricken and driven by pain, anger, or something else, the Gator continued to attack the two pilots with an added vigor, despite its condition.

Mal had taken the chance seconds ago to draw her pistol, letting the carbine hang from its torso sling. She two-handed it and fired three rounds in rapid succession, into the Gator's eyeless head, before it could raise its jaws again.

The large creature slumped to the ground, its forelimbs splaying outward.

Eddie shrugged off his disarray.

"We appreciate the assist," Eddie said, to H. "Next time, though, give us a head's up, yeah?"

"Oops," H snickered under her breath.

Mal smiled and shook her head. The Gator started to twitch, or at least one of its spines did, and Mal was brisk in putting another .327 Magnum bullet into its skull. The creature went limp.

"Believe it or not, H," Mal said, proceeding toward the exit, giving the Gator a wide berth, "the Lasers didn't do the job."

"I didn't think so; I've noticed, these things are unnaturally tough." She sighed, frustrated. "Better than nothing, though, eh?"

"Absolutely," Eddie said, following Mal's path. She paused and spat on the creature's corpse, bitterness running through her veins. Eddie had not expected it, but was far from surprised. He cleared his throat and shielded his eyes against the sun as they exited the parking garage.

"SAR should be here in, what, twenty minutes now?" Mal asked, en route to her crouching *Bandit*.

"Uh, copy," H said. "Give or take."

"We're good to go, then," Eddie said, parting ways with Mal to reach his crouching *Adversary*. Looking upon it in that moment felt refreshing. "We ought to advise the other Wolves, if possible, to avoid leaving your Mechs unless an absolute emergency. These things, even the smallest ones, are too much to be handled by infantry means. Especially a lone pilot or two."

"Agreed," H said. "I'll try to reach Wally, but I tried earlier while y'all were inside, after I mopped up out here, and couldn't reach 'em."

"They must be...out of range," Eddie said, panting as he climbed his Mech and reentered the cockpit.

Mal was already ahead of him. Her hatch sealed shut and she happily relinquished her body of the carbine, pistol, and extra ammunition she had stuffed into her khaki pockets.

The heat outside, and what they had just endured, had her for once yearning for that coolant vest. And, of course, to be behind the controls of her *Bandit* again.

Eddie, likewise.

After stowing his weapons and disconnecting the earpiece radio, Eddie snatched a protein bar from the rations compartment. He unwrapped and chewed it like a cigar, hands-free, as he returned to his seat. His pilot's throne. He pulled the harness belts over his shoulders, secured it at the center, and plucked the half-eaten bar from his mouth. He then turned his head and took a swig of water from the supply tube, which was a little warmer than room-temperature, due to standby mode.

Any other time in combat he would have grimaced, but at that moment he hardly noticed. Then he returned the bar to his mouth, gnawing at the last half, while disengaging the *Adversary* from standby.

"Powering on to full capacity," the mechanically feminine voice announced.

Eddie's dried-sweat, strong hands found their home again on the Mech's controls.

The *Adversary* started to rise from its crouch.

He was facing the *Bandit*, and witnessed it do the same seconds later. Which meant that, despite having entered her cockpit sooner than Eddie, Mal had taken more time to return to her seat.

Eddie would not be shocked if she hadn't been privately contacting HQ for an update on Austin, Texas. Either the city as a whole, its status against the enemy and how its Clanners were faring in battle, or, if not all these things, trying to contact her parents directly.

149

He wouldn't be surprised if any of his fellow pilots were doing that, without telling him. Nor would he be upset. He himself had thought about it, though only in passing, in regards to his brother in London. After dismissing it the first—or was it the second?—time, Eddie took it on good faith that his brother was fine.

Optimistic or foolish, he refused to acknowledge either. He just put his heart into it, and left it at that. Meanwhile, he had to focus on preserving the health and lives of his Clan, and anyone else he could, within the realm of reason, strangers or otherwise.

"All systems online," the voice declared, its casual tone a constant.

It was supposed to be comforting. Sometimes he found it condescending. H agreed. Luke wished he could just mute it entirely. Or change the voice.

"H, how's your ammo holding up?" He asked, while glancing at his own HUD readings, already apprehensive of what he would see.

"Well…not great, Eddie," she sighed. "I used mostly my MGs and Lasers on the bodies around us."

Eddie didn't have to second glance to notice all of the slain creatures surrounding them, in front of the parking garage—but he did anyway, because it pleased him.

"And an occasional ACX," she continued. "LRMs are full, thank God, but my 20-mil is running low, and I'm about one burst away from drying out the fifty-cal."

Eddie knew every Mech inside and out, although their standard payloads weren't always the same, especially with veteran Clanners like H.

Most Autocannons of the same 60mm caliber as H's

Fenrir stored no more than eighty rounds, but given the cramped location of them on her Mech, it held about sixty. Which constituted fifteen trigger-pulls, given that both barrels fired simultaneously, two rounds each. Taking this under consideration, Eddie wanted to know specifics.

"Define low," he said. "For your ACX."

"Six shots," she said, referring to the amount of trigger-pulls, not the amount of rounds.

"Damn," he grimaced. "And your fifty?"

"The, uh, the MGs are at twenty-two rounds."

Eddie shook his head. "These damn things aren't the same as Mechs, not even tanks, by a long-shot."

"You're telling me. Tracking 'em with the fifty is a pain in the ass, with the ACX even worse. Except Gators, they make for a fat target, not as nimble as the Hounds and Boars."

"At least you've got all your missiles," he said, "and let's not forget about EBWs."

The importance of energy-based weapons in any Mech-driven battle was crucial. If a Mech's ballistic weapons—Railguns, Autocannons, machineguns, Vulcans, and even missiles—were depleted, it would still have its EBWs. Lasers and Particle Projection Cannons, although both of them produced more heat than any ballistic weapon, especially the PPC.

Nonetheless, they never ran out of ammunition.

"Checking in," Mal said with a heavy sigh, "and I'm running low, too. No EBW's, though, so feel free to hit me with a different speech of consolation."

Eddie kneaded his temple. She was right. The *Bandit* wasn't fitted with a single energy-based weapon. Part of its design flaw, as the *Bandit* was among the first Mechs to ever be designed. Its intention was meant to be a support Mech, though, in a small package. The chassis was designed for mobility, and use on reconnaissance missions. It was the perfect strafing Mech, still capable of sniping enemies from afar with its Railgun. The lighter tonnage prohibited more than eight heat-sinks at the most; additional units would be required if it ran any EBW platform.

This didn't make her the weakest link in their Clan, though. Every Mech served its own unique role in combat—with enemy Mechs at least.

Their new enemy today was testing limits they had never imagined addressing.

"Still," H said, as if reading Eddie's mind, "at least these monsters are easy on the armor."

"Got that right," Eddie said, Mech torso swiveling to face the *Fenrir*. He noticed no sign of armor damage, just some blood splatter around one of its feet, an arm, and the side of her cockpit. Their enemy's blood was a vivid red-orange, impossible to miss. There was something disturbingly beautiful about it, too, but Eddie would never admit this.

"Ahem," Mal cleared her throat. Eddie spun the *Adversary*'s torso to face her *Bandit* again. "So, the Railgun is tip-top, and that's where my good news ends. The .50 is down to forty-one. And the Vulcan's at ninety-four."

Eddie's jaw clenched. The three-barrel Vulcan fired at a rate of two-thousand rounds-per-minute; while that was only a theoretical number, since no Mech actually carried anything near a thousand 20mm rounds, the weapon was

fast nonetheless. Typically utilized by skilled pilots in le-
thal bursts, to chip away enemy armor, especially on
weakened limbs, and to neutralize tanks.

Their enemy this time was different, however, a biological species from, possibly, another dimension entirely.

Eddie didn't like to dwell on that notion too much. The
second he started to entertain some theories buried in his
mind, the second he started to lose grip on reality.

Insane as it had become, so fast.

"What about you, boss?" H asked.

Eddie ran his eyes over his HUD's ammunition
readouts once again.

"Honestly, not terrible," he replied. "Autocannons are
at seventy-percent and SRMs are full."

"But?" H said, detecting an unease in Eddie's voice.

"But," he sighed, "I'm thinking we exfil back to base
to resupply and then head out again. Check Sac off our list
and maybe join the Hawks in S-F. I hate not having an update for so long. Especially knowing that more of those
damn things are touching down."

"Big copy," H said.

"Wanna contact the others?" Mal said, knowing that
the *Adversary* had the best comms range of the three
Mechs.

"Yeah, I'll try to radio Wally. Shouldn't be out of
range, especially here."

He reached for his comms monitor, bottom left of his
HUD. Seconds before he was able to toggle an open broadcast, his comms crackled with life.

And it wasn't either of the two Mechs before him. He
shot a glance up at his comms display on his HUD, and saw

Wally's name blinking green. It had been gray, as were Luke and Nomi's.

"Come in, come in, do you read, Eddie?" Wally's voice, gruff as ever but even more so now, broke through.

Immediately, before even responding, Eddie connected H and Mal.

"Loud and clear, big guy," Eddie said. "What's your status?"

"Speak of the big, bearded, handsome devil," H muttered.

"Well, hello, beautiful," Wally replied, grinning in his Mech. He was pushing the gargantuan *Mastodon* faster than it ought to stride in an urban environment. Luke and Nomi were out in front of him, leading the way, her *Rottweiler* on point.

Wally glanced at his spinal cameras and his heart sank.

"Good, uh, *great* to hear your voices, really." Wally gulped. "Mal there?"

"Had a couple close calls on foot," Mal replied, smirking. "But I'm here."

"On foot? You crazy?"

"She is, copy," Eddie said. "I followed, though, so I guess we all go a little mad sometimes."

"Right, well, don't go doing that again."

"Saved some civvies that are gonna get an evac soon," Eddie said. "But shit yeah, I'd rather not again."

"That's great news, boss," Wally said, panting as if he himself was running. His impatience broke the ice. "But we're kinda in a pickle here. Got some mean things on our ass and we're disturbingly low on ammo. En route to the exfil for an airlift back to base. Just got off the horn with

HQ. They're having…radio problems with S-F, though. And bad news from Stockton; the other Clans have hit heavy contact."

"I heard a little here and there. What exactly is your status?" Eddie began accelerating his Mech away from the parking garage. Due northeast. "We're en route to my way-point, too. The Tungsteel factory."

"Copy, same. Nomi's got the lead."

"Luke, fall in!" Nomi suddenly barked into her mic. Although Eddie and the others couldn't see it, not even their arrow icons on their radar due to range, Nomi pulled her *Rottweiler* off to the side, out from their mobile column. Her Mech's legs agilely missed a building, but crashed through a traffic light. Sparks flew around its knees.

"Leading!" Luke shouted. "Keep up, Wally!"

"Trying!" The *Mastodon* lumbered onward.

They stuck to the main road, a four-lane path bisected by a grassy median.

"Can you get a shot?" Luke asked.

Nomi stayed behind, off to the side. "I…I think…fucker's fast, though."

Her target was a multi-legged, scorpion-like creature, the insectoid comparison only due to its six legs and arcing, barb-tipped tail. Otherwise the monstrosity, which was roughly as large as a firetruck—ladder extended—was incomparable. It had a fleshy composition despite a dark carapace on its spiked back, the base of its tail, and around its jointed six limbs. The face was eyeless, its jaws constantly snapping, lined with large canines and fierce incisors.

The barbed tail sporadically snapped forward, as a scorpion's might, even when it was clearly out of range. It kept itself from being engaged by the Mechs due to its agility and preference of pursuit—on top of buildings. Crawling up and over them, sometimes leaping from one to the next. All but demolishing their rooves and upper levels.

Worse yet, there were two on their trail.

And on the road between these creatures, a pack of four Boars and two Hounds.

"You're an Ember Wolf," Wally snapped, "fucking prove it!"

Nomi yelled incoherently and fired her Autocannon. The barrel recoiled with a clang, a muzzle flash temporarily blinding her. The impact was visible, though; one of the two Crawlers scampering over a squat building took the two 80mm rounds to what would be considered its face— a couple of feet before its carapace began. The jaws were decimated in a spray of blood and chunks of flesh, and one of the ACX rounds cut underneath its carapace, rupturing it from within. The creature tumbled into a parking garage, but not with enough momentum to crash through it.

Nomi magnified her aim as she breathed heavily and brandished a small smile. She saw its tail go limp, heavy like a flaccid oak tree, thumping to the pavement.

"One down," she said, and then her face became stern again. She looked to her hard left; the other Crawler was making progress, leaping instead of scurrying.

Nomi started to backpedal the Mech, and swung her torso to fire at the large creature, as it bounded from one roof to another. This time her ACX missed its mark—but not entirely. The first HEAT round clipped its tail, exploding and blowing off its barbed end. The creature shrieked splittingly, slowing its momentum. The second round streamed into the sky.

She began to spin her Mech around and follow Wally; she could pass his *Mastodon* in a few seconds. But she decided to lag behind a little, and try eliminating the creatures galloping after them, down the road directly at their six.

"Keep going, Luke," Nomi said. "I'm gonna hang back and cover our six."

"Copy, just watch yourself."

"Always."

Meanwhile, Eddie, Mal and H proceeded across west Sacramento toward the Tungsteel factory waypoint. Just a few miles outside of their HQ-designated exfil.

Listening to Nomi and the others exchange battle chatter was nerve-wracking for them. Simply because they could not actually be there to help.

It did, however, count as incentive.

To move faster. To make damn sure they reached their waypoint on time, if not before the others, so they could clear the area and be prepared for whatever followed their comrades.

Eddie had faith that they would be prepared, strategically.

Psychologically, however, was up for debate.

7

Titan or not, it fell. The trio of pilots had begun to think, and even joke out loud, that their moniker for these colossal creatures was a little too generous. In Greek mythology, Titans were Gods. But these abominations perished against the might of man and humanity's greatest technology.

They were far from Gods.

If anything, by slaying them, Charly, Brick, and Fox felt as if *they* had the godlike power.

Of course, none of them let that feeling go to their heads. It was, at most, a healthy power-trip. An ego boost for the pilots who were clearly overpowered by the giant creatures, no matter how many their Hawks put down for the count.

And although it seemed like a lot, five was hardly pushing it. San Francisco was a huge city, by population seventh in the United States. By area, twenty-second. So, a lot of residences packed into small districts. And the pilots had not even reached that part of the city. The three of them had a lot of ground to cover, but knew that soon—they hoped, very soon—their Mech support would arrive.

Mako and Onyx from the south, and their own Ember Wolves from the north.

Currently, the Hawks waged their war around central San Francisco.

After another Titan was killed, again by utilizing the assumed infrared organs as weak spots, the pilots assembled fifty feet above a dense metropolitan area.

"Well done, everyone," Charly said. She had since loosened up a little. They felt freshly invigorated every time they so much as wounded a Titan, let alone crippling it. That always heralded its finish.

"They don't call us a Clan for nothin'," Brick cheered.

"What do you think *they* are, huh?" Fox asked. "Clearly not a family. They don't attack like it. Less organized. More chaotic and shit."

"Here we go again," Charly rolled her eyes.

"No, come on, now. Let's give it a thought, for a fucking *second*," Fox insisted. "We're not robots, afterall. Shit, speaking of which, we've got a far better view and detachment from battle than any *Mech* pilot."

Brick said "oooh" as if they were at cadet school, and Fox just insulted Eddie to his face. Not quite, but behind his back. And the other Clanners for that matter. It was, of course, nothing sincere or personal; just the usual banter from Fox.

"Be that as it may," Charly chuckled briefly. "I just don't want to get into theories. It's not our job."

"Besides," Brick said, pivoting his aircraft to face Fox's. He and the others certainly felt more intimate with the fighting of their enemies without the canopy shields in place. The glass was UV protected, anyway, and shaded against the onslaught of unobstructed sunlight.

Brick could almost see Fox's face behind his own canopy, in his Hawk. They each hovered about twelve feet from one another's nose, thus forming a vague triangle of space between the front ends of their Hawks.

"You can't argue there hasn't been some semblance of strategy when these things first started touching down," Brick explained. "I mean, c'mon—over every major city across the globe? That takes coordination."

Fox nodded. "Yeah, okay, sure. I'll give 'em that. But so what? Whoever or *whatever* is in charge—*up there*—it's not these guys down here. Not even a Titan has the wits to plan something like a mass invasion."

"What about a horde of them? Like a senate."

Charly's voice was small, not wanting to give in to Fox's crazy theories, or baiting her thought on the matter. Ultimately, she couldn't resist, not with Brick chiming in.

"A senate!" Fox laughed. "A democracy of Titans! Oh, boy."

Charly started to retort and then Fox's laugh died down and he breathed a few genuine words into his mic.

"Well, it's possible."

She didn't know what to say.

"Anything is possible, Fox, at this point," Brick insisted. "But, Charly, I'm gonna have to disagree. Fox is right. But to an extent."

"So they're not devoid of strategy, but once they hit the ground, they become feral?" Charly said, confused.

"Exactly," Fox said, sounding delighted. Not in the concept they discussed, but the fact that they discussed it. Meanwhile, the mastered technology of fusion engines offered an unprecedented fuel supply. Their thrusters worked on a similar level that Mechs' hop-jets did, only with less tonnage, and more exhaust. For Hawks, thrusters were able to recycle molecules in the air, breaking them down to utilize the hydrogen needed to burn for propulsion, bolstered by a petrol supply to prolong flight time.

And oh, how grateful Fox was for this technology. He could discuss the nature of their enemy for hours! Of course, that would be excessive. But in his mind, anything theoretical could be in excess without issue.

"My guess is," he proposed, "some sort of hive-mind. A collective consciousness, wherever these things are from. Up there…a world, hungry for a new conquest."

"Us. It wants to…*eat* us?"

"Our planet, yeah," Fox shrugged. Now he felt ambivalent about sharing his ideas. Were they *too* insane? Or just the right amount?

"That would explain the gigantic Teeth…" Charly thought out loud, quietly. Her brow furrowed and she looked around, through her canopy. Vague silhouettes of other Teeth could be seen in the far distance.

"And the tendon things, like tongues?" Brick said.

"Or just that…tendons, or veins…oozing parasites—these smaller creatures—to neutralize us. Ripen our world for devourment."

Silence from Fox's comrades.

"I get it," he admitted. "Y'all think I've gone off the deep end. I under—"

"No, actually," Charly said, but was interrupted herself. Their comms frequency picked up a transmission from Headquarters.

"Ember Hawks, do you read?" The masculine voice was mildly frantic.

"Copy, clear as the weather up here," Brick replied,

trying to keep their mood buoyant, despite the bedlam.

"Good. Have been directed to relay some valuable Intel for you, from a Clan in Boston."

"How are they doing up there?" Brick asked, brow furrowed with concern.

The gravity of the situation was inescapable, ultimately. That what had happened to San Francisco was happening globally struck a chord deep in everyone, especially military personnel, which they couldn't mute. Only momentarily suppress.

"Dreadful. It's worse in condensed states like the northeast. But—there's been a glimpse of light."

The transmitter's voice softened a little. This injected some hope into the Hawk pilots.

"We sure could use some of that," Charly said.

"Our Intel from a Hawk team in Boston, with the help of their Mech crew, has revealed weak spots *on the larger enemies. They're calling them Behemoths."*

Already the pilots were scowling.

Charly shook her head and mouthed the word "Titan" to herself.

Fox gave in very quickly. His eyebrows raised and he nodded, as if to say "not bad."

Brick just rolled his eyes.

"The theory that our enemies use infrared to target us, and focus on larger population centers," HQ proceeded, *"has been confirmed. These* Behemoths *have heat vision organs located on certain parts of their bodies. It's fascinating, and very helpful Intel."*

Charly all but sighed gutturally into her mic. She certainly wanted to.

After a pause of silence from all three pilots, the HQ transmitter cleared his throat.

"Are you there, Ember?"

"We read you, HQ," Brick said. He started to add to that, with a lick of attitude in his voice, Charly could tell, but she chose to take the reins.

"We appreciate the input," she said, albeit blandly. She then remembered just how grave the situation was, world-wide, and that it was apparently worse in regions where large cities were closer together. So she changed her tone to one of sincerity. "Give Boston our best. And spread the word. We're in this together; it's the only way we'll triumph."

"Loud and clear, Ember," he said, with his own inflection of hope. *"Godspeed and happy—"*

Hunting? The word was abruptly chewed up in white noise. It cut into their comms channel like a dagger of static, making the pilots grimace and recoil.

As they moved to decrease the volume on HQ's transmission, a different sound stole their attention. Ear-splitting, a roll of thunder enrobed in the cacophony of lightning cracking. The weather remained clear, and the absence of clouds—

They pushed apart, all but dissipating from the sky. The atmosphere gaped violently, in the wake of something big falling. From above. From the exospheric tear. What descended threw a huge shadow over the pilots; but it wasn't uniform. It spun and fell wildly, without the linear direction of its predecessors.

A Tooth-structure.

It landed some eight-hundred feet from the hovering

Hawks, demolishing an entire block, and then some. The shockwave destabilized their VTOLs but they reoriented quickly, cursing into their mics.

"Look!" Fox exclaimed, spinning his Hawk to face a particular direction. The others looked, and saw the nearest standing Tooth in the distance move. Toward its peak, which was not fully visible through the clouds surrounding. But surely, it moved—slowly, sluggishly, cumbersomely. With its movement came a splitting sound, indescribable.

The pilots looked around them. Tooth structures in the distance, every one they could spot, moved like that one. Churning from above. Dragging its massive point through the Earth.

And then...they stopped.

"What the hell is going on?" Brick said, raking in breaths.

"I don't know but maybe we should—" Charly was interrupted by a grand sight.

The tooth-like monoliths began to fall. With a crack of thunder that sounded for miles from each, they tore away from the sky and toppled. Some of them cracked as they did, and Titans crawled out in a panic. Whole blocks were demolished as the structures fell, some of them even gained momentum and rolled a few hundred feet, bulldozing buildings.

Brick exclaimed in awe.

Charly accelerated in the direction of the nearest Tooth, hoping to take advantage of the disoriented Titans crawling out of it.

She announced as much into her mic, her voice frantic, but her hands steady at the controls.

Brick clenched his jaw and followed suit. Fox didn't hesitate, either.

They had a job to do, a duty to uphold.

Moreover, their rage was a constant flame.

"Charly, bank right!" Fox shouted all of a sudden. She reacted in an instant, complying with trust. Her VTOL jerked to the right, and a giant Tooth in freefall plummeted through the sky, missing her by ten feet. The pressure alone pushed her craft but she readjusted safely.

Brick exclaimed and witnessed the structure hit the ground ninety feet below them, on its side. The sound was deafening, the effect devastating.

"They're falling, more are falling from above!" Fox exclaimed, awe and terror in his voice.

The three pilots paused in flight to hover and peer up, through their canopies. To witness with their own eyes. And sure enough, from the fissure in the sky above the planet, as far as their naked eyes could see, things fell. Their proportions varied. From the giant Teeth-structures to Titans and smaller creatures, too.

It wasn't just San Francisco, either. From their perspective, the others were merely specks in the sky, but they rained the Earth wherever the giant Teeth had touched down previously.

"It's like," Fox breathed, "their world is dying."

Charly's brow furrowed. She wasn't sure she had heard him clearly.

She started to say "what" into her mic, and suddenly a vast shadow covered their VTOLs.

"Scatter!" She snapped.

The three of them banked in a panic, narrowly evading

a Hammerhead plunging through the sky. It howled piercingly as it passed them, and their crafts angled to witness its descent. The giant creature landed on the square roof of an office complex, blowing out the windows of the top three floors. Metal groaned and some of the building crushed under its weight. It flailed until it fell off, demolishing a parking garage below.

It rolled, either dying or out of breath, they couldn't tell which.

There was no time to observe, unfortunately, let alone engage it.

More shadows loomed over them, and the surrounding buildings.

"Evasive maneuvers!" Brick shouted.

The pilots watched their camera feeds, keeping an eye on their blind spots as they dodged the falling objects. Most were creatures, dozens of Hounds and the occasional Titan. For every tenth Hound that fell was a Boar, and for every three of them, a Gator.

They didn't make these deductions, though.

It was pure chaos in the air.

However, Fox's mind raced to other places, too. He pondered ventilating his thoughts, but wasn't sure it would do them any good.

Something heavy struck Brick's right wing, and bounced off. His VTOL tilted in that direction, and alarms wailed in his cockpit. He glanced up and around frenetically, but was able to level out the craft.

What she glimpsed as a Hound, in Charly's starboard camera, fell onto a thruster. She immediately reversed propulsion, while it scrambled to cling onto the wing. Heat flushed out, ablating the creature's barbed face. Its flesh melted away, and it tumbled off the thruster with a whimper.

"Nice one!" Brick cheered.

They were not staying in the same area. They flew when they could, occasionally diving and climbing, banking and rolling. Doing whatever they could to evade the downpour of creatures, and even an occasional chunk of "tooth."

The shards were enormous but never more than a quarter the size of their source.

One fragment of a Tooth fell so fast that it stopped spinning and just plunged, but at a slight angle. It ultimately impaled a skyscraper diagonally, showering glass and debris onto the streets below.

"I hope nobody was hiding in there," Fox said quietly, gulping.

They all hoped with the full weight of their hearts that no populated shelters, makeshift or otherwise, were among the impact zones.

"I think," Fox said, finally thrusting his inner voice outside. "I think their world is dying! I think…they attacked us as a last-ditch effort to survive!"

"Yeah, but they underestimated us!" Charly shouted.

Fox couldn't tell whether she was pulling his chain or actually submitting to the theory.

At any rate, he agreed.

"Goddamn right!" He said with a fierce certainty.

"They bit off more than they could chew, eh!?" Brick added.

Everybody nodded fervently. The anger in their veins,

the determination like a conflagration.

After a few minutes of evasion, the amount of falling creatures diminished. But not entirely.

Suddenly a cluster landed on Brick's VTOL, after he evaded the freefall of a lumpy-backed Titan, its feelers lashing out to no effect. Two Hounds and a Boar panicked for traction on top of his VTOL. The latter was the most ungainly and graceless, but managed to find some purchase just behind his canopy. Its wretched shadow fell over the reinforced glass, darkening his cockpit briefly.

He rocked his wings while hovering, trying to rid the creatures but afraid of losing balance.

"Hold still, dammit!" Charly said, locating him and hovering herself. She levitated her Hawk about six feet above Brick's, facing the left side of his fuselage.

"Trying," Brick growled, frustrated as he fought for stability. The Boar on top was not as much of an issue as the two Hounds; one on his right wing, and the other trying to make it from his tail to his left wing.

Charly risked using her Lasers, knowing that they were less likely to cut through the Hawk's armor than a HEAT round from her Vulcan.

Still, glimpsing those twin red beams not thirty feet away, was unsettling for Brick.

And then a thick orange goop splashed the top of his canopy, directly above his head. He glimpsed the video feed from his tail-mounted camera, and witnessed the Boar slide off his Hawk, in separate pieces.

One of the two Hounds had managed to leap from his tail to his left wing, momentarily destabilizing his craft. He cursed under his breath and suddenly rocked his wings to the left, making one of the Hounds skitter off but still cling on, while the one on his right rose into the air.

Charly hit it with both Lasers, decapitating the creature before it could compute what was going on.

"Whew!" Brick cheered.

"Incoming!" Fox announced, his Hawk's nose climbing through the air, both Lasers and Vulcan spitting at the same time. He managed to neutralize two creatures midair, but a few got through his salvos.

Brick evaded by clinging his VTOL onto a tall building, its magnetic skids deploying and attaching himself like a squirrel.

Charly darted out, spinning around, but a Boar clunked her tail and sent her into a spin.

"You got this, hang on!" Brick exclaimed, spectating upside-down.

"I'm trying, I'm trying," Charly said through her teeth, the panic in her voice unnerving to hear, especially for Brick.

And then he looked forward—which, in his current position, was skyward. From the gaping fissure in Earth's exosphere, stretching thousands of miles long and hundreds wide, still, more creatures fell. Far less than before, but a continuation nonetheless.

"Fuck me," he muttered, and disengaged the VTOL's magnetic skids. His thrusters pulsed and he rebounded off the building, rattling windows and frames in his wake.

Meanwhile, Fox was above, but not for long.

Below, Charly had regained control of her craft, only thanks to a Gator that had fallen laterally on top of it. How its back had not broken across the upper ridge of the

169

VTOL, behind her canopy, she didn't know. As heavily as it vibrated under the impact, she was shocked her craft survived, too.

Somehow, though, the creature's haphazard landing gave a semblance of balance to the Hawk.

She engaged her hover-thrusters so she could focus on the controls, but the damned thing wouldn't stop thrashing. Not unlike a real crocodile, or alligator for that matter.

The alien beast salivated and snarled as it wildly rolled on top of the VTOL, either in a frenzy or trying to actually find traction.

"Fuck, that thing's big," Brick mumbled, in disgust, as he approached her right side.

"Hold back, Brick, I got it," Fox said, descending, both of his wingtip thrusters inverted. Once dangerously above Charly's VTOL, he interrupted her exclamation with a swift rotation of his thrusters.

Fusion heat pulsed out, setting the Gator on fire. It uttered a disturbing sound before flopping off, and continuing its freefall. It would not go much farther before crashing through a street lamp, its partially melted body breaking in half.

"Gross," Fox said, with a chuckle.

"Real slick, Fox," Charly said, smirking and shaking off her disorientation. She guided her VTOL to the side, and picked up her nose to match Fox's hover height. She started to thank him more genuinely, but the blocked sunlight above their VTOLs stole the show.

The falling Titan robbed her of breath, and Brick's cry out garbled their team frequency.

It all happened so damn fast.

The Hammerhead roared like thunder as its colossal body flailed through the air. Its arrow-shaped tail end tore through a building before the mass of it came close. The VTOLs tried to scatter and evade, but a massively clawed hand lashed out with success. As if it could grab them and keep itself from hitting the ground. The hand merely clipped Fox's VTOL, scarring his canopy but not breaking the glass. The claw tip, like a sickle-shaped boulder of bone, briefly snagged the nose of his Hawk, and the sheer pressure overwhelmed his thrusters.

In the next instant, the Titan fell away, beneath them, a heavy victim of gravity.

"Pull up, Fox, pull *up*!" Charly screamed in a panic.

"Eject, eject!" Brick shouted at the same time.

Their voices collided over the airwaves, which were already mauled by static.

Fox struggled to yank on his ejection handle, between his legs. It wouldn't function. Alarms blared as his craft spiraled violently. One of his thrusters was shot, spewing smoke through the air.

"Canopy damaged. Canopy damaged."

The automated voice repeated, ever so calmly, amid a cacophony of alarms.

Fox looked up. The canopy was more than just scratched, it was warped around the seal.

He wasn't going anywhere.

He looked through the panel to his left.

"Their world is dying!" he shouted into his mic, laughing madly. "Their world is dying, don't let them take ours with—"

Brick and Charly watched his VTOL spin into a high-rise apartment complex. Glass exploded and the aircraft burst into flames. In the same instant, the Hawk's fusion engine went critical, ballooning into a white-hot sphere before exploding concussively.

No more than ten seconds from the moment that his craft was clipped by the falling Titan.

Which was either dying or dead on the streets and buildings below them.

They hovered a hundred feet in the air, sobbing and snarling and muttering incoherently. Disbelief and rage unlike any other flowed through them, an otherwise indescribable storm of emotions.

The futility of what they felt was easily the most exasperating.

More shadows and falling creatures forced them to put a pause on their lamentations, and take flight. This time, they did so with aggressive haste.

Nothing to bury. Just ash and debris.

"Where are we going, Charly?" Brick asked, sniffling but growling the question. He blinked rapidly as he pushed the throttle, knowing he couldn't properly evade if he had to see through a curtain of tears.

"Hydro is low. Need to refuel and..." Charly shook her head and repeatedly punched her instrument panel, or rather the dashboard above it. Her hand hurt but nothing broke; in her, or on the panel. She sniffled and gritted her teeth. "Need to refuel and resupply the Vulcan."

"Yeah, I'm low, too." Brick paused. They rocked their wings and banked pendulously, evading creatures that continued to plummet in their own panic.

The pilots moved faster now because, apparently, the

amount of creatures falling was significantly less than minutes ago.

"But that's not your only reason, is it?" Brick asked. The channel hummed with silence. "Is it, Charly?"

"I get it, Brick. Intel can't feed us a damn thing about this mess. It's a whole different ballgame than actual war. I ain't mad at 'em."

She had gone off on a tirade in the past, during the Great War, about bad Intel that cost them lives of ground and air support crew.

"Then *what*?" Brick pressed, pushing his VTOL to catch up to her. If he pressured it too much more, and if they didn't let up off the throttle at least a little bit soon, then they would burn through their hydrogen reserves and drop like twenty-ton flies.

Charly's breath was gravelly.

"I want to see my family."

Brick knew she wasn't referring to her biological family, as much as he could feel that urge in her, and himself, to reunite with their loved ones amidst this chaos. No, he knew what she meant.

They were a Clan for a reason.

And all of them had just lost a little brother. In H's case, like a son she never had. And for Wally, the second one of the day.

It was only three in the afternoon.

As climactic as the falling of creatures and their giant structures was, as relieving as it could be in theory, it had come with tremendous collateral.

Both pilots played Fox's last words over and over in their heads.

Their world is dying. Don't let them...
Take ours with it.

8

Much to Eddie's chagrin, the rest of the Ember Wolves did not peacefully assemble. They had enemies trailing them, which was no surprise considering their last transmission with Wally. Staccato bursts of static plagued their comms, which confused them as they got even closer to each other on radar.

It certainly wasn't good news for whenever they tried to contact HQ again.

Which, Eddie hoped, would be extremely soon.

"Sensors are tracking six, is that right, Wally!?" H asked, skirting around a squat building to Eddie's far right. Her *Fenrir*'s torso swiveled to the left, while her legs continued forward.

Nomi was in the lead, Luke at her *Rottweiler*'s heels. Behind trailed Wally, lumbering at eighty-percent his top speed. The *Mastodon*'s steps shuddered nearby buildings, shattering some windows and even sending small tremors up some of their Mechs' legs.

"Uh, copy," Wally replied gruffly, glancing at his spinal camera. "Four Hellhounds and two Warthogs."

Eddie and Mal smirked at their slightly different monikers for the creatures. Meanwhile, H was unflinching in battle-mode.

"Don't bother engaging, I'm gonna light 'em up," she

said aggressively.

"Maintain stride, Wolves," Eddie commanded, his sightline of the approaching Mechs clear over the tops of shorter structures. This block in the industrial district of Sacramento was home to mostly open roads, squat out-buildings, and the occasional refinery tower, all surrounding the Tungsteel's primary factory.

He and Mal stood forty feet apart, their Mechs like inert gargoyles on either side of the factory's property gate. The once sturdy, eight-foot-tall chain-link fence with razor-wire was now warped debris under the Mechs' feet.

"Be with you in ten," Nomi declared.

"Following," Luke said, and rotated his torso to the left, glimpsing the fiercely painted *Fenrir* stride onto a narrow backroad between refinery towers.

"Keep forward," Wally demanded.

Luke spun around to focus on his and Nomi's arrival in the company of Eddie and Mal.

Meanwhile, the *Fenrir*'s arm cannons lit up. Dual Lasers converged on a pair of Hounds pursuing Wally. They would have just about caught up thanks to their agile maneuvering of rooftops had it not been for the Lasers. Their perfectly seamless beams cut through carapace and flesh in an instant, killing one of them and wounding the other. The second Hound lost a back left leg and its right hanged on by a thread of muscle; blood and entrails oozed out of the wound where cauterization didn't occur. The creature let out a whimpering sound of pain, but not defeat.

It continued pushing forward, until it came to the edge of the roof and had to dismount. A crippled attempt, the creature fell through scaffolding in a cloud of dust.

H swung her torso and backpedaled, lining up with an alley between outbuildings. Her Lasers shot out again, and her lead on a Boar aligned perfectly. The two beams converged on its bulky left shoulder, splitting it in half.

"Three down," H said.

Luke and Nomi had just arrived at the factory, dividing to fan out and cover Wally's approach.

A Hound got past H's aim and leapt onto the *Mastodon*'s narrow lower back. Its large, fierce claws acted as grappling hooks to the giant Mech's armor, clinging successfully.

With each lumbering step the *Mastodon* took, though, its hundred-ton carriage vibrating at twenty miles-an-hour, the Hound was almost shaken off.

"Wally," H said briskly, "torso-twist left, hard!"

He complied right away, just as the Hound was trying to climb around the left side of the *Mastodon*'s narrow waist.

Its enormous, inverted-triangle torso spun in that direction, and the Hound's left arm got caught in the pivot. Metal grinded flesh and bone; the creature howled and lost its purchase, slipping off of the Mech's back. Wally's continued pace swung the Hound around the left side of the *Mastodon*'s waist, ripping its arm off at the shoulder. A succeeding foot crushed the creature against asphalt, one-hundred tons sufficing to flatten its existence.

"Did I get it?" Wally asked, glancing at his camera feeds. His Mech slowed as it reached Mal and Eddie.

"Where are the other two?" H thought out loud, indirectly answering Wally.

"Nomi, H, seek and destroy," Eddie commanded.

"Happily," Nomi said, and strode back into the industrial labyrinth of outbuildings and refinery towers. H joined her, albeit on the other side of the block, circling around.

"Mal, cover Wally," Eddie said. "I know these things seem powerless against our Mechs, but I don't want to give 'em any hope."

"Copy," she said, her Bandit circling Wally, but she was immediately puzzled at why exactly Eddie had attached her to Wally.

"Uh, and what will you have *me* do, boss?" Wally asked.

"Hop on the comms. Raise HQ. I want immediate exfil, and an S-F update on our Hawks."

Eddie's voice was nothing less than assertive.

"Copy, on it," Wally replied. He was relieved to immobilize his Mech, and not be on the move after so long. Better yet, not have to watch where he was stepping. He took a quick swig of his water tube and gasped refreshingly while tapping at his comms keyboard.

"Team channel if you can," Eddie added.

"You got it."

"Where the hell did they go?" Nomi said. "You seeing anything, H?"

"Negative. They must be hiding. Strategizing."

"So they're not as dumb as they look," Nomi said, half a question and half a statement.

"We've noticed," Mal chipped in, "that they can be quite cunning. But still not a full toolbox, if you catch my drift."

Mal tapped her temple as she said the last part.

"Right," Nomi smirked. She dabbed sweat from her

brow with a knuckle. The coolant vest did its job, at least, but she wouldn't be devoid of perspiration in the snug confines of the *Rottweiler*'s cockpit.

"Luke, on me," Eddie said, leading the *Rhino* away from the factory gate. Luke followed Eddie's *Adversary* toward the entrance of the factory, which was made for people, not Mechs. There was, however, a Mech entrance in the rear, for testing and the like.

Eddie stopped outside of the entrance, as if what he said would literally be just outside of earshot from the others. Of course, she contacted Luke over a private channel.

With a glance at the comms display on his HUD, Luke noticed this.

"How y'all holding?" Eddie asked. "I didn't notice any damage. But Nomi—"

"It's been stressful, to say the least," Luke said, thumbs hooking the sleeveless gaps in his vest and briefly pulling it away from his chest, to the extent that his harness would allow. Air swept in, complementing the coolant, and he smirked briefly, crescent dimples on either side of his mouth. His head tilted back and he took a deep, husky breath.

"Likewise," Eddie replied. "But it's clear we're the dominant species. So long as we don't get out of our Mechs."

Luke chuckled. "Yeah, no shit. I mean, what kind of nut-job would do that?"

Eddie cleared his throat. "Mal. And, well…"

Luke straightened in his seat. "You crazy bastard. You went after her, didn't you?"

Eddie shrugged. "How could I not have?"

"Why'd she dismount in the first place?" Luke's brow furrowed.

Eddie sighed. "Spotted a Gator in a parking garage full of civvies hiding."

"Damn. That's tough. She's a brave chick."

"No shit. And a little batshit, too."

"Y'all are perfect for each other, then," Luke smirked. Before Eddie could deflect, Luke did it for him: "Hold up. You call the Croc-things "Gators"? Ha. That's cute."

Eddie grinned, shaking his head.

H's machineguns fired, the reports vaguely audible from where Eddie and Luke stood. Their Mech torsos spun to face the buildings in front of the factory, and all they could see were muzzle flashes from the *Fenrir*'s MGs, its torso pitched down slightly.

Opposite her, Nomi's *Rottweiler* levitated over a building, its hamstring-mounted hop-jets punishing the roof with fusion propulsion. Airborne, she howled into her mic as she opened up a clear line-of-fire to her target. The bewildered Boar turned its ugly head, gawking up at the aerial Mech, its infrared pits flaring.

It made a howling sound a nanosecond before the *Rott-weiler*'s Autocannon opened up. One after the other, two 80mm HEAT rounds popped the Boar like a red-orange flesh balloon.

Nomi exhaled as she eased up on the hop-jet thrusters, and brought the Mech down thirty feet away. Its digitigrade feet came to a rest on pavement, and Nomi briefly rocked in her cockpit seat.

"All clear," H declared. She swung her *Fenrir* to face the *Rottweiler* at her two o'clock. "Nice shooting, baby."

"Hell yeah," Nomi grinned. She followed H back to the factory, where Mal circled Wally, who remained quiet on their comms.

"They never disappoint, do they?" Eddie said to Luke, in regards to H and Nomi.

"Not once," Luke replied, smirking.

Eddie led Luke back to the front gate. Eddie's light-heartedness and patience was about to evaporate in the blink of an eye. It occurred to him that he still had not heard from Wally about HQ.

The *Mastodon*'s torso turned on stagnant legs, to face the approaching *Adversary*.

"Sorry, boss. They're not responding. Nothing's getting through."

"Fuck's sake," Eddie grunted. He shook his head and kneaded his temple.

"Suggestion," Nomi said, punctuated by a drag on her water tube.

"Fire away," Eddie said.

"We move to HQ's exfil waypoint. Open ground, clear of the city. Better comms, probably."

"Yeah, was thinking that," Eddie said. "But then we'd be deserting Sac, before confirmation."

"Eddie, I think we're done here," H said bluntly, albeit with a tone that carried a form of defeat.

"I second that," Luke added. "Coming from the other side of the city, we mowed 'em down good. Seldom a sign of survivors, except here and there. Sac had better prep than San Fran and the other bigger cities."

"Right, more time to get underground," Eddie thought out loud, in accordance.

181

"Besides," Wally added, "we're all low on ballistics. Armor's up a hundred-percent, for once, which is something to be said, but not for granted."

Eddie nodded repeatedly. "Alright, alright. But I'm still not crystal about leaving Sac entirely, not before aerial confirmation."

"I'll hang," Mal volunteered, already knowing where Eddie was headed.

"Negative. You're ballistics-reliant. H will hang back, with Luke—"

"I'm set," H said. "I don't need a babysitter. No offense, Luke."

"None taken. I know you can handle your own. Besides…I'm ballistics reliant, too."

"I can't object," Eddie said. He looked at the *Fenrir* through his canopy. It was maybe forty feet away. He could vaguely see H through the rounded, UV-protected canopy. "Stay keen, H. As soon as we get word, I'll have Mal send for you, if we can't raise you on comms."

"Copy," H said, checking her radar and sensors. Nothing moved within a two-hundred-foot radius.

Eddie turned his Mech away, to face the westward direction of HQ's synchronized waypoint. It was a blue caret on everyone's radar.

"Fall in, Wolves," he said, and took a step.

He stalled his *Adversary* the split-second that their comms burst to life. Through a sea of static came a transmission from Headquarters.

"Son of a bitch," H said quietly, half-smiling.

The relief of hearing from HQ was bittersweet. The

white noise surrounding the transmission, and the distressed voice of the man on the other end, was reason enough.

"...read...Ember...there's...Francisco...interference...do you..."

"Wally, hotspot the transmission and bounce it to us," Eddie said. He turned his Mech around and faced the open road just outside the factory gates. "On me."

"I'm reading outside interference," Wally said. "It's not base."

"That's a relief," Nomi said softly.

They assembled just outside the factory gate, or what was left of it, trampled. The cluster of six Mechs had the *Mastodon* at center.

"Rectifying the signal," Wally said. "Should be coming—"

"—scans are positive, I repeat—"

"Hold, HQ, we read you," Wally said, his voice booming for clarity. "Had a comms issue. Please repeat full transmission."

"Copy, Ember. Brace for bad news, and good news. Care for which first?"

"Good," Eddie said. His subconscious rationale was simple—he didn't want to crush whatever the good news was, with his anger about the bad news.

"Well, Sacramento aerial scans are reading positive for enemy neutralization. Scattered threats are slowly heading to your location. The Mechs are the largest active output of heat in the city. Bunkers hold their own, and other groups of civvies are currently being evacuated via helos with gunner support."

183

Eddie and Mal were particularly relieved, and delighted to hear that. Nomi even cheered and H chimed in with some reassured positivity.

It all died down rather quickly, though, as they waited to hear either more good news or the bad.

"On another good note," the voice from HQ said, taking everyone by surprise, *"we've established comms with Onyx, Mako, and San Francisco."*

Some cheering all around. It lasted maybe two seconds, before the transmitter's solemnity crushed their spirits. And then what he had to say was the real blow.

"Unfortunately," he continued, sighing heavily, *"the last bit of good news comes with heavy collateral. Reports surrounding S-F, from news copters before their radios cut out, relay what we believe to be an early sign of defeat for the enemy. Their massive structures are collapsing, and breaking apart. The larger creatures crawling from them are either injured or disoriented. More fall from the skies above S-F, and other major cities* worldwide. *It's a climactic phenomenon that's been given the name* Skyfall.*"*

The pilots, had they been standing in a circle and not within their Mechs, would have muttered amongst themselves. As it were, they merely mumbled, not into active mics. Or, in their heads bustled a tumult of thoughts.

"What is the collateral?" Mal asked.

"Our Hawks, isn't it?" Eddie hated to make such a bold guess.

"Affirmative," HQ replied. The transmitter cleared his throat. *"We, uh, haven't been able to establish stable contact with them. The last time we did was about half an hour*

184

ago. The link broke up and that's around the time we received reports about Skyfall."

Now, some audible mutterings over the team channel. As HQ tried to get in a word, Eddie shook his head firmly and then expressed the same gesture with his voice. It could be shockingly smooth when he wished, but under duress or when strained in anger, it was a carnivorous, gravelly tone.

Which was now.

"We're at the exfil, if you've got helos evac-ing civvies from Sac, and aerial scans give us the green-light to go, then why the *fuck* don't I hear thrusters in the distance!?"

"W-We read you, Ember, we're just, we're short-staffed and running around with our heads chopped off. The base is a chicken coop and everyone's just trying to, to—"

"Christ Almighty," H exclaimed, "is there someone there that can fly us outta here or *not*? Our birds are probably being pelted by who-knows-what from above, likely low on hydro and ballistics, *as are we*, and—"

"H!" Eddie snapped, cutting her off. As much as he valued her tirade and energy, he could tell she was nearing the deep end herself. If anybody was going to go off, it would be him. As their tacit leader, it was his burden.

"Sorry, boss," H muttered. She understood, and was grateful for Eddie speaking up. She knew, of course, that her outburst wasn't underappreciated.

"Listen, HQ," Eddie said through a deep breath, "we are in need of an ammo resupply and nothing else. Send us an airlift to our location, at your predesignated waypoint, and we'll rearm en route to S-F."

The transmitter stumbled on his words before getting the statement out.

"That's a, uh, that's a negative, Ember. The dangers in S-F are too great to risk you, or any of our birds. We've been trying to sync a waypoint to the Hawks, just north of S-F, a safe place to evac to."

Eddie laughed irately. "Are you fucking kidding me? The *dangers* are too great? Who do you think we are!? Cadets!?"

"Of course not, Ember, but my CO has made it clear that—"

"And what do you mean a *safe place*?" Eddie continued. Despite the coolant vest and the inert Mech, his skin was starting to heat up, his tanned face turning pink with frustration. "You just *said* that the risks—"

"Onyx and Mako have hit an impasse in Stockton. They managed to clear the city of hostiles but not without taking great losses." The transmitter now spoke with firmer conviction. Clearly, enough to successfully interrupt Eddie. *"Their* entire convoy *was wiped out. Tanks, sir,* tanks. *Your own convoy has since been recalled to base, but are trying to redirect traffic out of Sacramento, and away from San Fran. The* survivors *of Onyx and Mako are being airlifted back to base as we speak. They, too, are low on ballistic ammo and some need medical attention."*

He took a deep, haggard breath. Eddie did not butt in, nor did anyone else. They felt a grave weight settle on their shoulders, and in their hearts, at this news.

"We should have been clearer," the transmitter said, regret palpable in his voice alone. *"That, under no circumstances, you are to leave your Mechs. But...we also*

understand that the drive to protect others is what makes you Clanners who you are. And all of us who aren't pilots respect that from a deep place. However…it has cost two lives from Mako, one from Onyx, and injuries sustained by others.

"Now…three airlifts have been sent to your exfil way-point. Two miles from your current position. They should be arriving in…about seventeen minutes, now. You'll be brought back to base for debriefing and rearmament.

"We here have faith in the Ember Hawks. Unfortu-nately, even their transponders aren't reading on our radar. But we strongly believe that's because of interfer-ence from Skyfall, nothing else."

Nobody really had anything else to say now. Whoever the nameless HQ transmitter was, had done a great job at getting a hold of himself and telling the Clanners like it was, no bullshit.

No matter how much it hurt to hear.

"One more thing," Eddie summoned the boldness to say, "you have to give me your *word* that we will be air-lifted to the waypoint you set for our Hawks, as soon as we're debriefed, if they aren't back by then. Whoever your bravest, or craziest, pilot is—just take us as far as they will go."

"You have my word, Ember," the man replied, without hesitation. There was a soundness to his voice that didn't make Eddie dubious. *"Now double-time it to that waypoint and keep an eye out for any hostiles that may be tracking you from within the city. Airlift is fourteen minutes out. Godspeed."*

Eddie nodded. "Solid copy, HQ."

187

Wally terminated the transmission and Eddie didn't waste a second. He spun his *Adversary*'s torso in the direction of the exfil waypoint, and then aligned the Mech's bird-like legs.

"On me, Clanners. Mal, if you would? Lead the way."

"You got it. Want me to keep pace?"

"Negative. Slingshot ahead, paint any targets that you might cross. Shouldn't be any this way, though."

"Copy."

"Let's move out," Eddie announced, leading the others off the factory property, trailing behind Mal at three-quarters the speed. "And hope that our wingnuts get their tails outta S-F without any trouble."

"If HQ's got that much faith in 'em," Nomi said, "*I* got faith."

"I second that," Luke said.

"We all do," Eddie nodded.

Instead of circumventing an L-shaped outbuilding ahead of him, he hit his hop-jets and thrusters built into the back of his Mech's torso levitated it over the structure. The pronged toes established a secure landing on the other side, pancaking an empty security booth in the process.

There was no treading softly around harmless collateral damage like that. Especially when time was of the essence.

Behind him, visible in both his spinal cameras and on his radar, the rest of the Ember Wolves, except for Mal, followed him closely. Only Wally lagged behind a little, simply because of the *Mastodon*'s cumbersome design and weight. All things considered, he was pushing it to the max, and likely thinking of Farooq with every hundred-ton step.

Ahead, Mal was making great progress real quick. She weaved around structures like a jaguar, or an Oviraptor, which was the name of the *Bandit*'s prototype. Of course, not anyone could hop into such a light and nimble Mech, and be able to maneuver it so agilely.

Wally had tried, before, on the training course at base. And it had been fuel for many laughs in the weeks that followed.

Mal had developed a special talent with the *Bandit*, and was as attached to it on a personal level as H was with her *Fenrir*, and as Eddie had quickly become with his *Adversary*.

Of course, nobody could rival the unique connection that Wally had with his *Mastodon*. No matter how many of them came off the production line, his belonged to him—and Farooq—exclusively.

"Motion sensors are picking up zilch," Mal announced, as she passed a Sacramento watertower at the outskirts of the city.

"Copy, same. Wally, how's it reading back there?" Eddie asked.

"Uh, just a little hot."

"Inside or out?" Eddie raised an eyebrow.

"Bit of both," Wally replied. "Nothing to be alarmed at, though; inside, at least. I'm counting, uh, ten…no, eleven…hostiles on my six."

"Which ones?" Eddie asked. "We *did* notice you three gave 'em your own names. Kinda off from ours."

"Right, well, call 'em what you want, they're all ugly and fast. Even the Crocs when they wanna be."

"Eddie and Mal call 'em Gators," Luke laughed.

"Though I bet H was the one who dropped that name."

H scoffed audibly. Playfully.

"Anyway," Wally said, getting back to the nitty gritty, "I've only got 'em on motion sensors right now, no cams. But…they're starting to fan out, and might circle around to try hitting us from the front. I think Mal will see a few in-the-flesh before any of us do."

"Thinking they're smarter than us," Nomi said, belligerently. She shook her head. "We'll show 'em."

"Fucking right, we will," Luke practically snarled. His brow furrowed. "Can't believe Onyx and Mako lost pilots. And their whole goddamn convoy."

"Burn that spite like kerosene, Luke," Eddie said. "Use it. Get ready to slaughter any fucking thing that isn't human. Clanners are Gods on an open field."

Typically, in Mech-on-Mech combat, especially one-v-one duels, urban environments or anywhere that had obstacles, such as mountainous regions, were ideal. For taking cover, both to avoid getting sniped by an enemy Autocannon or Railgun, and to strategize heat maintenance.

However, their enemies here weren't Mechs.

And they had that much to be grateful for, despite the insanity that entailed the situation.

These creatures were soft-bodied, when it came to Mech weapons. And in an open environment, which was what awaited them outside of the city, they could cull the creatures with superior firepower.

Eddie itched for that moment to come.

And before he knew it, with great relief, it had.

His *Adversary* breached a chain-link fence as if it were a strip of paper, and he strode out into a vast pasture of

190

rolling hills, painted with greens and yellows. The latter was thanks to sweeping swathes of Bermuda buttercup, which gave the fields a beautiful tone, complemented by the mid-afternoon sunlight.

As delightful of a sight as it was, especially one for the sore eyes of the Ember Wolves, who had been waging a strange war in the dull urban sprawl that was Sacramento, Eddie knew the beauty would be short-lived. While the colors would remain, their combat and bloodshed would enhance nothing; if anything, it would scar the terrain.

More collateral damage.

"Spread out, prepare to engage—" Eddie started, but Mal interrupted him, and about sixty feet away started striding to his ten o'clock.

"Contact, at your seven," Mal announced. Her Vulcan lit up, tracers streaming through the gentle sunlight. The rotary cannon made a *bdddt* sound, in bursts. She added, with a lick of excitement: "Look alive, Clanners."

The rest of the Mechs, which had cleared the city's outskirts and trekked into the open field, continued striding forward at a slower pace, while pivoting their torsos to the left.

Nomi paused, tracking enemies to her right.

"At our four o'clock, too," she announced. "Little fuckers."

"Light 'em up," Luke said, pairing up with her.

Although low on ballistic ammunition, they knew how to burst-fire effectively. However, in the open, the Hounds proved annoyingly agile. On the other hand, Boars and any Gators foolish enough to approach were easy pickings.

And then there were the Crawlers, which were brand

new to Eddie, Mal, and H.

Two of them had been pursuing Ember toward the edge of the city. Now they leapt free, alarmingly nimble. Their six legs definitely assisted this, the arched tail providing additional balance even when striking.

"What the living hell is *that*!?" H exclaimed, as she marked the targeted Crawler on her HUD. It linked up with everyone's, and within five seconds their heads-up-displays were a swirl of red markers. Whichever one a pilot targeted, a red triangle outline formed around it, and remained until neutralization.

"We call 'em Crawlers," Nomi said. "For obvious reasons."

"No shit," Eddie said, glancing at the one that H engaged.

Meanwhile, he had his own targets.

The *Fenrir*'s dual particle projection cannons slashed blue lightning downrange. The PPCs had a distinct sound that was not unlike the crack of lightning, paired with a violent hiss as charged plasma electrified the air. And scorched through whatever the helical beam struck, whether it was a tree, window, concrete barrier, or epidermal layer of Tungsteel on a Mech.

In this case, a pair of Boars galloping together. Instead of suffering devastating wounds that cauterized instantly, the power of the PPCs obliterated their bodies. Red-orange mist, tinged azure from the beams, spewed into the air. Alien gore, splattering Bermuda buttercups.

Eddie followed H's same strategy—focusing on his EBWs instead of ballistics. Even when taking under consideration that their airlift was due in ten minutes, so

192

theoretically they didn't need to worry about ammunition conservation.

If something went wrong, though...

So Eddie stuck to his guns, literally, his energy-based weapons. In his case, that came down to chin-integrated Lasers and shoulder-mounted PPCs.

Using PPCs, or even a single one at the moment, seemed gratuitous. H neutralized their larger targets quickly, alternating between the heat-sensitive PPCs and the .50-cal, with an occasional Laser thrown in when she could afford it.

The two Crawlers, fierce as they were and revolting as they looked, were less intimidating in the open. An array of Lasers downrange cut through their legs, even where bony protrusions armored their joints. It took more than one slice of a Laser to cut through, but it was satisfactorily dealt with before they could close on any of the Mechs.

More to the pilots' advantage, they had virtually end-less space to backpedal.

H then utilized her dual PPCs to neutralize the Crawl-ers, with the help of Wally's Railguns.

They were down to three Hounds when all of a sudden the creatures stopped juking and stood still. Had it not been such a strange sight to witness, the pilots would have simply blown them away. Instead they watched as their en-emy sniffed the air and exchanged sweeping, eyeless glances. Then they snarled into the air and made choking sounds, eventually pulling back.

Toward Sacramento again.

"I don't know what the hell that was all about," Eddie said, befuddled, "but don't let 'em back into the city!"

Everyone knew he didn't have to say it twice.

Mal's right arm-mounted Railgun split one of the Hounds in half. A diaphanous trail of smoke left a thin trail through the air, where it had passed.

"Beautiful hit," Eddie remarked.

Luke and Nomi's Vulcans sputtered out rounds after the other two. Streams of ejected casings littered the grass, trailing smoke in their wake. The brass was ultimately trampled into the soil by the pacing war machines.

Both creatures were effectively evasive, outmaneuvering every bullet, even the HEAT ones that blasted the earth at their heels.

Eddie lined up his PPCs, but paused when Wally stepped into his line-of-sight. Before Eddie said a word, the *Mastodon*'s two Lasers split the creatures from hindquarter to shoulder, both at once.

"Uh, I've got big readings on my radar," Eddie said. "Sensors are labelling 'em as enemy Mechs; gotta be at least fifteen tons to make that limit.

"How many and where?" Nomi asked, rotating her *Rottweiler* to look in the *Adversary*'s direction. Southwest of Sacramento.

Eddie gulped, once he saw the giant beasts lumbering down the fields from a distance. About half a mile and closing, distressingly fast with each massive stride.

"It's…It's looking like three. They're…two, three times as big as the *Mastodon*. Get ready to…stack up."

Eddie knew he had to get a control of himself to properly lead this battle.

Once the other Mechs turned to look in the same direction that he was, they witnessed the enormous monsters come more clearly into view. The pilots used their magnified reticles to observe, in unparalleled awe, the Titans' approach.

Every crushing footfall announced their arrival, even up in a Mech cockpit.

"Uh, boss?" Luke gulped, cycling his weapons. "We're gonna need bigger—"

"Egos?" Eddie interrupted, nodding briskly. "We sure are. Ember? *Open fire!*"

9

If he and his pilots lived to see the drab interior of a debriefing room after this engagement, he was afraid he wouldn't have the adequate words to describe their targets. Surely, he imagined, that others had seen them elsewhere. In San Francisco, most likely.

Back of his mind, Eddie was certain of it—that these gargantuan beasts were the same monsters that had broken out of the giant Tooth-structures first seen on the screen back at base. And those same structures, now reportedly collapsing as well as falling from the sky—a good sign, no debate.

Although clearly there were some consequences. Among them, the dangers that his aerial comrades— friends—must still be facing, and then there was *this*.

As with any conflict, when one side began its descent into the L column, troop morale tended to plummet, too. And with that went things like strategy, sanity, and composure.

Especially when the enemy was already a feral legion of abominations dispelled from a rip in space.

So, they were bound to stray from the path.

Eddie of course would keep all of that to himself, in the recesses of his mind, until after the battle.

Supposing he survived.

Each Titan was about a hundred feet tall, so, a little over twice the height of Wally's *Mastodon*. And that said a lot, moreover because they each had a slightly hunched posture. God forbid one of them were to rise up on its haunches, the four-legged Hammerhead like a bear, or use its tail for further support as a kangaroo could. There were two of those, whose terrifying tails were their most evident weapon against the Mechs, hence Mal's constant state of movement.

And Eddie's command to stay mobile, even if not especially for the slower Mechs like Wally and Luke.

"Don't let them get within striking range!" Eddie shouted into his mic. "Take advantage of their close-quarters limitations!"

That said, the two Hammerheads had one hell of a reach. With their forelimbs, let alone their sweeping tails. The third, at least, was a lumpy-backed behemoth that was much slower, and yet far uglier.

Although it had long feelers snaking from its back and stout neck, they seemed more interested in licking the open air surrounding it than lashing out at the Mechs. Occasionally two or three would curl around in an attempt to cover its pulsing cysts, a lighter color than its dark flesh, which made Eddie pay even more attention to them.

"H! Skirt around Lumpy and target the cysts on its back! PPCs and Lasers only."

"Weak spots?" H asked, already on the move, disengaging from the Hammerhead. Her path arced around, behind the pacing *Adversary*, to get a clearer shot of the Titan's backside.

"Might just piss it off more, but yeah, I'm hoping so,"

197

Eddie said. "I'll keep it interested up front."

"Copy."

If Eddie was right about these things having come from San Francisco—or that region at least, this side of the Golden Gate Bridge—that would mean they passed other smaller cities en route. Woodland and Davis being among them. Despite their slow pace, their strides were immense and there was no accounting for their motivation.

Perhaps those smaller cities, likely with most of their population in bunkers or safely hiding, posed no great interest to these beasts. Especially if Intel was right, and their vision was in fact based on thermal imaging.

A gathering of six Mechs in the middle of an open field, backdropped by the city of Sacramento, however? A prime target, especially if their infrared organs—wherever they were located on their massive bodies—had an impressive range.

It wouldn't be shocking, especially at this point.

None of this was comforting.

And yet for that reason, Eddie was all the more motivated. He had to wonder what was going through his comrades' minds, too, at the time, but he wasn't given much time or focus to go down that road.

He had to stay composed, mildly at least, enough to keep Lumpy distracted while H circled it to get some clear shots at its cysts.

Eddie figured the best case scenario was that its bubble-like lumps were really housings for its infrared sensors. It had enough on its neck and shoulders to constitute some form of forward vision.

"You'd think that HQ would've been able to scan the

region and spot these godforsaken things coming from at least *a mile out* and notify us, huh?"

Wally had a point.

"Especially seeing as how sensitive they are about where their birds go," Nomi added.

"Woulda, coulda, shoulda," Eddie said, shrugging. "Let's just focus on bringing these things down, fast as we can, before our rides get here and flip it back to base."

"Nah, they wouldn't *leave us* out here," Luke said, but there was incredulity in his voice.

"Those airlifts have a machine-gunner at best," H said. One of her PPCs zapped the air, an oblique blue streak lashing at Lumpy's back. She missed her target, but did sear off a feeler and some superficial flesh in the process. The creature was not happy about it. H took the little victory and kept trying; she also continued her thought. "They aren't built for combat, not like a Hawk. And they're slow as fuck. I wouldn't necessarily blame the pilots for making a U-turn in the sky if they saw these things on the horizon."

"With or without us at their feet," Eddie said, sighing. "She's right. So let's get to it, Clanners. They're slow and seem as confused about us as we are about them. Only...with less firepower."

It was all the reassurance and encouragement the pilots needed to kick it into high-gear.

Eddie continued trying to keep Lumpy's focus by slashing its raggedly toothed snout with his Lasers, so H could line up better PPC shots.

In the meantime, about eighty feet to Eddie's right, Wally sporadically fired at one of the two Hammerheads. He began to stride with his torso turned, however, away from the fight.

"I can't get anything in," he griped. "Not even my big AC's are getting through. And this thing's starting to act up, y'all might be able to hop around but I can't."

"Don't worry about it, Wally, just get to a safe distance and see if you can snipe it," Mal said.

"Snipe it where, though?"

Mal kept juking in front of, and below, the giant beast's hammer-like skull, which casted the yellow and green field in a sweeping shadow. Her intermittent bombardments seemed futile until moments ago, when she started aiming at its forearms. The flesh was a different color there and, unlike most of the rest of its body, actually flesh—not bony carapace.

She didn't have to be an extraterrestrial zoologist to see that her shots there were having an effect on it.

"The upper forearms," Mal said. "It seems to be reacting when I land there, but I'm a few bursts from going dry."

"Copy, just keep it distracted."

"Right," Mal said. She temporarily muted her mic and shook her head. "Easy-fucking-peasy."

Eddie glanced in Mal's direction. He hated seeing her skirt so close to the lumbering beast, and hearing that she was low on ammo, but at least her *Bandit* was nimble and he had no reservations about her as a pilot.

Plus, it did help that the two Hammerheads were, despite their magnitude and imposing tails, not moving much. They each kept about a hundred feet apart, occasionally sidestepping a stride or two, but nothing major.

A swing of their tails here and there, none of which came close to connecting with any of the mobile Mechs.

200

It was as if they were either studying their enemies, these new opponents, or—if not both these possibilities—they felt genuinely befuddled.

Afterall, the Mechs were prominent heat signatures, and were assailing the Titans clear as day, but their size and mobility likely confused the creatures.

Eddie wondered if they even had that level of brain-power.

Regardless of the reason, he and the others took advantage.

On that note, Eddie thought of something.

He glanced at his radar, while H zapped a second bubble on Lumpy's back. Like its predecessor, the sort of cyst burst filthily and the Titan's reaction was nothing shy of *pissed off*.

Eddie noticed that his Clan was, although spaced apart, still far too clustered. Especially given the scope and potential threats that their enemies were.

"Clanners, spread out!" Eddie shouted. "Take advantage of the open ground! Nomi, see if you can give that freakshow a run for its money, maybe juke it out. When it falls, you and Luke hit it with all you've—"

"Eddie, hop back!" H blurted.

He didn't think, he didn't analyze, and he didn't look around. He reacted; he obeyed. He trusted.

Both feet on the pedals, Eddie throttled the *Adversary*'s hop-jets, while directing himself backward. In the same instant, Lumpy's huge, thick, slug-like tail swung across the field, right where he had been. It would have crushed his *Adversary* with ease, or at least flung it off its toes.

201

The Titan was bleeding profusely down its back.

It slowly pivoted, its tail mowing down swathes of flowers in its path, to try and track H.

Eddie eased his Mech down to the ground again. It lurched into a half-crouch on its hocked legs, actuators grinding loudly but only naturally.

"Whew," he exhaled. "Appreciate it, H."

"I saved your eighty-ton ass, now do me a solid and save mine, yeah?"

"You got it," he said, determined.

Meanwhile, the other pilots were heeding Eddie's advice, which had of course come across like orders. Whatever they had been, the trust in each other was unquestionable. And as soon as the pilots began to fan out more, while Nomi did to her pursuer what Eddie had suggested, they reaped the rewards.

More or less.

The Hammerheads were each about sixty feet taller than most of the Mechs. That didn't seem like a whole lot except when its length was considered. Shoulder-to-shoulder alone was a terrifying tower of jagged bone, like indestructible armor.

A glimpse of vulnerable underbelly was never more than just that—a glimpse. From the end of its concave "snout" to the tip of its Ankylosaurus-like tail, the Hammerhead was nauseatingly huge and posed too great of a threat if it ever decided to utilize its weapons.

So, all anyone could do was evade, while their wingman attacked from afar.

Nomi thought she had her and Luke's Titan on the

verge of slipping and plummeting a few times, but its agility despite its bulkiness proved frustrating.

Not wanting to deviate too far from the others, she kept looping back toward the rest of the team. All the while Luke tried concentrating fire on its forearms or lower sides.

"Gotcha, motherfucker!" Eddie growled, both shoulder-mounted PPCs converging their helical beams on a recently destroyed lump. The devastating energy seared into the deep wound, and the creature's chest pushed forward, its head whipping back. A geyser of vividly red-orange blood spewed from its wretched jaws.

"Timber!" H cheered, her hop-jets flaring as she leapt back a hundred feet.

The Titan lumbered in pain, disoriented and experiencing death throes, aimless.

The others would have cheered, too, had they been given a chance. Everybody was warring their own battle, all at once, with little more than a breath between squeezing triggers and waiting for a weapon to reload or recharge.

And then the Titan that seemed intent on catching the evasive Nomi suddenly stopped in its tracks. Giant patches of earth and grass were chewed up in its clawed wake. It turned its head around on a thick, lithe neck, and eyelessly witnessed one of its own kind fall.

Lumpy toppled, and the ground quaked.

The Hammerhead made a snorting, guttural sound, and then trumpeted not unlike an elephant. Given its proportions and atrociousness, the vocalization was more equivalent to at least *ten* elephants. An ear-splitting, yet thunderous crash of a sound.

Disturbing in its own right, too.

"That can't be good," Wally muttered into his mic.

The other Titan, which was formerly distracted by Mal, stopped as well. To listen, and then react.

It roared, next, its skull brought low to the ground. Patches of flowers and blades of grass were ripped up against the brutal exhalation. Mal's *Bandit* rattled in the concussive wake, and in her cockpit she could hear leg actuators violently vibrate. Even the reinforced glass of her canopy shuddered.

"Mal, get outta there!" Eddie shouted.

"Bounce, Mal!" Wally added, and began approaching the Titan, a risk he dared to take, while engaging it with his enormous Autocannons. The giant bores flashed white-hot and slammed the Hammerhead's right neck with 180mm high-explosive anti-tank rounds. Each shot was worth a cluster of three impacts, and Wally was damned if he missed such a big target.

After the first two, however, which equated to six explosive rounds, the Titan shook its giant skull like a wet dog, and then looked in Wally's direction.

The *Mastodon* slowed to a stop.

Mal redirected, to the Titan's left, and tried to steal its focus by burst-firing at it…from below.

Now *she* was taking the risk. An even bigger one, too, given her route and comparable size.

She strode her *Bandit* beneath the Titan's belly. Her Mech's torso pitched back, and her Vulcan rotary cannon spun. Explosive rounds chewed into the behemoth's stomach, splashing her small canopy with red-orange gore.

The Titan flinched and bellowed in pain.

"You crazy fucking bitch!" Eddie exclaimed, his face

204

warped between a big grin and a terrified expression.

Mal just clenched her teeth and growled through them as she squeezed her joystick's red trigger. Eventually the Vulcan ran dry, its three linked barrels burning orange from heat expulsion, spinning on empty.

"Move your ass, Mal!" Wally shouted, and fired both of his Railguns simultaneously. The *Mastodon*'s right arm recoiled, but he barely felt it in his center-mass cockpit. The Hammerhead was about to slouch on top of Mal, who was only just then beginning to accelerate, when a pair of high-velocity tungsten slugs slammed into its right shoulder. The bony carapace cracked like a tectonic plate, as the shoulder had already been battered by Wally's ACX. Now it split, and one of the two Railgun slugs pierced the wound.

This was a bonus for Wally.

His intention was to simply knock the giant creature over, and give Mal some free space to escape.

This was a success. The impact from Wally's dual Railguns pushed the Titan over. The shoulder wound was complementary to the disembowelment executed, insanely, by Mal.

Her *Bandit* emerged, clearing its collapse.

The small Mech was doused in vibrant red-orange gore, appearing as if it had been dunked in the goop, but not completely fallen in.

Mal laughed maniacally, and toggled her canopy protection. This heated the reinforced glass, melting away any residue.

Cheering for the victory commenced and ended in the same moment.

The remaining Titan had stopped its feral, fruitless

pursuit of Nomi in exchange for engaging her directly. Horizontally, it swung its skull at her, which she perceived now as more of a massive, bony pickaxe than hammer, and she missed what was actually the second attempt at that point by crouching her *Rottweiler*. Previously she had hopped and dodged it, but couldn't a second time in lieu of her thrusters recharging.

Concurrently, Luke tried to grab the Titan's attention by striding to its right and firing at its forearm. He managed to wound it enough to vex the creature, but its swinging tail in his direction triggered his own evasive maneuvers.

"Everyone, engage!" Eddie shouted. Ordered. "Pull its attention away from them!"

He and H were too far away to get within effective range anytime soon. Wally, too, and his slow speed exacerbated this.

Due to the Mechs' positions, they couldn't acquire a clear shot of the Titan's limited weak spots with Luke's *Rhino* to the right of it.

"Jesus Christ, what in the fuck is—!?"

"Turn around, turn around!"

Two voices crackled onto the team's frequency.

Eddie looked around, just as a pair of blips appeared at the southeast edge of his radar. He didn't slow down, though, not a single percentile.

He, H, and Mal witnessed the approach of the two airlift craft against the backdrop of Sacramento's outskirts. From whence they had come.

An airlift was a clamp-shaped VTOL transport about twice as big as a Hawk but with significantly less armor and weaponry. Its own thrusters, however, were far superior, and also connected to a fusion engine.

"No, don't leave!" H demanded. "Fall back to the watertower, wait for us!"

The pilots didn't say anything at first. They were already at a safe distance, about an eighth of a mile away, but they still banked their aircraft in the opposite direction.

"Wally, concentrate fire on its neck!" Eddie yelled, returning his concentration to the matter at hand.

Wally complied, while the Hammerhead continued to swing its dangerous skull at Nomi. She barely had time to juke or accelerate every time her Mech adjusted from its previous maneuver. Whether it was crouching or hopping, neither action not as instantaneous as it might be for a person.

The Titan was adamant it was going to get her.

So much so that it forced itself to ignore the huge-caliber shots it suffered from Wally to its neck.

"Buy her some goddamn time to get outta there!" Eddie hollered, in reference to Nomi.

"Right knee actuator is fucked!" Nomi exclaimed, her voice cracking. Bad news on top of bad news.

The constant hopping and landing, in addition to the vibrations from her pursuer's stomps, had taken a toll. She tried not to sob as she anticipated being demolished or even speared by the Titan's skull.

Her *Rottweiler*'s all-terrain tracks could drive her but not fast enough to elude this attacker.

"Arms, hit its fucking arms!" Luke snapped, clearing that area as his *Rhino* accelerated toward the back-end of the Titan.

"No, Luke!" Nomi shouted.

"Luke, goddammit, steer clear of that fucking tail!" H demanded.

"Hit the arms!" Luke insisted, his voice ragged. "Arms and belly! Put this piece of shit in the dirt!"

Luke drove his *Rhino* under the Titan's rump, behind its back legs. He had successfully evaded the tail, for the time being. As Mal had just done, he now aimed up at the Titan's vulnerable underside, which was theoretically its—

"How's this for an enema?" Luke growled, and his short-range missile pack lit up. Exhaust smoke poured out behind the *Rhino*'s left shoulder, and all three warheads detonated less than fifty feet from the Mech's canopy. The close-quarters blast spiked the *Rhino*'s heat levels and splashed simmering alien blood on the outside of the reinforced glass in front of Luke. It also sufficed to rock the Titan, making it lurch forward.

Nomi was in the process of landing as her hop-jets settled. The Hammerhead's skull hit the ground twenty feet away, horizontally, plowing through grass and flowers. Her *Rottweiler* shuddered and the damaged leg actuator blew, sparks flying around the right knee. The Mech tilted to that side and Nomi exclaimed wordlessly.

"Her right knee blew out!" Wally announced.

Not even the *Rottweiler*'s tank-tracked feet could move her now.

"Keep hitting it!" Eddie growled through his teeth, and everyone except for Luke and Nomi fired at its right side, between its shoulder and hindquarters.

"Get outta there, Luke!" H shouted, and the Titan's tail swung toward her and Eddie. She screamed on impulse, hopping back. The *Fenrir*'s thrusters engaged, scorching green and yellow to black. The sharpened boulder of bone at the end of the Titan's tail missed H by twenty feet, and Eddie by maybe a yard.

His teeth chattered briefly, the canopy glass rattling in its frame.

A violent *whoosh* could be heard just outside his Mech, and then the tail retracted.

The Titan's right side dripped blood and chunks of flesh, as did it between the legs, onto Luke's *Rhino*.

"We need to—" Eddie started, but Luke interrupted.

"Fall back!" He shouted. His voice dipped into a growl. "That tail's gonna wipe you out. Fuck this."

"Luke, whatever you're thinking," Nomi said, tears on her cheeks. In the spinal camera feed displayed below her HUD, she saw the Hammerhead's atrocious skull lift from the ground, soil and vegetation crumbling from its other-worldly jaws.

"Nomi, love," Luke chuckled. "I don't think."

Luke fired his Railgun into the missile-ruptured wound between the Titan's legs, and the slug actually exited through the carapace at the base of its lower back. The Titan yowled and kicked at Luke's *Rhino*, but missed.

He let his Vulcan rip, pouring 20mm HEAT rounds into the open wound.

The Titan sat down.

Into the gaping, spilling wound, Luke's *Rhino* was enveloped.

"Fuck, this thing just won't die!" He shouted into his mic.

Eddie didn't know what to say. Perhaps in some other

version of the scenario, he would have laughed at the sight. But the severity of the predicament was too tremendous.

"Save the gay jokes," Luke added, as if reading Eddie's passing thought. The *Rhino*'s legs kicked below it, visible from where Eddie and H stood.

Wally's Autocannons thundered, both firing simultaneously. The *Mastodon* juddered where it stood, its inverted-triangle torso recoiling appropriately.

The high-explosive clusters struck the Hammerhead's right skull protrusion, closest to the alcove at the center. Part of the bone broke away, although no blood followed.

Still, the beast roared in what they could only deduce as pain.

Nomi was in the process of limping away.

"Eddie," H said, her voice hollow.

"What?" His eyebrows hiked.

"Good God, there's another one!" An airlift pilot exclaimed under his breath. "Clanners, on your six, there's—"

Eddie glanced at his spinal camera feed.

His heart sank, in the same manner that H had said his name a second ago.

The Hammerhead didn't lumber toward them from the distance. It *galloped*.

Within seconds of noticing it, the blip of its presence appeared on his motion sensors, and then the ground thudded from its rapid approach.

"What's that?" Luke asked. There was a slight echo to his transmission.

Meanwhile, the wounded Hammerhead turned to face Wally.

"Nomi's in the clear!" He announced, targeting the alcove, his Railguns selected. "Taking a killshot!"

"All of that and I'm not gonna get the—"

Luke was interrupted by the reverberant thunderclap of the dual Railguns firing simultaneously. The two eight-pound, thirty-inch-long, fourteen-inch-wide tungsten slugs traveled at a velocity of two miles per second.

Here, from a hundred feet away.

And Wally's aim was pinpoint. The projectiles split the Hammerhead's skull in half. A plume of red-orange gore erupted into the air. Fuchsia brain slop rained the ground in chunks, and the Titan's body went limp in the same instant.

"I'd say that's a weak spot," Wally said with an almost calm indifference.

Luke's *Rhino* staggered free of the slain Titan's rear wound, coated in orange slime head to toe, dripping it in thick excess.

He activated his canopy protection so he could see what he swore was the announcement of yet another massive enemy.

As the gore cleared from his canopy, he witnessed the Hammerhead's fast approach, now less than four-hundred feet from Eddie and H, who were about a quarter of that from him.

He glanced at his radar, without turning his torso, and saw Nomi's icon moving. Slowly, but moving; and still lit up.

A weak smile formed on his face.

He went to accelerate his Mech.

There was so much slime and gore on the *Rhino* that it

had gotten into the crevices of his torso rotator, and limb joints.

Alarms blared in his cockpit.

"Movement impeded. Movement impeded. Clear obstruction to proceed. Movement impeded. Movement—"

The automated voice continued.

Luke's brow furrowed. "No. No, wait."

Eddie's dual PPCs fired and he lashed out with his Lasers as he strode the *Adversary* to his far left, and H reacted similarly, but to her right. The impending Titan slowed only slightly as it continued to charge forward, utilizing all four limbs to gallop fiercely, its hammer-head lowered as a bull would do.

"It's not stopping!" Eddie exclaimed. He glanced at his radar. Wally and Nomi were, very slowly, walking away from the head of the slain Titan's corpse. Mal made a U-turn, having begun to leave the area, only now heading back.

Luke's *Rhino* was immobile.

Eddie's heart raced and his brow furrowed. He looked at the comms window on his HUD. Luke's name was flashing, but he couldn't hear anything.

"Luke, move," he said, and his *Adversary* stopped.

"Luke's joints are jammed," Mal said, relaying the information as she deduced upon nearing his *Rhino*.

"I can't...I...nothing will respond," Luke kept mumbling, the panic building.

He looked up. The charging Titan would reach him in six, maybe seven seconds.

Mal was completely out of ammunition. She could not distract the Titan if she tried, unless she—

Ran across its path.

Little time to act, she had to—

The Titan roared and veered sideways last-second. Its tail swung toward H's *Fenrir*. She exclaimed and reached for her ejection handle.

Eddie's voice fell in his throat as he watched the *Fenrir*'s conical cockpit get wedged in half by the impact of the tail's end. The Mech was slung off of it eventually, tumbling across the field in pieces.

Gasps of shock spilled into the team's comms.

Eddie wanted to search for a possible ejection chute but had his own evasion to conduct. The Titan's skull swung toward him, and he engaged his hop-jets. The *Adversary* ascended, narrowly dodging the pendulous skull.

As he came down, Eddie tried angling himself away from the Hammerhead. It lifted its ugly face and tilted its head sideways, jaws agape.

It was going to eat him.

His Mech, anyway.

He launched a flight of eight missiles at it, their small warheads exploding around its crescent-shaped mouth. It flinched and shook its head, while his Mech landed sixty feet away.

As the war machine adjusted from the controlled landing, the Titan's tail swung behind it. And then its feet pivoted, turning the giant beast around. The tail whipped with terrible speed, forcing Mal to evade by hopping into the air.

The tail's trajectory curved toward Luke.

Still imprisoned by his unresponsive Mech, he engaged his thrusters, too.

They were clogged.

His *Rhino* had become nothing more than a fifty-ton paperweight, low on ammunition and incapable of targeting.

"Ejecting!" he announced, and yanked on the handle between his legs. The coolant line to his vest disconnected. Simultaneously, the canopy popped off with a series of bursts, and then his cockpit seat thrusted airborne. Below, he witnessed his *Rhino* get demolished by the bludgeoning tail, which still had slivers of metal clinging to the jagged bone, from H's *Fenrir*.

Despite the two Mechs' complete destruction, Luke was slightly grateful neither had gone critical. This occurred when the fusion engine was explosively compromised, achieved by penetrative damage from enemy firepower.

Structural demolition, however, wouldn't cause a critical blast unless stored ammunition blew, or some other flammable agent was involved.

A parachute billowed out from Luke's headrest, and he braced as the seat lurched in the air, before commencing a floating descent.

He had a great view of the "battlefield" from up here. About two-hundred feet in the air. What was once an utterly beautiful southern Californian landscape was now scarred by troughs in the grass from claws and the like, scorched flowers, and the corpses of enormous, malevolent, otherworldly beasts.

A column of black smoke ascended from H's destroyed *Fenrir*.

From his *Rhino*, too, which had been slung across the

field, in the direction of Wally and Nomi. Her *Rottweiler* limped, but was intact.

He felt relieved about that.

He looked toward the *Fenrir*, though, and a pain in his chest throbbed. H—

Luke's eyes widened.

A glimpse of white against the sunlit sky, and far horizon. He thought it was a cloud at first, but no: a parachute. And dangling below it, a small black pill shape, from this distance. H's cockpit seat, with her harnessed to it.

Relief flooded through Luke.

His gaze fell upon the still alive Hammerhead, however.

Eddie faced it down, his *Adversary*'s weapons going off, alternating in a frenzy.

Mal had spotted H's seat, and tracked her descent so she could pick her up soon as she landed.

Much to Luke's surprise, and undeniable joy, one of the two airlifts was en route to Wally and Nomi.

When he looked back down at the Titan, which was now about a hundred feet from where he was proceeding to land, any happiness dissipated.

"Aw, shit."

Meanwhile, in Eddie's cockpit, a squall of heat alarms rang out.

"I can't keep holding its attention!" He exclaimed, slowly backpedaling the *Adversary* while alternating between a PPC and his remaining SRMs. If he pushed the *Adversary* any further, weapons wise, the Mech was going to automatically shutdown to protect the integrity of its engine and systems, which would, in this case, be the certain death of him.

The Hammerhead's ferocious shape loomed over the Mech.

Before Luke touched down, he throttled his seat forward, using a lever on the right side. It pushed through the air, his boots some forty feet off the ground.

The thrusters were designed only for short bursts, to help the ejected pilot land safely.

Specific direction and elevation were not options.

Luke wasn't connected to the team channel anymore. But that didn't matter. He was seen by some of them, and in all of their hearts, he knew he was felt.

For however long they wished.

Eddie, withdrew the *Adversary*. Heat generation was redlining, at 87% and very slowly dropping. At ninety, his Mech would automatically shut down. He shook his head as he watched the Titan's jaws loom toward him.

"Mal, I—" He started to say, but choked on his own voice. His eyes dropped to see an object a couple of feet lower than his canopy come toward the Titan. It turned its head to its left, Eddie's right, and he realized the object was Luke in his ejected seat. Eddie screamed Luke's name, scrambling the channel with static.

Even though he wasn't on comms, Luke's expression was visible from where Eddie sat.

He was laughing.

No—cackling.

The Hammerhead's skull snapped forward, its jaws closing around Luke's seat, midair. With Luke Shaw harnessed to it. The destruction of the seat ignited the petrol-fueled thrusters. It was a small explosion, but it sufficed to

216

obliterate the Titan's lower jaw, and from the wound gushed a cascade of saliva and blood.

As enormous as it was, the Titan faltered, just like that.

Eddie's heart pounded faster than his tears fell.

And far faster than his Mech's heat levels dropped. But the instant they were in the yellow, he fired both PPCs—his ACX ammo reserves were empty—into the monster's skull. One of the clusters missed the alcove. The other struck, consecutive HEAT rounds bursting through the inner, exposed flesh.

The Hammerhead's bony skull split open and chunks of it fell to the ground.

Along with the rest of its limp body.

Eddie was beyond speechless, incapable of processing the death of two of his teammates, two of his closest friends.

Luke Shaw and Helena—

"You gotta be fucking kidding," Mal's voice stumbled into the recovered radio frequency. It was tired and near surrender; only in tone, not intention.

Eddie looked around. All of a sudden his motion sensors lit up.

The *Adversary* turned.

In the direction that the Hammerhead had come. Another Titan approached. Another godforsaken Hammerhead.

Except that it didn't charge. It occasionally turned to swing its tail into the sky.

Eddie's brow wrinkled.

And then a new yet familiar sound occurred in the

background of Mal's transmission. The hissing and clamping of a hatch closing.

"I got H," Mal said.

Eddie's head jerked so hard he hurt his neck. His *Adversary* swung its torso at his control, to face the direction of Mal's *Bandit* on his radar. But the heap of the Titan's corpse blocked his view. He strode clear of it, and saw the *Bandit* begin accelerating in the general direction of Wally and Nomi.

Back towards Sacramento.

"Care to say anything?" Mal asked.

Eddie started to, and then H's stressed yet distinct voice sounded on the channel.

"Happy to be alive," she said. "And killer shooting, Eddie. We're watching Nomi and Wally get picked up by one of the airlifts, now. I think they're out of radio range."

Despite the residual distress, and exhaustion, in H's voice, it was devoid of grief. If anything, she sounded heavily relieved.

Eddie realized she and Mal had not witnessed what he did. They saw the fall of the Titan, but not what preceded it. And not the most crucial part of its death.

The orange-splattered *Bandit* strode past Eddie, about a hundred and twenty feet away. Then it came to a stop, its torso pivoted to face him, or, more rather, the approach of another Hammerhead in the distance.

It was still about eight-hundred feet away, at least. And it kept pausing to swing its tail airborne.

"What the hell is going on?" Mal asked.

"I don't know," Eddie said. His voice shaky.

"Look, let's just go," Mal said. Her *Bandit*'s torso

swung around, as if looking for something. Inside, Mal observed her camera feeds, and the view through her canopy. H gripped the cockpit seat, hovering over Mal's shoulder. Soot caked to her sweaty forehead, cheeks, arms and hands. She had since discarded her useless coolant vest.

"Where is he?" H asked, under her breath.

"Eddie, where's Luke?" Mal's inflection wavered. "H said she saw his chute before she landed. But I'm not...I'm not seeing his seat transponder on my radar."

"Get to the airlifts," Eddie said, swallowing.

"Eddie," Mal said, and put a hand to her mouth.

"Get to the fucking airlifts," he barked. "I'm right behind you."

H staggered back, a hand raised to her head. And another on her stomach. She felt sick.

New icons appeared on Eddie and Mal's radars.

And then familiar voices echoed until balancing out on their team channel.

"Coming in hot, Ember," Charly said.

"Whipping around, topside," Brick added.

Their voices were curt and to the point. Rugged. Pained. Angry.

"I fucking *knew* you wingnuts were gonna—"

Charly interrupted Eddie, as was almost customary when they shared the same battlefield. Except there was no sarcasm or laughter in the background this time.

"Get your asses to the airlift," she said bluntly.

Brick's Hawk thrusted high above Eddie, and whipped around, leaving a U-shaped smoke trail in his wake. His VTOL propelled forward, Lasers engaging the imminent Hammerhead, which paused to lash out at a hovering

Charly. She evaded, agilely, and Eddie could tell that they had gotten used to this.

He was impressed and as overjoyed as he could be, given the circumstances.

Already he began backpedaling.

Mal's *Bandit* had not budged, though.

"Where's Fox?" She asked, her voice thin.

"Y'all remember the halo joke?" Charly asked, while raining SRMs down on the Hammerhead. Her tone had taken an oddly casual turn.

"Uh, yeah," Mal said, brow creasing a little. She glanced over her shoulder but didn't see H. She heard her crying in the back of the cockpit, into her hands.

"Fox would insist that we Hawks fly so high we're deserving of halos," Brick said, his voice mucousy.

Eddie shook his head. His eyes scanned the skies. He didn't want to accept it.

"I'd say," Brick added, his VTOL pushing forward and volleying the annoyed Titan with Vulcan rounds. Yet his voice was as calm as the surface of a lake. "I'd say that halos were only for angels."

Charly laughed. It wasn't her usual cackle. It was a genuine snicker, but stifled under something else.

"Yeah, and he'd just say…*oh, right, hard pass*."

She and Brick laughed.

The Hammerhead staggered from its wounds and then resumed its forward gallop, now a slowed lope.

"Where's Fox?" Mal asked.

"He'd hate how cheesy that was," Brick added.

"Get to the airlift, Mal," Charly said, sniffling. "We've gotta bring this thing down. Can't disappoint an angel."

10

Make that two. Eddie wanted to say it, but bit his tongue. They could mourn Luke's death, and Fox's, once they were safely in the air. While the so-called wingnuts performed combative acrobatics to take down their remaining enemy, a monster of an organism from some other realm, the Mechs assembled at the exfil.

Above which hovered two airlift VTOLs. They had already magnetically lifted the damaged *Rottweiler*, but Wally refused so long as he had teammates still on the ground.

He remained below, ready to be lifted as soon as Mal and Eddie arrived.

Far beyond them, about a quarter mile away from where he stood in his *Mastodon*, the Hammerhead sustained salvos of Lasers, missiles, and gunfire from two Hawks. Wally beat himself up over pondering which two pilots they were; Charly and Brick or Charly and Fox or—

He knew they were Ember, at the very least. His magnified HUD reticle established the Ember emblems on the aircraft. Onyx and Mako did not have Hawks attached to their Clans. So it was already obvious that the VTOLs were Ember Hawks, and they weren't close enough for his systems to identify them.

Wally wished he was wrong. A very small part of him

221

wished he did not know the pilots. Only because he knew that if there weren't three, it meant one had perished some-where along their journey here.

Incapable of overlooking the reality of the situation, and the immeasurable numbers of casualties suffered worldwide, including his own son in another state, Wally was the opposite of ignorant.

He was as deep into the tragedy as its hooks were in him.

And he refused to let any more of his teammates suffer or die as they already had. Whether that was in his control or not was another issue entirely, one that he felt he *could* in fact ignore.

This was a *Mastodon*, afterall.

He didn't mind pretending that it was a godlike ma-chine of sorts.

His witnessing of Luke's heroic death was kept from Nomi for obvious reasons. Even when she barraged him with questions of his status, and the others'. Wally hated lying to those he cared about, but had nothing except lies for Nomi at the time.

"He ejected, he'll be picked up," Wally had eventually said. In theory, it wasn't exactly a lie; except that he re-peated that statement moments after magnifying his reticle and bearing witness to Luke's sacrifice. An act that saved Eddie from certain death.

In a way, Wally liked to believe, Luke would still be picked up.

Just not by any of them.

Eddie's voice came through Wally's comms, banked by static. It quickly cleared once his *Adversary* was within

222

range.

"...right behind you, Wally. The hell are you waiting for?"

"Say again, boss," Wally said simply.

"Go on up, we're right behind you," Eddie repeated. Mal's *Bandit* led him by a few paces.

"Where's H? Wally asked, his voice thick with fear. "I saw a chute but—"

"I'd say save your tears, Wally," H's voice came through, on Mal's frequency. It was as far from composed as he had ever heard it. "But Fox and Luke—"

"S-Save it, H. Let's get you all off your feet, first."

He tried interrupting H before Nomi caught on. There was little that Luke's name could be misinterpreted as.

The *Bandit* arrived below the second airlift and through a series of non-verbal commands via her control panel, Mal confirmed her readiness. The airlift lowered its magnetic cables and proceeded to lift her Mech off its soil-embedded feet. Blades of grass and crushed yellow petals fell from the metal toes as the *Bandit* ascended.

Inside the cockpit, H clutched onto the back of Mal's seat. With one hand. The other gripped Mal's, their fingers interlocked and knuckles white. H pressed her brow against the back of Mal's headrest. She resisted the urge to slam her face into it as many times as she imagined doing it.

The frustration and grief bubbled in her veins.

"No, wait, we've gotta go back for Luke," Nomi said, through a curtain of tears dripping past her lips. "Uh, W-Wally said he ejected. He's probably down there some-where, terrified—"

"Nomi, Nomi, *Nomi*!" Eddie ultimately shouted to get

her to listen. Meanwhile, his *Adversary* was being raised under the same airlift as Mal's. "Nomi. Trust me. Luke...he didn't die terrified."

Nomi's voice crumbled into a messy lamentation that was ultimately muted on her end. In her cockpit, she threw a fit of anger and grief, the pain of the unyielding harness against her chest, covered by the coolant vest, reminding her she was alive.

And that only maddened her more.

"Wally, get your ass up here," H said, her voice gaining strength.

"Sending confirmation now," he replied, tapping his controls.

The airlift complied and, though slower than the others, hoisted him up with twice as many magnetic cables. He raised beside the *Rottweiler*, whose wounded leg dangled below the damaged knee actuator. It wouldn't fall off unless it got caught on something, and was certainly repairable.

Supposing nothing worse happened to it before they reached the base.

"What's the deal with the Hawks?" Wally asked.

"And where's Fox!?" Nomi blurted.

"He's no longer with us," Eddie said, grimly. "Charly and Brick said as much. We'll get the full details as soon as we—"

A rumbling explosion caught their attention some eight-hundred feet away. They looked, but as soon as Wally's *Mastodon* was secure, the airlifts commenced flight.

What the Clanners witnessed was the rupturing of the

Hammerhead's distinctive skull, from a series of well-placed missiles. The blast scarred the sky, and rained upon the fallen Titan its own vibrant bloodshed.

The two Hawks looped around each other before rapidly catching up with the airlifts.

"Y'all clearly have had practice," Mal said.

"We're not on our A-game, though," Charly admitted. "Can't stop thinking about Fox."

"Ballistics are empty, too," Brick said dryly. "That was the last of our missiles."

"Yeah," Charly sighed. "And our hydrogen levels are alarming. Literally."

"You'll burn less going slower," one of the airlift pilots chimed in. "Escort us at our speed and it'll work out for everyone."

"That was the plan," Brick said.

"In whose Mechs are H and Luke?" Charly asked. "We noticed during our flyby that the *Fenrir* and *Rhino* were destroyed, but saw chutes."

"I'm, uh," H cleared her throat. She hovered over Mal's shoulder. "I'm in the *Bandit*. Mal picked me up. But…"

"But what?" Charly asked in a chuckle, her voice cracking. Her brow furrowed and she began to ask in a more demanding tone.

"Luke's dead," Nomi blurted, hard. And then her tone, which was initially stiff, slackened with anguish. "Apparently, he uh…"

"He sacrificed himself, last-second," Eddie said, the pain his voice unmistakable. He hated saying it out loud. "To…To save me."

"After saving me, too," Nomi said. Her inflection weakened. "Again…"

Brick and Charly were speechless. Their emotional agony wrung them out from the inside, though. If their hearts could speak without articulation, and be traditionally heard, they'd be screaming now.

"These…These fucking *things*, they just…" Charly said, angrily, through gritted teeth.

"To say he was a good man," Brick said, struggling to focus on the positive, "would be an understatement."

"We are all good men and women," H said. "Trying to be great." She sniffled. "The same of Fox and Luke can be said about the pilots who died in Stockton, today."

Brick and Charly perked up.

"Mako and Onyx. They got hit, too?" Brick asked. "How bad?"

"HQ said…there were three casualties. And a fourth sustained bad injuries. Their entire tank convoy…wiped out."

H took a deep breath.

"That it's gotten so bad on the ground, miles outside of San Francisco, is heartbreaking. The loss of civilian life, nevermind us, has been…tremendous."

She sniffled and shook her head. A hand rose to her face. Mal noticed, and took over before anyone else could on H's behalf.

"But Sacramento's been declared safe," she said. "Any straggling enemies will be mopped up by SAR teams. We should be seeing 'em pass us shortly."

As it was, the airlifts were flying Ember back to base,

226

without going directly over Sacramento. They circumvented it, favoring rural routes.

"Uh, we hate to interrupt," an airlift pilot said, "but the lady is right. Search and rescue oughtta be two to three minutes out, tops. We're already past Sac. Won't be seeing 'em from here. To, uh, to our understanding, though, Sac is secure. Thanks to you all."

"Copy, and great to hear," Charly said, trying her damnedest to focus on the positive.

"And Stockton?" Brick asked.

"I believe," the pilot answered, his statement carried on a heavy breath, "it's in the running. Might require another flyby; ground forces are questionable. And unfortunately...Modesto, Fremont, and San Jose were all hit bad, too."

A few of the Clanners cursed under their breaths. The two Hawk pilots mostly kept quiet. Inside their heads, of course, was another story.

"What the hell *were* those things, anyway?" Another of the airlift pilots asked, his voice shaken.

"Did you not see the footage at base?" Mal asked.

"Glimpses. But nothing holds up in person."

The airlift pilot had a point. Nobody could contest that. They all nodded in implicit agreement.

"We call 'em Titans," Brick finally said with a shrug. "Those particular bastards, Hammerheads."

"Well, nobody can debate that," Eddie smirked weakly.

"What about the fatter one with the bacne?" H asked.

A few of them chuckled out loud. It was so quiet and sullen that the sounds barely transmitted.

"*Lumpy* is all we've got right now," Charly said, feeling silly saying it out loud like that.

"No shit," Eddie said.

"You, too?"

"Great minds, I guess," Eddie shrugged.

"Yeah, sure."

Brick took the liberty of restricting their comms to an Ember-only channel, thus shutting out the airlift pilots. He had good reason.

"Speaking of which," Brick said, with a heavy heart and an even heavier, huskier voice. "Fox had some things to say before…before his Hawk went down. When the things were falling outta the sky."

"Was there ever a time he *didn't* have something to say?" Nomi chuckled, sniffling.

Everyone smiled one way or another.

Brick continued. "In the hours leading up to this "Skyfall," Fox theorized that the enemy's world—*up there*—was dying, somehow or another. And that by coming here, attacking us the way they did, was like a last-ditch attempt to save themselves. To *devour* Earth, and, I don't know, assimilate us or something. *Feed* off our atmosphere, our people, the planet itself. We, Charly and I, I…I thought he was nuts. Fucking Fox, ya know?"

He chuckled unevenly.

His and Charly's Hawks flew about a hundred feet in front of the two airlifts. Their maximum speed was ninety knots *with* Mechs in tow. The Hawks were capable of twice that if needed; of course, as the airlift pilot mentioned, pushing their thrusters now would be brutally detrimental to their low hydrogen reserves.

228

So, they cruised just out ahead of the two airlifts. The pilots kept a watchful eye on their route ahead, both through their own canopies, monitors, and radars.

Unfortunately, the airlifts couldn't exceed an altitude of more than three-hundred feet with the Mechs in tow. Which made them potential targets if any other Titans were to show.

Hence the Hawk escort.

"It's not totally absurd," Wally said. He was the last person any of them would expect to nibble at one of Fox's crazy theories.

In his cockpit seat, Wally twisted a little and finally detached his harness. He kept the vest on because, even with the Mech on standby mode—a requirement to be transported by an airlift—it was still awfully hot inside.

Wally then leaned forward, elbows on his knees, and ran it through his head.

"I mean, the huge Teeth…those pink, toothed tentacles…hell, even the enemies themselves. Diverse as they've been, they all share a very…fleshy biology. Maybe…I dunno, maybe…"

"Well, spit it out, old man," Nomi said, not as belligerently as it would've seemed to a third party.

Some light laughter.

"Maybe," Wally said, with a rising vigor in him, "our enemy's homeworld *is* an organism itself. It feeds, and it must be fed. It hungers, but on a much larger scale than any human or even animal stomach."

"That would explain the Teeth," Eddie thought out loud.

"And the creatures," Charly said. Part of her could

229

barely believe she was biting at this. However, deep down, a voice not unlike Fox's told her it was true. "They...They're like *parasites*. To take from us, and feed to their host. Their...their world."

"If that's the case, these things aren't *just* aliens," Mal said, with a grunt of a laugh, an I-can't-believe-I'm-gonna-say-this expression. "They're from another *dimension*."

Some gasping and muttering from pilot to pilot.

Eddie couldn't help but think: Fox would have loved this. And Luke, he would have been the voice of reason, but then again, so would Charly and Wally. The others were more susceptible to believing farfetched theories, albeit nobody as easily as Fox.

Mal enjoyed entertaining his ideas, too, no matter how crazy they got. For her, though, it was more of an amusement thing.

For Fox, he wasn't stupid. He could see through her skepticism, but he enjoyed being humored nonetheless.

Mal recalled some fun memories of her teammate, her friend, and felt her heart break.

Just when she began to focus on being grateful for the lives of her other comrades, memories of Luke crashed through her mind. And her heart, already broken with sadness, began to crumble into finer shards of pain and disbelief.

They all went through this process during the ride back to base, some more intensely than others.

Their discussion wasn't over yet, though.

"Wherever they came from," Eddie said firmly, "we cannot allow them to return."

"I don't think we'll have to worry about that," Brick

said. A sort of cunning grin appeared on his dark, tear-glazed face. "If what Fox was saying is true—and even if it isn't—Skyfall is proof enough…that our enemy is staring defeat in the eye. And we're the *lid*. We can close this thing once and for all."

Eddie nodded, liking the sound of that.

"How?" H said, leaning over Mal's shoulder.

"We debrief," Eddie said. There was a simplicity to his tone that was, however, not undermined by a lack of gravity. Mal wondered if Eddie would ever sound nonchalant after this day. "Then, we take our repaired and rearmed Mechs *back* into the fight. Our Hawks cover us from the sky; we get rid of the infestation in San Francisco. We do whatever the hell it takes."

"And then some," Nomi said, more aggressive than before.

"And when we're done with S-F," Wally said, hopping on the bandwagon of boosted morale. "When SAR sweeps it for civilians, we resupply and hit the next city. With Onyx and Mako, we'll retake So-Cal by tomorrow's end."

Eddie wanted to cheer. They all wanted to celebrate this wild, whimsical strategy that their hearts pounded for.

"We're coming up on Headquarters," Charly announced.

Just then their HUD comms windows flashed with a message from the airlift pilots.

Brick opened their channel.

"Base is in range, Ember," one of them said. "Setting you all down outside the Mech hangar. ETA, two minutes."

"Copy, good news," Eddie said.

"Thanks for the lift," Mal said.

"Happy to help. Our condolences for your losses. As soon as we're cleared, and given escort, we'll return to that site to retrieve those Mechs."

"We appreciate you," Charly said. "Fly safe."

"Likewise, ma'am."

"We've been told by HQ," the other pilot said, "to instruct all of Ember to DB-Room C2, as soon as you're ready."

Eddie assumed that meant, after a visit to the nearest restroom. A splash on the face, the use of a toilet, scream in the mirror or throw up, any of these things. They were all within reason after what had happened.

"Solid copy," Eddie said.

"Should we set down outside the Hawk hangar or—"

"Negative," the pilot interrupted Brick. "It's too far from C2. Land on the tarmac with the Mechs, there should be Hawk techs standing by, too."

"You got it."

The two airlifts reached the base, and slowly lowered the Ember Wolves to the tarmac. Mech feet touched down, and magnetic cables released. The VTOLs flew off, rocking their stubby wings in a farewell gesture. Before setting down themselves, Charly and Brick responded the same way.

The instant the Ember Wolves had lowered to the tarmac, about a hundred and fifty feet from the open hangar doors, a horde of Mech-techs drove out in UTVs to reach them. One hauled a large cart that would be used to transport any Mech that had leg damage. In this case, Nomi's *Rottweiler*.

Just behind them, a smaller team of technicians specifically trained and equipped to work on Hawks, followed. They drove larger vehicles that hauled supplies for the VTOLs, including a reservoir for refueling.

Brick and Charly were especially happy to see them. Although, "happy" was an arguable term.

Seeing their own teammates, their own longtime friends and comrades, in the flesh and not just their voices, was the biggest reunion of all.

They really were a Clan.

And their emotions were shared.

Big smiles quickly warped into frowns, eyes lit up with joy and relief before welling with tears, and then shedding them onto sweat-stained cheeks.

Coolant vests were discarded as soon as the Clanners had debarked from their cockpits, knowing they would be replaced by fresh ones from the Mech-techs.

After a frenzy of hugs and collective sobbing into shoulders, the pilots thanked their technicians in passing. They had survived their mission, but they knew full well that it was only part one.

A battle that had been waged and won on many fronts, but also lost on others.

The war awaited them.

And with great haste, the nine that were now seven, proceeded with the spirits of Luke and Fox fueling their determination.

11

Dull orange, like a rotting tangerine, their enemy's blood was far from beautiful on a forty-foot war machine. The Mechs undergoing rearmament in their respective bays within the hangar belonged to Onyx and Mako. No repairs were being made, fortunately; just ballistic weapons to re-supply, and the cleaning of joints, thruster exhausts, and canopies.

Many of them were more than just blotched by enemy gore, but caked in it. Especially the arm cannons of a par-ticular Onyx *Pluto* and the feet of a Mako *Tyrant*.

"Looks like Carmine waded through the enemy quite a bit," Eddie had said, as the pilots passed the Mechs.

"Glad to see his *Tyrant* came back," Wally said. "Not that I'm surprised."

"The *Fenrir* they had isn't here," H said, shaking her head. "Goddammit."

"Nor is the *Tarantula* and *Rottweiler*," Nomi said. "Must've been their casualties. I wonder how bad it was in Stockton."

"HQ said they got out of their Mechs," H added. She glanced at Eddie and Mal after saying it, and gave them a suggestive stare.

"Can't say I don't blame 'em," Eddie confessed, shrugging.

"Hell of a time *that* was," Mal sighed.

Everyone who wasn't H suddenly gawked at Eddie and Mal.

"Let me guess," Charly said. "Civilians."

Mal nodded. "And a big, fat, spiky gator-looking piece of shit. Turns out, some Hounds, too."

"I'm gonna go out a limb and say," Brick flashed a lopsided smirk, "we're all on the same page with callsigns."

"More or less," Wally nodded.

After exiting the Mech hangar and entering the base's inner corridors, they made a beeline to the nearest restroom. They had to pass through two different auto-doors before reaching it, nevermind all the personnel bumping into them en route.

Most of the base crew that were in the corridors and exchanged glances with the stone-faced Ember Clan were speechless. Some tried to say something moving, or express gratitude for their service, but the pilots were moving too fast.

Rude as it might have seemed in hindsight, they didn't have the luxury of stopping. For anything.

Except the restroom.

Once inside, the pilots disseminated to take care of themselves individually. Although unisex, the large restroom offered nine stalls, four urinals, and eight sinks.

The first person back outside was Wally. He immediately turned a corner and got on a base phone, which could not dial out, but only call specific rooms. He knew the number for the Communications Center on the top floor of the compound.

He had to get confirmation on the status of Farooq and his fiancé.

Meanwhile, Brick, H, and Mal exited the bathroom and proceeded to pace in the corridor.

Inside, the other pilots handled themselves less swiftly.

Knowing what was at stake, and that they could mourn better through the aggression of combat, the men and women didn't take much longer. They washed up and exited like waves in a storm.

A few shoulder slaps and sullen nods later, the Clan proceeded around the corner. Wally stood with his back to the phone, and the look on his face alone said enough. He had not gotten good news.

H hugged him, and they touched foreheads. The other pilots hung arms over shoulders, huddling together in consolation.

"We," Wally said through a deep, hoarse voice, and the pilots parted. "We have work to do."

Everyone nodded firmly, resolutely.

In unison, with equal vigor, they made their way to the debriefing wing of the compound. Specifically, DB-Room C2. Spacious but less so than the small auditorium they had been briefed in by Captain Bonheur, it had a large rectangular table, twelve pedestal chairs, and a seventy-inch screen centered on the left wall.

Entering the room, the pilots were relieved to find it occupied.

With space to spare.

The pedestal chairs had mesh backs, and swiveled. Some of them were still moving, as if whoever had just been in them left in a hurry.

"Who did we miss?" Eddie asked out loud.

There were four people at the head of the table, on the other side of the room. An older man in an AMF uniform, whose badges alone indicated he was high in the command chain, Captain Bonheur herself, and two younger personnel; Eddie guessed, communications crew. They held holo-tablets; one of them had it returned to her by the older man. His white hair, what little of it remained, had seen better days; so had his rough, clean-shaven face.

"Please, have a seat," Captain Bonheur gestured. "And I presume you mean Mako and Onyx. Or, what remains of them."

"That'll be enough, Captain," the officer said firmly. He cleared his throat while Bonheur's eyes lowered from Eddie, and bowed her head.

"Yes, Major."

Suddenly the pilots stiffened, and saluted.

"At ease, Ember," the white-haired man sighed. He beckoned the pilots, and they quickly took seats closest to his end of the table.

"Pardon me, Major," Eddie said, trying to sustain the bark in his bite, "but why can't we know more about our other Clans? We may not be as close to them as we are each other, but—"

The Major raised his hand.

Eddie stopped and lowered his head. His strong eyes, however, lifted up after a moment.

"You may know as much as you already do," the Major replied. "But that is all, and why is that all, Captain?"

Bonheur turned, rigidly, to face the sitting pilots.

237

"Because time and strategy is essential, not emotions," she said. The look on her face showed that she didn't wholeheartedly agree with this statement, but at the same time she grasped its sentiment.

Nomi did not.

She stood up, pounding a fist into the wooden table at the same time.

"I'll be *damned* if I bury my emotions, *sir*," she said through her teeth, tears glazing her eyes. "We may be Mech pilots but we are not Mechs ourselves. We are *not* robots, sir."

The Major sighed deeply. Emotionally, one could interpret.

He lowered his head, and closed his eyes. Nobody said a thing and suddenly Nomi felt terribly uncomfortable being the only one standing, except Bonheur.

"We fight for those who choose flight," the Major said, quietly but audibly, his head still down and his eyes still shut. "We battle with weapons of war…"

He lifted his head, and his chin.

As he spoke the next line, so did every single pilot in the room. Captain Bonheur mouthed the words. It was almost entirely in perfect unison.

"For those who battle with heart."

Nomi sat down, her lip quivering.

"I apologize for sounding blunt and cruel, Ember," the Major said. "But this *is* war, make no mistake. Losses have been suffered on all fronts. From tanks to Mechs to entire convoys, and the men and women that formed them. Not just here. All over this planet. *Our* home. Not…theirs."

The Major stood, and the pilots began to stand, too. He

immediately gave a wave, motioning for them to stay seated.

He put his hands behind his back, clutching a forearm as he spoke.

"My name is Reigart. Major Gene Reigart. I've flown up from the AMF Hub in Anaheim."

This compound outside of Sacramento was just a forward operating base. There were many AMF FOBs scattered throughout the United States, each one strategically positioned outside a major city. An AMF Hub, however, was exclusive to higher ranked personnel and strategists. They were not as active as FOBs, since the end of the Great Mech War.

There were only four in North America.

Every continent on the planet had at least two AMF Hubs.

So to hear that Major Reigart flew up from the Anaheim Hub said a lot in so few words.

Not that any of them were doubting the gravity of the situation as a whole.

A vast, global whole.

"That said," Major Reigart continued, "I bring the highest commendation for your efforts in Sacramento, and the achievement of taking back the city. San Francisco, Los Angeles, San Diego, and many other large cities in our great nation, however, are still captive to our enemy. But! Our enemy…is dying on their hill.

"Ember Hawks, I know you have seen this. Your audio and visual reconnaissance of San Francisco are testament of the enemy's capabilities—and their weaknesses. Other

Clans across the country, as well as Paris, Istanbul, Mombasa, and more, are rallying their greatest efforts to defeat this terrible enemy."

Reigart's voice climbed to an aggressive yet triumphant crescendo. Then he gathered himself and his tone continued at an even pace.

"What I need from all of you, Ember, is trust and devotion. Trust in AMF intelligence, and devotion to the AMF creed. That we do in fact fight for those we love, to preserve our way of life, against anything that threatens it."

He took a rugged breath and leaned forward, fingertips extended to the table.

His voice sank a little.

"Your Sacramento convoy has already been dispatched to escort Onyx and Mako to Berkeley and Oakland. All non-Mech ground vehicles are, from here on, forbidden from entering an occupied city, due to the close-quarters threats. We cannot risk another Stockton. Onyx and Mako lost their entire convoy, and suffered losses themselves, because their pilots left their cockpits for…for noble reasons, albeit."

The Major seemed to get choked up for a moment. It didn't last, but it was nonetheless powerful and sincere. He stood up again and straightened his uniform.

"So, no Mech pilot is to leave their cockpit for any reason, unless absolutely *goddamn* necessary to the progression of their mission. Is that understood!?"

"Sir, yes, sir!" A unified, stern response.

"Excellent. There is little else I can tell you all at this crucial moment in our species' history. This is not an American conflict. It is a global struggle. But the enemy

240

is…dying, we believe."

Charly and Brick exchanged glances. There was a weight of sorrow, and respect, in their eyes.

The other pilots remembered Fox in the same fashion. Although they wished they had been there, not to witness his death, but his valor.

And while Eddie believed he had been the only one to see Luke's sacrifice, Wally had, too, though from afar. Certainly over time, this would come to light, but for now it was Eddie's burden to carry. Yet, also, his blessing.

There wasn't one breath he took from that point forward that was not reinforced by the love and *undying* support of Lucas Shaw.

"I can only fathom that you all have questions regarding our enemy," Reigart continued. He cleared his throat. "I unfortunately cannot divulge much information. Not because of some NDA with AMF and NASA, but because, well, frankly…we are in the dark on the matter. Due to the threats, there have been no successful attempts at investigating the opening in what we believe to not only be space but time itself, above our skies."

The men and women at the table adjusted in their seats and exchanged befuddled looks. It certainly wasn't comforting to know that neither AMF nor NASA had made any headway into investigating their enemy's source.

Or as they had secretly come to believe, their enemy's actual homeworld.

"Felix Kowalski," Charly said, startling her comrades, Brick especially, "believed that our enemies descended from their own realm. Possibly even another dimension. And that…their world was dying, hence the falling of their structures and...*troops*, if you will."

Charly looked around the table and realized it might not have been the best forum to pose this theory. Her brow furrowed with an iota of regret in hindsight, but when her eyes reconnected with Reigart, she didn't back down.

She had read curiosity in the older officer's gaze. A genuine, even patient, curiosity.

She remembered Fox, what he had said, the passion behind it, and the commendable pilot he was. The man, the friend, which he would always be to them.

"It was the last thing he said to us, before his Hawk went down. No quip or words of inspiration. Just a...a statement, Major."

"That our world is dying," Brick said, his voice unwavering. The weight and grief behind it, however, was unmistakable. "And to not let them take ours with it."

Major Reigart nodded twice before clearing his throat. His gaze lifted, to nobody in particular. Ultimately he walked over to stand beside Captain Bonheur, whose face looked worse for wear, subjected to the emotions subtly bubbling within the debriefing room. Not to mention what it had been like in the company of Mako and Onyx.

"It is to my understanding that Kowalski, and Shaw, were both laudable pilots," Reigart said. "Veterans of the Great War, and in ways nobody will truly understand, except for you all here, *heroes*, of this one."

Everyone nodded, firmly.

"Ember," Reigart declared, and immediately Eddie stood up from his seat, saluting. The others followed without hesitation. Reigart nodded. "You shall carry their spirits with you, in your valiant return to the warzone that has become our beloved San Francisco. You will fight with the honor, courage, discipline, and *brutality* that is demanded of you in this trying time."

"Nothing less, sir," Eddie said, arms at his sides and chin up.

"I'd like to advise you all not to fight with vengeance in your hearts," Reigart said with a heavy sigh, "but I understand that would be a silly thing to expect of you at this point."

He turned and looked at Bonheur, who lowered her head. He then looked at the closed doors, at the clock on the wall behind Eddie, and at the black screen a few feet from that. Then he looked up, at the ceiling, or beyond it in theory, and shut his eyes.

When he lowered his face again, his eyes opened, and his brow stiffened.

There was no mootness to his gaze.

"However," he said, "we are *all* avenging those fallen on this fateful day."

His eyes rested on Wally.

"Some family, some friends, but in the end," he scanned the faces of every pilot in the room, "all casualties of the human race. That is what we are protecting. And this day, it began beautifully. A gorgeous sunrise."

Major Reigart's tone softened for those last few words. In his ensuing sentence, however, his voice gradually built into a crushing crescendo, a herald of victory.

"Let us end it, with an unforgettable sunset, and not let these *abominations* witness a *single tomorrow*, here on Earth!"

With the energy of a coach at halftime, tenfold, Major

Reigart had managed to rouse the pilots into a cheering outburst. If their morale had not been monumentally lifted, he would be shocked.

At the absolute least, he knew it was an effective adrenaline shot, and hoped it wouldn't be short-lived.

"Now get out there and give 'em hell!" Major Reigart punctuated, and like a group of footballers the pilots exited the debriefing room in a storm.

Behind them, Reigart gently elbowed Bonheur, who was already smiling. The old man's face slowly lit up with pride and confidence, not just in himself, but his pilots, too.

"Told ya, Captain," Reigart smirked, "the Major's still got it."

12

Eddie had never seen Mech-techs speak and move with such vigor, at least not since the last days of the Great War. They clearly had unparalleled faith in Ember Clan, which they knew was well-placed. Whether the AMF technicians were tenured and experienced or novices at their jobs, Ember's reputation preceded them.

Now most of all, that they defended more than just their country, but in essence, their species.

It was not lost to Eddie and his teammates that elsewhere in the world, other AMF pilots—among military, police, and even strong civilian men and women—were taking the same stand. Fighting, standing ground, and risking their lives to ensure the longevity of others.

All in the name of humanity.

Their fight wasn't selfish to one nation.

But to all.

Reentering his *Adversary* was almost as rejuvenating a feeling as Major Reigart's speech. Which he had taken to heart, just as he trusted his teammates had, as well.

Perhaps more so for Wally and Nomi. He knew how close Nomi was to Luke, their friendship closer to a father-daughter bond. Luke had saved her life once, and now twice, and Eddie knew what it felt like, only for him, there would be no repaying.

Not traditionally, anyway.

He certainly wouldn't waste the gift.

"How's that *Rottweiler* look?" Eddie asked.

Their comms were crisp and devoid of any hint of interference.

"You saw it, she's standing proud again," Nomi said.

They all occupied their Mechs now, outside of the hangar where they last left them. The knee actuator of the *Rottweiler* had been adeptly and swiftly repaired. There was some scarring to the armor around the joint, above the Mech's unique digitigrade feet, but the actuator itself was brand new.

"Glad to hear it," Eddie said. He pivoted his *Adversary*'s torso to face the newest addition to the Ember Wolves. "I know it's no *Fenrir*, but how you doing, H?"

"My *chest* is bigger than this thing," H said.

Eddie couldn't resist laughing. The whole crew gave in.

"Don't undersell yourself, H, you're a fucking vet," Wally said.

H had to remind herself that she did, in fact, have more experience as an AMF pilot than anybody present.

"Yeah, well, I guess, then..." She took a deep breath, not sounding too excited. "I'm adjusting."

"You'll be a *Pluto* master in no time," Eddie said.

"No choice there," Eddie said, glancing at his radar. Two blips appeared, incoming. "Airlift is on approach. Can't do much off your feet, H, but I know you'll get the hang of it once we reach S-F."

"Yeah, copy," H sighed. "I just miss her is all."

"We all will. The *Fenrir* is iconic for a reason."

"A pilot makes their Mech, not the other way around," Mal said.

"Oh, Christ," Brick said, from the cockpit of his grounded Hawk, eighty feet away. "Is she really quoting Snow again?"

Mal chuckled, shrugging. "He is a wise man."

"He is a rich man," Charly added.

"But we are richer," Eddie said. "In camaraderie and experience."

"Amen," Charly nodded, her voice sincere.

"Ember, this is Javelin Niner, we were never properly introduced," an airlift pilot said, his voice familiar on their comms.

"Howdy, cowboy," Charly smirked.

"Ignore her, Javelin," Eddie said lightheartedly, but only at first. "Happy to have you two back. This is Locke. You've been instructed by the Major himself, I assume?"

"Affirmative," the man replied, a slightly blithe tone underlying his professionalism. "We're honored to be your escort once more."

"It's appreciated, Javelin, got you in my sights."

The two airlifts came into view, flying low.

"We've been green-lit, Eddie," Charly said.

"Copy. Pave our way, wingnuts."

"Follow the corpses," Brick joked.

The two Hawk VTOLs lifted off the tarmac, their tilt-wing thrusters burning freshly refueled hydrogen.

Before the pair of airlifts arrived, Brick and Charly flew off, thrusters searing the air in their wake. Their crafts looped around each other's flight path like a helix, a fancy maneuver that Fox would sometimes do himself, around

Charly.

Eddie grinned, shaking his head, and saluted.

"Unfortunately, we can't follow suit," Javelin said. "But we'll definitely get you there."

Eddie chuckled. He started to say something but Wally beat him to it.

"Grateful," he said. "Better that way, in fact."

"I concur," Eddie said.

The two airlifts descended stably, their magnetic cables dangling to connect. The five Mechs were hoisted, safe and sound.

"Heavier load this time," Javelin said.

"H's *Fenrir* got scrapped in the last battle," Eddie took the opportunity to save her from explaining the predicament. "She had been riding in the *Bandit*, so we were down one Mech. Well, two technically."

Eddie took a deep breath.

"And," he concluded, "the *Pluto* was the only Mech available on reserve."

"This thing's less than half the tonnage as my *Fenrir*," H griped.

"Faster, then," Javelin said. Eddie imagined him shrugging as the airlift pilot spoke.

They had begun their controlled flight toward San Francisco from the AMF base. Despite the revitalization from Reigart's speech, the Ember Wolves were now subjected to relaxing in their snug coolant vests and lingering in their cockpits.

Which, for H, was almost torturous. The *Pluto*'s cockpit was a third the size of the *Fenrir*'s. It protruded from the Mech's ovoid torso in a conical fashion not unlike the

Fenrir, but was nonetheless remarkably smaller.

"Yeah, much faster," H said, agreeing but not sounding thrilled about it. "Which means it's easier to topple, has less armor, less armaments, and—"

"Higher speeds, more maneuverability," Mal said, "longer hop-jet duration, and is a harder-to-hit target."

"Yeah, 'cause your enemy's barely flinched from the damage you've inflicted," H retorted.

Mal and Nomi laughed.

"Simmer down, H," Wally said. "You and I both know that a great pilot makes the most of their Mech. Even if it was as small as a *Pluto*'s fucking *leg*."

H sighed. She knew full well.

"Just look at Mal," Eddie said. "Survived our entire excursion without suffering any damage, helped take down a Titan, and even when she was out of ammo, picked up *your* sorry ass."

"Right, right," H nodded. She shrugged. She then dialed a private frequency with Mal. "Told you. His heart's got your name written on it."

Mal caught herself from replying on the team channel, and adjusted her comms to respond to H privately.

She laughed first. "If you say so."

"He's practically drooling," H said.

"No, no." Mal smirked. "That's coolant fluid."

"Or something else," H said, and Mal scoffed.

"I'm just excited to have my reserves maxed out again," Eddie said.

H let out a laugh into her private channel with Mal before she backed out of it and returned to the team frequency.

"I've never met a pilot more obsessed with the particle projector cannon," Wally said. "Yet you're going on about your ballistics."

"Ammo is ammo," Eddie shrugged. "And sure, yeah, the PPC is the single best invention this side of the century, but…"

A few laughs echoed over the channel.

The airlift pilots weren't excluded.

"*But* it produces more heat than a *Colossus* going critical," Eddie continued.

The exaggeration wasn't criticized for good reason. Despite the famed and praised damage potential of a PPC, let alone a Mech with two of them, its standard heat generation was notorious to say the least.

Make that a *pair* of PPCs on a Mech that didn't have the heat-sink configuration of a Support Class model, and you had a problem. Any pilot who favored their PPCs on such a Mech would face serious challenges in the battlefield.

Eddie, however, was always game.

"Be that as it may," Wally said, "I'm sure you could've lasted another hour without resupplying."

"Could've, sure," Eddie said, with a hint of dramatized arrogance. "But ideally? Nah."

"Well, *ideally*," Wally huffed, "we'd all be living in a parallel dimension where ammunition was *infinite*."

"EBWs are infinite," H squeaked.

"Can we not talk about parallel dimensions, please?" Nomi said, disgustedly.

Although she did bring the carefree conversation down

a peg, nobody blamed her. The source of her pettiness literally hung over their heads.

Punctuating what she said, almost all of them leaned forward in their seats to peer up through their canopies. They could see a faint impression of the sky's rupture past the clouds, but clearer from their current airborne position than when they walked the ground below. Still, they assumed it was a much bolder sight from cities such as San Francisco.

How the tear in space—and time?—managed to umbrella so many metropolises, and only those, was beyond the pilots' understanding. They had long since given up trying to grasp the science behind their enemy's capabilities, and sheer existence.

It was all too confounding.

All too terrifying.

The team sat in tension-thick silence for over ten minutes. Some of them took the time to meditate and collect their thoughts, their composure, and what this battle really meant for them. Not just on a personal level, but on a worldwide scale.

Reigart's words resounded in skulls and hearts. There was flair for the sake of flair and then there was actual wisdom.

What Reigart had said was not spewed simply to boost morale and stir their spirits. It was a combat-geared sagacity that struck the warrior chords in every pilot present.

Eddie believed this was a shared mindset for Charly and Brick, too.

And as problematic with authority as H had been in the past, especially before the Great War, he knew that she felt

251

this, too. Deeply, even. The same went for Luke, in theory; he had always been dubious of higher ranked uniforms sharing sentiments with troops and field pilots.

Eddie knew Luke well, and well enough that he believed the man would not be incredulous of Reigart.

He was ready to disappoint nobody in their encroaching battle. Which meant, too, that he would have to be even more brazen in combat than ever before.

Especially in the horrid face of such an enemy.

"We've an incoming message of high priority from HQ," Javelin announced.

Everybody sat upright in their seats. Wally had been pacing his cockpit; he quickly returned to his seat. Those who had disengaged their harnesses now strapped themselves in again.

"Patch us in, Javelin," Eddie said.

A spurt of static surrounded a voice from base. The transmission slowly clarified. There was a hoarseness in the man's speech that took Eddie by surprise; not the usual HQ transmitter.

"Ember, listen up," the masculine tone said. Immediately, Eddie and the others perked, attentive.

Meanwhile, outside their canopies, it was clear that the airlifts were adjusting their course. Nothing severe, just taking a different route in the same direction.

"We've received valuable Intel from the Tidal Wolves up in Seattle. After assessing the information, we've chosen to alter your current strategy, as it would greatly benefit your team and, with any luck, the endgame."

Feeling a little defensive, and wanting to be as gung-ho about their original plan as possible, Eddie impulsively countered.

"What might have worked up in Seattle may not down here," he said, trying to regulate the attitude he gave off. "Besides, we don't want any shortcuts. Tell your Intel team—"

"This is Major Reigart speaking, pilot!" The transmitter snapped.

Eddie mouthed an expletive and kneaded his forehead with all five fingers. He was embarrassed and surely his teammates felt the same for him.

"Now," Reigart continued, assertive as ever, *"you will comply with these orders as they are in you and your team's best interest! I understand your frustration and skepticism, but this is a matter that could potentially solve our problem on a massive scale."*

Eddie resisted exhaling, not wanting a sigh to be misinterpreted over the channel.

Instead, he spoke with apologetic conviction, and the devotion of his Clan.

"My apologies, Major. I understand. My team and I will give our all for any strategy that shows such promise."

Reigart cleared his throat over the frequency. It was a grating, more than audible expression that conveyed his acceptance without actually saying it.

"Excellent," he finally said. *"Because I wanted to give this information to you all* personally.*"*

"We're all ears, Major," Eddie said. He then saw the distinctive skyline of San Francisco appear against the horizon. For once, not a single Tooth-structure stood amongst the high-rises, so few of them still intact. Eddie's right hand gripped his joystick. "All ears and trigger fingers."

"That's the spirit, pilot. Hang onto it, 'cause this strategy will call for some guts. And I know the Ember Wolves have plenty of that. Rest assured, your Hawks have already been notified."

"I take it Fallon and Knight took the news with more confidence than I did?" Eddie said.

Reigart actually snickered over the channel. Eddie counted that as a small victory he would take to his grave.

"That's correct," the Major replied, and paused. *"Locke, is it?"*

Eddie nodded. "Yes, sir."

"Your Hawks should be arriving shortly, if not already, judging by your current location."

"What's the plan, sir?"

"The word's spreading, this may be our best bet of eradicating the enemy once and for all. As it worked in Seattle, and reportedly Winnipeg, hopefully more to come, this has been designated Operation Subterfuge."

"Subterfuge, sir?" Eddie asked, brow furrowed.

He pictured the Major nodding before answering, with poise.

"Correct. Your new strategy will be to infiltrate S-F as originally planned, but only for the sake of attracting attention. Your Hawks will help herd the big ones, which I believe you've come to call Titans."

"Affirmative."

"How fitting. And so will these Titans fall."

"Yes, sir."

"Mind you, your primary goal is not to engage these

Titans to kill *them, but to* lure *them."*

"Out of the city," Wally thought out loud.

"Correct, pilot," Major Reigart said. *"Mechs are huge heat signatures, especially your* Mastodon, *so your Clan will be the best targets for the enemy's infrared. You'll engage the Titans sporadically, enough to keep them interested, ultimately baiting them to a specific waypoint, vacant of civilian life."*

Eddie spotted a yellow caret appear on his HUD, and toggled his satellite view of the surrounding area. The waypoint was to be their drop-zone, near the tip of the San Francisco Peninsula. He magnified the radar. Specifically, they would be landing outside the Presidio of San Francisco, on the south side of the Golden Gate Bridge. Although ruptured halfway across, the Bridge still stood, its red towers piercing clouds as distinctly as ever.

Eddie's hand gripped his joystick so firmly that, in the back of his mind, he feared it would break under the pressure.

"Where will we be leading them, sir?" Nomi asked.

"Not far from your infil," Reigart replied.

"The Peninsula," Mal said. Half question, half statement. She, too, was just then observing her radar. And, lifting her eyes, she and the others could see their approach of the Golden Gate.

"Correct," Reigart said. *"Pacific Heights, specifically. You'll drop down just outside the Presidio, in the National Park. The Californian in me would suggest you watch your step, but the military man in me has to admit— that it won't matter in an hour or two."*

"Sir?" Nomi asked, brow furrowed.

Major Reigart sighed. *"You'll lure as many Titans, in one wave, to your waypoint at the Presidio Golf Course. As close to the end of Veterans Boulevard as you can manage. There, they'll meet their fate."*

"MOAB?" Wally asked, his throat dry.

"God, no. Negative. Carpet-bombing. We'll hit 'em hard and fast, bury their noses in the dirt. Supposing they'll have noses after the first few detonate."

"Yield?" Eddie asked.

"Each payload will be about a ton's worth of TNT," Reigart said. *"So, think three Tomahawks."*

Wally did a low whistle.

"How many bombs in each payload?" Mal asked.

"Four Mk-85s. Depending on your Hawks' report from the air, we'll adjust our delivery. But the first three bombers will be ready to strafe as soon as you give the signal, Ember."

"What signal?" Eddie gulped.

"The second your lead Mech steps foot on that Golf Course, you tell one of your Hawks. They'll radio our bombers for a rapid response. ETA from their position to yours, expect a window of twenty to thirty seconds."

"Jesus," Eddie muttered.

"Precisely. So as soon as that signal is given, you and your Wolves maintain speed. Hoof it as far as the Peninsula will take you, but I can guarantee that you won't come close to the water. Let alone the Presidio itself. Your Hawks will be your eyes in the sky. They'll tell you when to brace."

As Reigart spoke, the airlifts carried the Mechs over

Winfield Scott Park. And then the Presidio of San Francisco, another decommissioned military base converted into a national park.

"It is imperative that I reiterate my last point," Reigart said, and took a deep breath. *"Regardless of your proximity to the targets, those bombs* will *drop. Be grateful you're in AMF Mechs, and brace for impact. Due to the bombing method, the shockwaves should be minimal, depending on your range. As soon as the bombs deploy, I recommend crouching your Mechs to avoid tipping over. If you are in fact too close when they start whistling, eject and propel yourself as far north as possible."*

Eddie knew it was a lot to take in, but in theory it was a much simpler strategy than those he had been thrust into last-minute during the Great War. At least their enemy here, while enormous and indiscriminately barbaric, were more or less mindless. They might not be scientifically stupid, but their reliance on heat vision gave them a huge weakness that could and would be manipulated.

"Javelin Niner, your airlift crew…" Reigart's transmission was suddenly clouded with interference. *"…informed of…Subterfuge and…be back…exfil when…confirmed…"*

The airlifts paused over a large baseball field that shared property with a tennis court, soccer field, and basketball court.

More static made the transmission unlistenable.

"Stand-by, Ember," Javelin said. "Running communications filters. Interference should be expected this close to the city, even with the enemy's structures no longer standing. Skyfall or not."

Eddie slackened his harnesses and leaned forward in his seat, peering up through his canopy. He could just barely see the sky directly above the airlifts, from under their open cargo holds.

The fissure in Earth's exosphere looked narrower than he remembered.

He leaned back and secured his harness.

After a drag from his water tube, he started nodding to himself, collecting his thoughts. Rallying his hopes, ambitions, and courage.

"They're dying, alright," he mumbled, barely audible.

"What's that, boss?" Wally asked.

Eddie opened his mouth more. "They're dying, man. Fox was fucking right. And Luke helped prove it, too. These things are mortal, *weak* even. They're just *flesh*, end of the day. Like us, but with no tech. They're exposed, and right now, their morale is *fucked*. Look up. Their little slit in space is sealing. Their world isn't retreating, it's slipping away. From existence."

Eddie nodded more. A wicked grin dominated his features.

"It's returning to the void. Death has claimed their kind. It's time we escort the rest of them."

In their other Mechs, Eddie's teammates nodded and slowly absorbed his words as wisdom. Whether or not they fully understood his perspective, or necessarily believed him, they could tell *he* had faith in what he said. And that sufficed for them.

"Forget Snow," Mal said. "From now on, I'm quoting Locke."

Eddie's lips closed but he still grinned.

"Patch up those comms, Javelin," he said, hand on his joystick. "And put our feet on the ground. We've got a fucking duty to fulfill."

13

Home plate. Just missed by a half-ton toe belonging to Eddie's *Adversary*. The rest of the Mech's foot pancaked the turf. In the outfield, Wally's *Mastodon* and H's new steel-blue *Pluto* touched down. It was a softer landing than their previous descent to tarmac, outside of the Mech hangar. Here, they were at the outskirts of densely residential San Francisco.

Landing on the pitcher's mound was one of the *Bandit*'s feet. Mal grimaced, but it quickly transitioned into a sarcastic smirk.

"I know you hated playing softball growing up," H said, "but damn, that was harsh."

Mal chuckled. "I'll take it."

"H, weren't you a home-runner?" Eddie asked. It was insane to remember that he, Charly, and Brick went to the AMF Academy together in 2048. Eighteen years ago, the three of them met H, who was thirty at the time. And already a pilot, before any of them knew how to operate hopjets.

"They called me the Babe," H said.

"They called someone else that, eons ago," Wally said. "And it wasn't a woman."

"That's the joke."

"I know," Wally grinned.

H rolled her eyes. "Double-entendres. How lovely."

"Focus, Wolves," Eddie said. He turned his *Adversary* to face the greater San Francisco area. A few hundred feet from the edge of the outfield was a row of small houses.

Miles beyond that, a metropolis visible to the high-seated Mech pilots.

The skyline of downtown San Francisco was currently cast beneath the afternoon sun. It would still be a few hours until sunset, which was something to both be grateful for and nauseated by.

Eddie was thankful that this conflict would be waged in the expanse of a day. Although, more realistically, the threats wouldn't be completely neutralized for days to follow, and rebuilding wouldn't begin for months.

SAR teams and other infantry crew would be tasked with mopping up potential stragglers in the coming weeks.

The nausea came from a simple acknowledgement: that such sweeping, grave losses of life and structural destruction were the result of less than a day's assault.

Assuming—praying—that they were in fact on the cusp of victory, for good. Any thought that their enemy might return or attempt to prolong the attack was mind-boggling.

A reason why none of the pilots, not even Major Reigart, acknowledged this possibility.

Not at the moment, in any case.

Their focus was the present, and immediate future.

"Sir," Javelin said. "We've got Major Reigart back on comms. Much clearer now, but don't know for how long."

"Copy, we appreciate it," Eddie said. "Patch him through."

"You read? Ember?" There was hesitation in Reigart's voice. At this point, it was undeniably his voice.

Eddie still kicked himself for not recognizing it earlier.

"Crystal," he said. "We got cut off, sir. You were last discussing our exfil details."

"That's right. And the interference should be expected with—"

"The structures and all that, yeah," Eddie nodded, waving his hand. "Even though they're not standing. Regardless of Skyfall."

"I take it you've been out of practice, talking to someone who not only outranks you but also out-experiences you, Locke," Major Reigart said, with more amusement than anger.

"I, uh…apologies, sir."

"Right, well, before you interrupted me, I was going to say—the comms interference should be expected with the recent developments. It seems that tear in our exosphere is closing. *NASA estimates that it'll be as if it didn't exist in the first place, in less than six hours. They're currently trying to lob a satellite or probe up in there, but every time they try, it gets fried. Some kind of cosmic distortion, or uh…"*

Reigart trailed off briefly, mumbling the rest.

"I dunno, frankly, it all went over my head."

"Literally, sir, and we're with you," Eddie said, although he was taking the reins of speaking for the rest of Ember. He of course knew that if Fox was present, he'd be all over *that* conversation.

"Right, well, that's that," Reigart sighed. *"As for your exfil…Javelin will be—"*

"Hold up, sorry sir," Wally blurted.

Movement had caught his eyes before anyone else's. His *Mastodon* served as a sort of lookout tower, tall as it stood. All of the Mechs had clear sightlines above the residential districts sprawled before them, but there were some trees that only Wally could just barely see up over.

He now grimaced at what he witnessed.

"I've got two Titans trudging toward us. Half a mile." He gritted his teeth in anger. "Careless footing, boss."

"Major?" Eddie said. "I hate to be rude for a third time in half an hour, but can you make it snappy?"

Although not audibly laughing, there was a grunt of a sound that made everyone picture Reigart smiling.

In the next heartbeat, his inflection stiffened, and his delivery accelerated.

"Copy, now listen up. Javelin's gonna come back for ya after *your Clan confirms kills, from the bombing. You do not seek confirmation until your Hawks give you the green light. Clear?"*

"Got it, sir."

"It seems our heat-signature plan is working already," Wally said. "They're still coming. Angrily."

"Not as angrily as we will be, Wally, sit tight," Eddie said. "Major, anything else?"

The punch of thrusters scorching the air caught the attention of everybody in the field, not just Wally. Although, from where they stood, only Wally could actually witness the pair of Hawks soar through the air, strafing the two Titans with precise Lasers and Vulcan bursts.

"What's that, what am I hearing?" Reigart asked, as their sound-dampened cockpits still picked up the distinct

noise.

"Our Hawks givin' 'em hell, sir," Wally grinned.

The Clanners cheered quietly. As if they weren't already fired up for battle, that certainly did the job.

"Excellent," Reigart said. *"Was gonna say, downtown has been cleared of major threats, especially with the cessation of Skyfall. Both big and small, our enemy has started pushing to the residential areas near the Peninsula, where the majority of civilians are."*

"Early Intel stated they'd be in bunkers, mostly," Mal said.

"Correct, but that probably only accounts for an eighth of the population. At least a quarter has already been...killed. Then there are those hiding, above-ground. I can't say which houses do or don't have bunkers. Most of 'em have shelters of some kind, which should by now survive a trampling."

"So what you're saying is, don't mind our footing?" Eddie asked, hating to pose the question.

"As much as you can afford, mentally. Try to focus on your targets, and the plan. Keep 'em interested in nothing but you*. Don't get out of your Mechs, and stay mobile."*

"Copy, Major."

"Your Hawks will remain in the city to mop up smaller targets to the best of their abilities, fuel, and ammo, after Operation Subterfuge has run its course."

"They're already doing a great job now, sir," Wally said. He paused and frowned. "Although they don't seem to be luring them this way."

"That's their plan; to herd 'em, as much at once, to your exfil. We wanna avoid the risk of these things wising

up."

"Right. Makes sense, sir."

"Eventually, albeit on a smaller scale, Mako and Onyx will conduct the same operation on the south side of S-F, once San Mateo is designated safe. We are almost there, folks. Once we relinquish the Bay Area of enemy presence, we can face tomorrow's sunrise with a slightly less heavy heart."

Everybody nodded. It felt like all the motivation they needed.

"We'll be back, though, won't we, Major?" Eddie asked. "Tell me…that we'll be back."

"You'll be sent wherever you're needed, Ember. Wherever you're willing to go."

"For California? For America?" Mal said. She shook her head. "For *humans*? We're in it, Major."

"That's what I hoped to hear, pilot," Reigart said. He proceeded to speak vociferously. *"Because this is it. Word is being spread, across the globe, that they're falling; not just from the sky, but from their high horses. Many of them die on impact, too. It seems that San Francisco has seen the worst of it, but these monsters, they haven't seen the worst of us. It's time to go out and there and give it to 'em.*

"Prove that we never stopped trying. And will never truly rest until their scourge has been wiped off the face of the Earth."

"Weapons ready, sir," Eddie said.

"Clear to engage, Ember. Over."

Reigart's transmission ended.

The thrusters to the hovering airlifts above them tilted, and propelled them away.

"See you soon, Javelin out."

"Fly safe," Eddie said, and then looked at his Mechs. "Wally, take the lead. Nomi, on his left. I've got his right. Mal and H, push forward, both sides, post routes."

Everyone "copied" and started to advance.

Started to.

"Boss, I can't do this," Wally said, the blocky toes of his *Mastodon* mere feet from the edge of the nearest house, having already crushed its tiny backyard.

The homes were so tightly packed, like sardines, and rows upon rows of them, for hundreds of square miles.

"Switch to thermal," Eddie advised. The *Mastodon* is the only one among us with precise infrared tech. We can only detect intense signatures. You should be able to—"

"It's working. Haven't had the need for this, not even in training."

"That's 'cause no Clanner is mad enough to bring the fight to suburbia."

"Right. But *these* things…"

"Completely different," Eddie said, irascible. "So what's it reading?"

"Uh, good and not good. I mean…half the city's already been leveled. Most of these houses have been walked on well before our arrival. None of the Teeth landed here, at least, but I'm seeing some tentacles where houses should be."

"The smaller creatures come outta those, right?"

"I believe so." Wally paused and tapped one of his monitors. "Infrared is reading some of those, too but…shit, I could be seeing this wrong, but…I think the rest of our civvies are below deck."

266

Eddie exhaled with relief.

"Makes sense," Mal thought out loud. "Those who survived the first onslaught of feet and quakes, went to their bunkers and shelters."

"Seems that way," Wally nodded.

"Can you mark us a path?" Eddie asked.

Explosions rocking the Titan less than half a mile away caught their attention. The cumbersome cyst-backed abomination teetered and fell forward, crushing two whole blocks in its wake.

"You're supposed to lure, not kill!" Wally shouted into his comms.

If Brick and Charly heard him, they didn't acknowledge.

"Wally, I need a path or I'm gonna start taking leaps of faith," Eddie said, urgently.

"Judging by my readings, we don't need one. At least, we can't afford something that precise."

"Operation Subterfuge," Nomi said, "calls for the luring of those giants *back* to our exfil. The Golf Course, it's about four-hundred feet to our right. So, we'll be retracing our steps anyway."

"And bringing those monsters with us," Mal said. "So it's unavoidable collateral. I hate to say it."

"Empty homes that'll need rebuilding," Eddie said, nodding. Gulping. He directed his Mech forward, and said it again, this time slower: "Empty. Homes."

His *Adversary* strode through a small house, demolished from the ground level by the forward step of a two-ton foot. Then came the next.

"We're not behemoths," Eddie said. "If you can—

Nomi, Mal, H—try to stick to the roads and yards. But don't stress it too much. Our focus is the enemy. We're gonna have to retrace anyway, like Nomi said."

"Copy," H said, and before Mal advanced, piloted her *Pluto* with unsurprising skill into the suburbs.

Mal sighed and proceeded, too.

Wally was last. He didn't care to advance at all, but knew he was especially needed. The heat his Mech gave off, even when inert, was too remarkable not to include in this plan.

Suddenly their comms crackled with new life.

"There are some taller buildings at your two o'clock, Wolves," Brick said. "See 'em?"

"Copy," Eddie said.

"Banks, hotels, gyms. Shit like that. Some of the Titans are that way. Others are pulling in from up north. I think your presence just saved SFO."

"Good timing. Did any of the airport get hit?"

"Parking lots got it pretty bad. Terminal, barely. I mean it. You guys just saved a lotta lives just by showing up. Those Mechs really do put out some heat. Comparably, anyway."

"Especially Wally," Charly said.

"Wonderful," Wally mumbled.

"Oh, and sorry 'bout that Titan," Charly said, the regret in her voice palpable. So was the frustration. "He was being a particularly big pain-in-the-ass."

"We're hoping most of the civvies in the area are underground," Nomi said.

"It looks that way. We did a few flybys and didn't notice anything moving, except some Hounds and Boars."

"These tentacle things, man," Brick said, grimly, "they keep spewing those creatures."

The horridly toothed scarlet and sometimes lighter pink-colored tentacles squirmed lazily around, and sometimes right through, some of the homes they navigated. Many were entirely unmoving, but their exposed tendon-like composition was impossible to ignore.

A reminder that their enemy was at least of the flesh.

"Now that they're cut off from home-sweet-home," Brick continued, "I think they're the enemy's dying carriers. Once they're empty, they wilt and—"

"Two o'clock, Ember!" Charly exclaimed.

She and Brick banked in opposite directions through the air, above the taller buildings a quarter mile ahead of the Mechs.

A Ramada Inn served as the podium of a Hammerhead as it crawled up the back side and mounted it like a gargoyle, facing the approaching Mechs. Its enormous claws dug into the building's anterior, crushing concrete and shattering glass with ease. Debris rained down on cars in the parking lot below. Structural chunks fell, flattening vehicles and demolishing the awning above the front doors.

Around the base of a Citi Bank to the hotel's far left, half a block over, another Hammerhead crawled. At first it just growled and hissed like a three-hundred-ton reptile, mindful of its cover. And then it roared, thunder rolling, and its bony hindquarters crashed through the bank with zero regard.

"Don't waste time and effort on hitting weak spots!" Eddie said. "Just lure these dumb fucks back to the exfil!"

"Incoming from the north," Charly said, her and

Brick's VTOLs keeping to the high skies. Their orders were separate—to merely survey the city, guide the Mechs, and avoid distracting the Titans themselves, beyond herding.

Their focus was to remain on the Mechs, now that they had arrived.

Worst case, if a Mech was in trouble, a Hawk could descend to help out. Momentarily.

"How many?" Eddie asked, hitting the mounted Hammerhead with both PPCs. His heat meter rose into the yellow, stirring a low alarm. The Hammerhead took the blue lightning bolts to the head, each impacting either of its skull protrusions. Electrified chunks of bone sprayed into the air, making the Titan's head recoil, but it didn't topple off the hotel.

"Four," Brick replied. "Two Hammerheads and two Lumpy's."

"Both moving awfully fast," Charly said. "They're either hungry, or pissed."

"Or both," Mal said.

"Or desperate," Eddie smirked, his sinister sense of confidence teetering on the arrogant. He didn't care, regardless. If anything, it seemed like it was about time that he felt this way.

"Should we turn back now?" Nomi asked.

"What do my eyes-in-the-sky say?" Eddie asked, and chanced another dual PPC shot. These two missed high, as the Hammerhead on top of the hotel descended down the front, ducking its head. Its fierce tail cut the hotel in half, making the pilots grimace.

"Got one more pulling out of downtown, guess it

wasn't as clear as anticipated," Charly said. "Another fucking Hammerhead. It's keeping low."

"No hiding now," Eddie said. He glanced at his team, fanned out before the approaching Hammerheads. The one from the base of the bank galloped with a slither to its trailing tail, faster than any of them would have liked to admit.

"I'd suggest pulling back," Charly said. "Reach the exfil, confirm location, and drop those fucking bombs."

"Solid copy," Eddie said. He whistled on impulse. "Wolves? On me!"

He spun his *Adversary* around, only after hitting the hotel-dismounted Hammerhead with a slingshot of his 90mm ACX. The Autocannon walloped the creature in its left shoulder with three successive HEAT rounds, each one producing a small fireball against its body.

They didn't penetrate.

For once, it wasn't necessarily part of Eddie's plan. He just wanted the ugly thing's attention.

"Got ya," he said, glancing at his spinal camera feed. It showed the giant creature rushing toward him, about eight-hundred feet away and closing.

Awfully fast.

The moment his Mech turned, one of its feet caught a Hound trying to sneak up on him. The half-ton toe speared the creature's underside and flung it through a shed.

"Oops," Eddie muttered, smirking.

A pair of Hounds leapt from opposing rooves at Nomi's stocky *Rottweiler* as she spun around. It startled her, given how low to the ground her Mech was; and if the two had latched onto it, they might have been able to topple it.

271

Fortunately, Wally cut them out of the sky with twin Lasers. The red beams converged on the beasts midair, decapitating them at their shoulders. Nomi gasped, hot red warmth splashing her canopy, along with a mist of alien blood that got through the cauterizations.

"Sorry," Wally said. He highlighted her Mech in his sights to glimpse her armor status and confirm that he had not in fact clipped her.

"Don't be," she said. "I appreciate it."

She and the others joined their retreat toward the exfil. Which Wally already stood very close to.

"I knew y'all were gonna outrun me, and didn't want to be the straggler to get picked off," Wally said. "So I hung back."

Wally's *Mastodon* turned on its heels, to face the direction from which they came. Despite this slow pivot, he already had a significant lead on the other Wolves.

"You won't hear us complaining," Eddie said. "Just keep hoofing it."

"You mean hobbling? I'm like a hundred-ton penguin in this thing!"

At least Wally said it laughing. Even if it was a heavily sarcastic laugh, it still showed that he was neither irate nor submissive to the flaws of the Mech. He knew it going into any fight, having chosen such a lumbering tank on legs.

Besides, it was his son's masterpiece.

And it really was a magnificent design.

"Your pals from the airport are catching up," Charly said. "Something fierce."

"Should we try to slow 'em down?" Brick asked.

"Negative, stay course and keep an eye on their progress, compared to us," Eddie said. He frequently glanced at his spinal camera feed, monitors, and radar, all while maxing his throttle.

His reticle lined up with an atrocious creature galloping toward him, down the center of a road between houses. It actually had the boldness to think it could take on his *Adversary*.

He shook his head and squeezed the trigger to his grouped Lasers. The twin beams caught the Boar in the snout, splitting it clean in half. His Mech jogged right over the remains.

A dry smirk graced his face.

It didn't last, which by that point Eddie took unsurprisingly. However, he was nonetheless beyond surprised when a blur of motion caught his eye, and he spun his torso to the right.

His comms crackled with a warning, but the sound of something large colliding with his cockpit kept him from hearing who it was. Not that it mattered in that moment. The Crawler had leapt off a building and clung to the side of his cockpit, three of its jointed, spidery limbs struggling to find purchase on the *Adversary*'s right arm and shoulder. Its tail whipped overhead and came down in a stabbing motion; the two barbs at the tip struck the canopy above Eddie's head. He flinched, and heard the reinforced glass shudder in its frame, but not break.

One more hit like that, and he couldn't expect it not to splinter.

"Some help, maybe?" Eddie said, half-laughing it as he struggled to keep his Mech from toppling. His left hand made sure to sustain forward throttle, so that he didn't lag behind and become easy pickings for the pursuing Titan.

"Everybody, keep moving," Wally said, having turned his *Mastodon* back around. "I've got this."

"Oh, Christ," Eddie muttered.

The Crawler's atrocious, eyeless face slobbered against the canopy, as its shockingly large teeth scraped glass. Fortunately, thanks to the *Adversary*'s moving legs and swinging torso, the *Crawler*—easily three-quarters the size of the forty-foot Mech—couldn't fully latch onto it.

"Stop swinging!" Wally said.

Eddie saw the *Mastodon* about a mile away. He was beginning to lag behind the other Mechs' advancement, which he knew he couldn't risk, given the dogged Titans on their six.

Eddie aligned his torso and almost wanted to close his eyes.

"Firing," Wally announced.

Two red beams cut off three of the Crawler's legs at its joints, making the creature slip. It fell, crushing at least two houses beneath it, and that was before one of the *Adversary*'s two-ton feet concaved its wretched face. A split-second later, Eddie corrected his speed and resumed max-throttle.

"Thanks, bud," Eddie said.

"Uh, you got it," Wally said, and turned to continued forward.

Eddie glanced at his spinal camera feed. The Hammerheads, both, were not relenting. At least the injured Crawler was fatally trampled in their path; he could be grateful for that.

"Well, I've got good news, at least," Charly said.

"What's that?" Eddie raised his eyebrows, taking a deep breath.

"Don't look now, and I mean it, but—that big-ass eye in the sky is just about closed up. Another couple hours, at most, and it'll be gone."

"For good, hopefully," Nomi sighed.

"Wonderful," Eddie said simply, almost in the same breath as Nomi.

"You think NASA is gonna get anything in there?" H asked, just as her *Pluto* passed Nomi. She had quickly gotten the hang of piloting the Light Class Mech.

"Fuck if I know, or care," Eddie said. "Keep pushing forward."

They had just about caught up with Wally, a few hundred feet from the edge of Pacific Heights.

"Fuck me," Charly muttered, barely audible. The grating sound of her voice was indicative enough that something was wrong.

"What is it?" Eddie asked. "What is—?"

His breath fell short as his eyes lined up with his spinal video feed. The two Hammerheads had paused their pursuit, and exchanged eyeless glances.

"So much for that," Eddie sighed, his voice inaudible.

The Titans' crescent-shaped jaws opened and closed, almost pensively he would say, as they looked at each other.

"Could they be that smart?" Wally asked, having stopped midstride and turned around.

"Or just not *that* stupid?" Mal sighed.

All five Mechs had stopped moving, and turned on

their feet to face the city again.

"We need to reengage their interest," Eddie said. "Charly, what's it looking like, with the others?"

She gulped, audibly enough.

Brick's VTOL, unlike Charly's, stopped hovering and whipped around in the sky, up above clouds, barely visible.

"They're fanning out. Two are taking your far left. Some taller buildings that way. More cover for them."

"If they can see that much, then maybe they can read topography, or—"

"Who cares what or why or how," Eddie said, annoyed. Not directly with Nomi, just with…everything.

Their enemy didn't make sense. And at times he liked them better that way. But it was beginning to be more of a nuisance than anything.

"Focus on your two Hammerheads," Brick said. "I'll pull Lumpy on the right, toward us. Charly, take the other two. I know you're up to it."

"You bet."

"Be careful, fucking wingnuts," Eddie said. "The Major didn't want you to engage them directly for a reason."

"A little too late for that," Charly chuckled, as she descended through the clouds and flew a couple hundred feet over the recently slain Titan.

Eddie shook his head and pivoted the *Adversary*'s torso to glance at his comrades; except for Wally. He remained nearest the edge of Pacific Heights. Standing in the middle of a road. The blocky feet of the *Mastodon* occupied the entire width of the two-lane street, toe to heel.

"Be our sniper, Wally," Eddie said, and piloted his Mech forward.

"Are you sure? I'll follow if—"

"Snipe, bud," Eddie said. "Those Railguns and AC's might come in handy."

"Copy."

One of the two Hammerheads roared as Eddie and Mal neared. H was at Mal's heels, and Nomi right behind her, to the right.

Gunfire and slashes of red Lasers cut down from the sky, at the three separated Titans. The Mech pilots witnessed these flashes in the distance, whether in their periphery or whenever it stole their eyes for a second. How close that distance quickly became was unsettling.

"Avoid the larger buildings if you can," Eddie advised.

The four Mechs reached a range of three or four hundred feet from the two Hammerheads.

One of them, pretending to be unfazed, suddenly whipped its tail at them. It swung around, curving, the boulder of bone at its tip decapitating the rooves off whole neighborhoods of houses in its wake. Nomi was nearest, and engaged her thrusters to dodge it. She fired her 80mm Autocannon while midair, and connected with her target. The cluster of high-explosive anti-tank rounds caught the Hammerhead in its left side. The Titan roared and flinched, retracting its tail.

As Nomi landed, struggling to do so without crushing a house beneath her Mech's tank-tracked feet, but managing to, Eddie and Mal lit up the other Titan. Mal's right-arm Railgun popped, and the slug chipped off a chunk of bone from its left shoulder. Almost in the same instant, Eddie's two PPCs connected with its chest. The creature had had its massive head lifted, thus exposing that area.

To Eddie's surprise, he caught a glimpse of blue-scorched flesh.

"Whew, killer shot, man," Mal cheered. She followed his *Adversary* as he skirted left, trying to favor streets as opposed to houses, naturally. Every six steps or so, he couldn't avoid wrecking a house in the process. It made him grimace but he concentrated on his primary objective.

Meanwhile, the Hammerhead with a more conscious tail tried swinging it at Nomi again. She kept hitting it with Vulcan volleys, but the monster wouldn't budge from where it stood.

"They're hardly flinching," Nomi grunted. "What's the deal?"

"They need better incentive," Brick said. "Stop toying with their bodies, and focus fire on their heads. You don't have to *try* hitting that sweet-spot, but they'll think you are."

"Copy," Eddie said, and did just that.

No time to waste.

A burst from his 90mm Autocannon smacked the Hammerhead in its chest wound again, and then it lowered his head. Mal struck the left protrusion from its skull with her Railgun, and half a second later, Eddie Lased the right with two red beams.

Not enough to cut through the dense bone, but more than sufficient to snag its attention.

And annoy it.

The Hammerhead made a snorting sound before lurching forward, but not sprinting. H spotted the swing of its tail from behind it, at an angle that the other two didn't. She hit it in the haunches with both Lasers, and made the call.

"Watch that tail!"

Eddie stomped his hop-jets just in time.

A three-story Travelodge hotel to his left got clipped by the rocky tip of the tail's end, and slung debris toward Mal. She had engaged her hop-jets in the nick of time, avoiding the arc of the tail by mere feet. A broken column from the hotel, sent airborne, struck her *Bandit*'s left foot, taking off a toe and denting the Tungsteel armor around the ankle.

Not enough to break it, but her landing wasn't pleasant.

"Clipped, going down hard!" Mal exclaimed.

Eddie couldn't spot her through the cloud of debris and the hotel ruins.

"Watch it, that tail's coming back around!"

Mal had to wait for her thrusters to recharge before using them again. Her Mech descended, a forty-foot drop. Being hit in the air had not made it any easier.

She braced in her compact cockpit as she glimpsed something dark move out in front of her, and below. From H's perspective, to Mal's right, the withdrawal of the Titan's tail narrowly missed her coming down. It didn't hit the hotel again, nor Eddie, who had retreated in an arc, to avoid just that. And in hopes of spotting Mal's *Bandit* among the dust cloud and ruins.

It had all happened dreadfully fast.

The *Bandit* landed, but awkwardly. Missing a toe would not have been so bad if that foot didn't touch down at a higher level than its other. And where it did, was a crevice between concrete debris. The ankle bent, not just the armor. The lightweight Mech was already scarce of armor in the legs.

A loud, wrenching, metallic sound caught Eddie and H's ears.

Eddie focused on his radar instead of his eyes. He saw Mal's arrow, and marked her on his HUD. A green triangle highlighted where, amid the dust cloud, she ought to be.

His eyes, however, were impulsively drawn to his left. The Hammerhead. It roared and lurched forward again, its massive clawed hands grinding half a dozen houses into the earth. At the same time, it brought its tail around again.

Closer, now.

"Mal, get outta there!" Eddie shouted. He bared his teeth and fired at the Hammerhead's skull, actually aiming for the alcove. His PPCs scarred the air with blue streaks of lightning, helical beams barely grazing the Titan's skull.

He cursed under his breath.

H hit it closer to the alcove with two Lasers, and a pair of short-range missiles. One plumed into fire and chunks of bone, the other grazed off, the warhead not detonating.

The tail came around.

"Outta here!" Mal yelled, and successfully ejected. The small canopy jettisoned and into the air she was propelled, a blink of an eye before her *Bandit* caught the brunt of the Titan's tail. It wrapped around the chunk of bone, and H had gotten so close that she had to hop-jet to evade it.

She pumped the thrusters to control her descent and make sure to miss it on its way back.

Eddie hop-jetted to miss its return, too, but didn't stop engaging the Hammerhead.

The other one had finally disregarded patience and began lashing out more boldly at Nomi.

"Bringing Lumpy around your way, Nomi!" Brick shouted.

"Groovy!" She said sarcastically.

"What's the status on Mal?" Charly asked, still struggling to pull the attention of the other two Hammerheads.

They had practically retreated to the edge of downtown. If she lost them to the high-rises, there was no telling when or how she would get them to come out.

"I'm going back for her, she ejected!" Eddie exclaimed, starting to loop around, and put his back to the Hammerhead.

"The hell you are," H said, spotting her parachute and thrusters about a hundred feet past the hotel ruins.

Eddie watched the steel-blue *Pluto* stride confidently down a street, and then his gaze lined up with the white of a parachute above the dust cloud.

"She's right, boss," Wally said, approaching the battle from far back. His massive shoulder-mounted Autocannons thundered. Two clusters of devastating 180mm HEAT rounds slammed into the Hammerhead's lower back, at the base of its tail. It had begun to raise its hindquarters to use the tail weapon like a scorpion. The impacts formed fireballs, and one or two cut through bone, making the creature bleed.

"How's that?" Eddie asked, already accepting it and staying away from Mal, leaving it to H, while engaging the Titan with Wally.

"You're the only other powerhouse Mech we've got down here," Wally said. He selected both of his Lasers, and converged the twin red beams toward the center of the Hammerhead's skull. They ablated an upper layer of bone, missing the precious alcove by maybe inches.

He gnashed his teeth in response, and angrily sent out a flight of four SRMs. He was a few hundred feet away, and knew that was pushing it for the short-range missiles, but dared it nonetheless.

His heat levels had nearly reached seventy-percent after that barrage.

Eddie accepted Wally and H's logic.

"Go get her, Helena," he said through clenched jaws.

"Locating her transponder," H said.

Meanwhile, Nomi played cat-and-mouse with the other Hammerhead, which felt dangerously familiar. She recalled the battle earlier in the day, dumbstruck that it was in fact all in the same day.

Mere hours ago, really.

"Stay with me, Luke," she whispered, and continued nimbly engaging the Titan.

"These things are giving me a headache," Charly confessed. "Might need a hand, Brick."

"If I do, I'll have to put this thing down," he said. "And I, uh, don't think I can do that myself."

"We need to buy Mal time," Charly said. "I've got that sold on my end, kinda outta my control, though, unfortunately."

"Then work on herding 'em," Brick said, "and I'll make this motherfucker chase its own tail."

"I'm going in," H said. Two seconds later: "Fuck!"

"Talk to us, H," Eddie said.

H saw Mal's stark white parachute caught on the corner of a townhouse. According to her radar, Mal's seat transponder placed her behind the townhouse, albeit out of sight, even from the *Pluto*'s cockpit, twenty-two feet off the ground.

The narrow spaces between the townhouses and surrounding homes made reaching that spot, in her Mech, impossible.

She paused, cursing under her breath, contemplating how to proceed. The pulsing green beacon on her radar, from Mal's seat transponder, was a relentless reminder of urgency.

Through her sound-dampened cockpit, H suddenly heard a few distinct sounds. Gunfire, screams, and noises that could only be described as "inhuman."

The gunshots belonged to a Corvin pistol, which were stowed into the back panel of every cockpit seat, along with a single extra magazine.

H's brow furrowed and she crouched the *Pluto*, putting it into standby, and released her harness. The belts whipped up, and she slipped out of the coolant vest. She stooped to take a quick drag on the water tube, licked her tattered lips, and leaned over the control panel.

"Mal's in trouble, shots fired, I'm going after her," she said bluntly, and then withdrew to cross the small cockpit.

She half-expected the Mech's comms to sputter with objections from her fellow pilots. Not a single voice came through at first.

However, more gunfire and sporadic screams from outside, twenty feet below her, continued.

She shook her head and hastily opened the small arms

hatch in the bulkhead six feet behind her seat. From it she snatched a radio earpiece, configuring it right away, while simultaneously arming herself. A Torrent SMG on a sling, which dangled below her chest, bouncing against her stomach as she slung a heavier weapon, A Hornet assault rifle.

H wasn't fucking around.

It felt much heavier than she remembered, and it had been a few months since she last used it at the range. Longer than that, in an exercise. The Mech-tech who had supplied the *Pluto*—or perhaps these weapons belonged to its former pilot—stowed a Corvin pistol, Torrent, and Hornet. Extra ammunition was scarce, unfortunately.

Moreover, she had no place to carry anything. Worst case, she could pack a Condor or Corvin magazine into her bra, as her pockets were barely big enough. But the Hornet's forty-round box-mag was too bulky, as was the Torrent's sixty-round drum.

"Fuck it," she muttered, and turned toward the hatch.

The *Pluto*'s fusion engine finally idled, and the Mech entered standby mode.

"H, you be fucking careful," Eddie's voice came through her comms. "We'll try to hold 'em off your position as long as possible."

"Appreciate it," she said, loudly, from the hatch. She depressurized it, and waited impatiently.

The screams and gunfire had ceased, which didn't necessarily make her feel any better.

Then her comms opened up again.

"I hate to even mention it," Wally breathed haggardly, "but the Major *did* say—"

"I *know* what he said," H's voice was loud, and adamant. The hatch hissed open and evening daylight made her squint, beneath a rigid, auburn-haired brow. Her hands flexed around the assault rifle, as a wind brushed her knuckles and exposed arms. "But nobody's gonna prohibit me from saving a friend."

14

Warzones differed in many ways. Variables included environment, enemy numbers, firepower, range, and more. Ultimately, they all shared one constant—an inescapable element of danger. Whether that contracted strictly fear, or was conducive of adrenaline pumping, varied on the soldiers themselves. Regardless, the threat factor was always unpredictable, which made any warzone unnerving to be in.

H felt this, without question. She could only fathom that she was experiencing a small fraction of what Mal did, given her aloneness and without proper firepower.

Then there were the civilians. If any were not in their bunkers, and burdened by being above ground, H couldn't imagine their anxiety. Incomparable.

One thing was certain, too—warzones of the past paled to those on this day. No matter the country, people suffered an unprecedented threat.

Which in turn stirred a sense of dread that crept under the skin like a parasite, dug a tunnel, and laid its eggs.

H did her best to compartmentalize this feeling as she slinked between townhouses. Toward where she believed Mal was. Unfortunately, that was all she could do—go on a hunch. On foot, she had no radar to track Mal's seat transponder. And her earpiece radio wasn't catching any signal

286

from her Ember Wolves, either; the Titans probably disrupted its weaker capabilities.

H at least assumed Mal was still in its immediate vicinity; that was protocol, anyway—to not venture far from the "crash site" of an ejection, so as to make SAR easier.

In this case, H was the search and rescue.

Above the three-story townhouses, she could hear the turmoil of Mechs engaging Titans. Buildings rattled audibly with every step of a nearby Mech, which H assumed had to be Wally or Eddie.

Or the Titans themselves.

She gulped and proceeded hastier than before. Time was of the essence for a few major reasons—all of which came down to Operation Subterfuge. They had to lure these beasts out of the city, onto the Presidio Golf Course, and then maintain being bait until the bombs dropped.

Last she recalled, unfortunately, not all of the Titans were taking the bait, and the ones that did now had to be stalled, so Mal could be retrieved.

There was no way around it.

H smirked at the irony of the situation. It hadn't even occurred to her until now: she was the one that would be picking Mal up in her Mech, as opposed to when Mal picked H up in the *Bandit* earlier today.

"Oh, how the tables have turned," she muttered to herself.

It seemed that anytime today when one of the pilots began to feel even a small bit of relief, it was crushed immediately.

Now was no exception.

Reality thrusted itself into H's realm without pity. The

snapping, barbed jaws of a Hound tore through a clothes-line and hanging sheets to her right. A waist-high chain-link fence clattered against the stumbling momentum of the beast, while H screamed on impulse and staggered to the left. There was very little space between the townhouses, and she found herself bouncing off another chain-link fence as she shouldered the assault rifle.

The Hound materialized through torn fabric and warped fencing, snarling like a revving V10.

Eight feet from her face.

H squeezed the trigger before she could properly aim, but at least the Hornet was firmly shouldered. Muzzle flashes lit up in the Hound's face, splashing H's own with heat. She hosed out seven or eight 6.5mm caseless rounds. Almost every single one hit their mark; afterall, her target was as big as a small sports car.

The Hound recoiled, vibrant orange blood splashing the grass and a ripped sheet impaled on one of its face-spikes.

H cursed under her breath and ducked, simultaneously running along the length of the fence. She glanced over her right shoulder, frantically, and saw the Hound begin to pursue her. Two full strides and it would catch up in an instant.

"Over here!" Mal cried out, followed by a gunshot in the air.

H's ears and other senses perked up.

She rolled to her right, sprung to her feet, and vaulted over the chain-link fence where it was still intact. Before her feet alighted on grass, her left hand still on the railing, she felt the metal vibrate. Her gaze shot right, and she saw the Hound charging her—

Plowing down the fence in its wake.

She gulped and knelt, the fence inches to her right. She shouldered the Hornet and took a deep breath, composing her aim despite what might very well be her impending death.

The Hound snarled, bleeding but not impeded, and closed the distance in three seconds.

H fired, and the full-size Hornet assault rifle shuddered in her hands, against her left shoulder. A six-round burst caught the creature in the chest, where its carapace didn't cover. The exposed, raw, dark red-orange flesh opened up, and the Hound let out a painful whimper.

It crashed into the grass, tumbling hard.

H rolled to her left, evading the beast just in time. Amidst her tumbles, the earpiece had dislodged somewhere. She didn't hesitate to look for it, as it had been useless anyway. Nor did she wait around to confirm the kill. She was almost certain that had not decommissioned the creature for good.

"It's H!" She called out. "Say something, Mal!"

"Here, I'm here!" Mal shouted. "Low on ammo!"

"Fire again, I got you!" H stopped moving to track Mal's voice better. And a gunshot, if she—

Mal fired her pistol again.

H's eyes narrowed, as her ears worked. She retraced her steps, passing another townhouse, realizing she had gone too far when the Hound chased her. Her route was different now, though, so she could avoid being in the same line-of-sight with it, supposing it wasn't dead. Now she moved between another row of townhouses, in the same block.

"Again!" H shouted.

"You're close!" Mal yelled, a lick of relief in her strained voice.

The unobstructed, open-air sound of two PPCs charging and then unleashing caught H's attention. Any nearer and it would have given her a static shock, let alone tortured her eardrums.

"So are they!" H called out.

She suddenly stopped in her tracks, boots chewing up grass and dirt. A big grin washed up on her tired, pale, sweat-beaded face. She leaned forward against the railing of a fence, briefly taking the pressure off her back and shoulders from carrying two weapons.

Mal stood in a backyard two properties away. She was just outside a small sunroom. Her ponytail was undone, several strands sticking to her soot and sweat-stained face. Her hair was frazzled but hung in its natural bob-style, level with her chin.

She had since discarded her coolant vest, which became useless after ejecting from the Mech.

In both hands she clutched a Corvin pistol, her arms extended, elbows locked. A gash on her left bicep caught the evening sunlight and glistened red.

"You good?" H asked.

"Peachy. Care to join?"

H nodded and looked around. "Coming to you."

"Be careful. There's a tentacle back a ways, and a couple Hounds prowling."

"No shit," H laughed crazily, just before withdrawing from Mal's line of sight. She lowered her shoulder into a side-door to one of the townhouses, breaking it in. Splinters burst and the square window in the frame shook but didn't break.

A man with dark hair and splintered glasses cowered in the corner of his kitchen.

H's eyes widened. She put a finger to her lips, and he nodded, whimpering softly. He was in his pajamas, and a dark circle stained his crotch.

H hated the emotion of pity but there was nothing else she could feel at the moment. Except for empathy, to a degree.

"Coming back for you," she whispered, and slowly moved to the other side of the kitchen. "I'm a Clanner. Just stay put."

"Oh, thank you, thank you so much," the man, in his low forties, began saying. His voice climbed in volume. He rose to his knees and trudged after her.

She reached the small living room, beside the stairs, and paused. She looked behind her, and her brow furrowed. She raised her hand, gesturing the man to stay.

"Stay put, mister. Will be right back."

He gulped and nodded, withdrawing to sit on his heels.

She exhaled with relief, and then turned to head down a short hallway beneath the stairs. She reached a side door and exited, using the knob this time.

The door opened to the right, and a glimpse of motion caught her eye through the small square window. It shattered and the door burst into fragments of wood, one of which was impaled by a curved tusk. The impact threw H onto her left side, and she tumbled head-over-heels. Her weapons stayed on their slings, which she was grateful for, and hated at the same time. It made her tumble even more painful.

Miraculously, H came to a stop legs-first, and managed to spring to her feet. She teetered briefly but pulled her back to the corner of the neighboring townhouse, as the Boar kept charging, barely pausing. She used a wall-mounted gutter as additional support for her aim, bent her knees, and squeezed the trigger.

No burst-firing this time.

The Hornet spewed a controlled stream of 6.5mm bullets. They hosed the Boar's face, which was unfortunately partially shielded by a large shard of door wood. A few bullets punched through it, and the others caught it in the pitted bone of its upper snout.

The powerful rounds were effective enough, even through wood, to penetrate the thin carapace.

It bucked and bellowed as it neared, slowing down. She didn't relinquish her squeeze on the trigger until the sixty-round box magazine ran dry. The weapon's recoil was adequately compensated through its design, leaving little vertical climb for the operator to handle.

It was still a full-scale assault rifle, though, heavy and cumbersome compared to the Condor carbine. H was not a petite woman, though. And while not a bodybuilder by any means, her strength was tried and true. She handled the AR until the muzzle smoked and the magazine clicked empty.

When she lowered her aim, she witnessed the Boar take a few cloven steps forward before collapsing in a heap. Its rough upper snout was previously pitted with infrared sensors; now, it was perforated with bullet holes, and bled profusely.

"Pig fuck," H grumbled, and stood up straight.

"Still with us?" Mall called out, tentatively.

"Solid," H took a deep breath. "Copy."

"The Mechs sound farther," Mal said worriedly. "Is everything okay out there?"

"Yeah, just stalling the Titans 'til I get you."

"Ready when you are." Mal's wit was still unscathed, at least.

H smirked and nodded to herself.

She had to reload, in theory; but didn't have anything else for the Hornet. Exhaustion had already taken over her. She took some deep breaths and unslung the nine-pound weapon. As much as she hated to, she let go of it and it hit the grass.

H put the Torrent submachine-gun in her hands as she spun around the corner. She put her back to a door. It was already ajar, which she hadn't expected. It gave way and she stumbled into a washroom. From the outside, the townhouse looked unbothered. At least from her previous position.

Inside was a whole other story.

Half the washroom was occupied by a massive tentacle, which descended from a destroyed ceiling. She guessed that it occupied the upper levels of the townhouse, and had wormed its way in from the opposite side. It appeared inert, but its pulsing pink-red flesh suggested it was very much "alive." The teeth lining it gave H the idea that it was more tongue than tendon, but then again nothing about these organisms made much sense.

She stowed her breath for fear of startling it.

Slowly, H began slinking through the washroom. She headed for a doorway that had been partially demolished by the descent of the tentacle. She could at least be remotely grateful for having more space to pass through. Which meant more distance she could put between herself and *it*.

A sound like flesh tearing and bones snapping caught her ear. She stopped staring in nervousness at the dormant tentacle in the washroom, as she exited, and looked into the living room to her left.

There was nothing *living* about it.

Except for the Gator, but H hated to apply the meaning of life to such an aberration.

Its similarity to an alligator was vague at best. It had merely become an agreeable callsign for the creature, by her team, to better accept its existence. And its mortality.

Most importantly.

Like molasses, H raised the barrel of her Torrent. The SMG had an integrated suppressor that muffled its shots. Although, in the moment, she wanted to do anything to defeat the sound she was hearing.

Let alone the sight.

The Gator was devouring a human body. Its second. The other, smaller corpse, was already mostly eaten. Currently, it wrenched away from the spine a dead man's arm, shoulder blade, and rib cage, all in one bite. Blood painted the walls, which were formerly periwinkle, and the beige hardwood floor.

H felt sick to her stomach.

The Gator's size was additionally nerve-wracking. The front door was gone, and its jambs had widened from the haunches of the creature. Its cylindrical body mass rested on the floor, occupying more than half of the living room's space.

Its stumpy, rigid snout turned to face H, and the bulbous end casually crashed through a credenza a few feet away. H flinched and backpedaled, squeezing the trigger.

The Torrent fired a burst, spitting from the suppressed barrel with a loud fizzing sound. Nowhere near the uproar of a Hornet or Condor.

Seemingly surprised by the attack more than anything, the Gator took a sloppy step to the right, its side crushing part of the staircase in the living room. Bullets from the Torrent raked its snout, some not even penetrating.

H gulped and shouted: "In trouble!"

"You're one house over!" Mal called out, at the top of her lungs. "Coming to you!"

H cursed under her breath and searched the Gator's appearance for a sign of its infrared organs. Except for where its dark blue coloration shifted to a bright orange on its cheeks and jowls, H saw nothing.

From the tip of its snout to the top of its head, above a stout neck, its hide had a pebbly texture. More than just carapace, she wondered, maybe between these bumps were its heat-vision pits…

H's scrutiny lasted maybe a few seconds.

It was all she had to take advantage of, before the annoyed Gator hissed at her, jaws gaping. She grimaced at the sight of shredded flesh dripping from its unnaturally large teeth.

The creature took a step toward her.

H backpedaled two feet, and raised the Torrent to properly aim. The bark of pistol fire erupted in the kitchen to the Gator's right, having mistakenly exposed its peripheral as soon as it faced H. She witnessed two rounds punch into its right cheek, before it shook its head and swung its snout forward. Its right clawed hand landed in the mess of bodies it had been feasting on.

H knelt and fired a steady ten rounds into the creature's left armpit. It snorted and tilted to that side, lowering itself.

"Hold your fire!" H barked, and braved herself forward. She stood upright and turned the Torrent in her clutches to achieve the best firing stance.

From Mal's perspective in the kitchen, H walked up to the left side of the fazed Gator, and then fired into the top of its head. The Torrent battered its pebbly forehead with over a dozen rounds, seven or eight actually penetrating.

Mal's eyes widened, taken aback.

H, meanwhile, gritted her teeth and kept firing until the bullets easily tore into the Gator's eventually-exposed orange flesh. Its chin hit the floor, crushing hardwood. Its stocky limbs splayed outward, with the exception of its left arm, which bent under its body.

H's chest and shoulders were heaving from deep, incessant breaths.

Seconds later she looked to her left, and saw Mal staring at her in the kitchen.

"Not a reptile fan, huh?" Mal said.

H smirked and shook her head. "Too cold for me."

Mal grinned, and a flood of temporary respite surged through her. She then sighed and beckoned H.

"Meet me out back," she said, "unless you wanna climb—"

296

H nonchalantly stepped over the fallen snout, reck-lessly one might observe, or bravely another could say. H would argue neither. She barely thought about it. And Mal just watched in shock.

More relief came when nothing happened.

The Gator really was dead.

"Wanna take me to your beloved *Pluto* now?" Mal asked.

"Bitch," H muttered, smirking. She led Mal out of the house and into the backyard. A sudden quake almost made the two women fall off their feet. An immense shadow was thrown against the next row of townhouses, followed by a gust of wind.

"That fucking tail," Mal said to H, brow rigid.

"Follow me."

Mal didn't argue. But she did eyeball H, and wasn't pleased with what she saw.

"Is that Torrent all you have?"

H reached the chain-link fence bordering the back-yard, some fifteen feet away from Mal's grounded pilot seat. She paused and looked back at Mal.

"Sorry, had a Hornet but ran out. Killed a Hound and Boar. Well…I dunno about the Hound."

"Shit, okay." Mal nodded. "Let's not stick around to find out, eh?"

H raised her eyebrows and nodded in agreement. She prepared to vault the fence, which would land her in the backyard of the townhouse where the man with glasses hid.

A disgusting sound stole her attention, however, and although Mal insisted she go, H was too captivated with horror. She looked to her left. Mal was guilty of shock, too, as the two women witnessed something revolting.

From inside the washroom where H had been earlier, the door still hanging open and accessible from the backyard, that large tentacle pulsed. Audibly. Its pink flesh peeled apart between rows of teeth, opening like a sleeve. Crawling from it was a Hound slick with viscous, saliva-like slime. It got to its feet, slowly at first, as if taking its baby-steps.

And it was a fast learner.

The Hound growled, and behind it, the tendon-tentacle wilted like a wretched flower. Drying and decomposing in seconds.

"You've gotta be fucking kidding me," H said, both deeply disturbed and casually annoyed.

"Go!" Mal shouted, pushing H in the back and firing her pistol at the Hound. Her first shot missed and the creature growled fiercely, darting forward.

She knew she only had a few shots left, max.

Her eyes squinted against the sun above, dampened by the billowing parachute caught on the roof. As the Hound neared the door, and H demanded she hurry, Mal collected her breath. She fired, two trigger squeezes, both bullets exiting different muzzles. They lined up, hitting the Hound in its exposed chest. It faltered for a moment, which was all she needed.

Mal stuffed the pistol into a pocket and vaulted the fence.

A scream erupted from the house whose backyard they were in.

"No, no, no," H said, her voice building in anger.

Mal was confused, but not for long.

A man exited the back door, screaming in terror. A Hound followed him, its broad shoulders crashing through the jambs and not fazing it even slightly.

H rolled to her right, springing up for a better angle. She fired at the creature's legs, the best shot she could achieve with no time to spare. A few bullets caught the Hound by its feet, but it seemed unaffected.

Mal, out of ammunition, could only watch in horror. It happened as fast as it took H to roll and spring up. Three, four seconds. The Hound caught up to the civilian, and his screams were interrupted by a gurgling cry of pain. Blood shot out of his mouth, and from impalement wounds in his left shoulder and below his left clavicle. Spines from the Hound's snout jutted through, and it lifted its head, hoisting the man off his feet.

He convulsed and choked on his own blood, impaled by the long barbs.

H was too awestruck with disbelief, and guilt, to react appropriately.

Another quake made the two women teeter. At the same time, the Hound faltered and the man slid off its rigid spines. He hit the grass with a wet thump.

H growled and stood and fired.

The Torrent was never not true to its name. With a high cyclic rate and a sixty-round drum magazine, it was capable of raining out rounds like a concentrated downpour. She pumped the creature's chest and throat with enough bullets to make a regular animal see-through. The large, vaguely canine creature finally lost its balance and fell onto the grass, bleeding out.

H breathed rapidly, and hoarsely, as she slowly

brought the weapon down. Mal caught up to her, tugging on her shirt, and then her arm.

"We have to *go*, H!"

H got up and followed, eventually taking her tear-stung eyes off the man's lifeless, bloody corpse.

The clear skies and unobstructed sunlight didn't help diminish the terrible sight. And it certainly wouldn't obscure it from her memory.

The sudden *whoosh* of a Hammerhead's tail sweeping by didn't just startle the two pilots, it almost knocked them off their feet. Rooves and windows rattled, an occasional tree shuddering.

Birds and any pets kept in the area, but not with their owners in a shelter, were smart enough to have relocated long ago.

The shadow that the tail took with it barely reached them, but the pressure in the air indicated that it was far too close for comfort.

H gripped Mal's shoulder and tugged, pulling herself in front, as she had the only gun.

"How many rounds you got left?" Mal asked, hating to pose the question.

"It's a drum, so fuck if I know," she shrugged.

"Nothing extra?"

"What's it look like? Wanna check my bra?"

Mal rolled her eyes. "Go. Our best bet now is haste."

"No shit."

They were both running ragged in more ways than one. Physically, mentally, and emotionally. A coolant vest was suddenly looking mighty fine right about now, for H. It had yet to cross Mal's mind but would once she was inside the

Pluto, assuming they reached it alive. If they did, she would regret not grabbing it from the lawn before leaving the crash site. In theory, she and H could alternate hooking it up to the coolant line in the *Pluto*'s cockpit.

H had failed to do so earlier, when Mal picked her up in the *Bandit*. Like Mal now, so had H discarded the coolant vest. Its burdensome weight and bulk became immediately apparent whenever a pilot wore it outside of their Mech.

Especially on a warm, arguably beautiful day in southern California.

As soon as they were within view of the *Pluto*'s feet, standing in the middle of a road in front of the first row of townhouses, the two women paused. They caught their breaths for a second, and then proceeded forward.

There was a rumbling sound to their left, like heavy breathing. Unnaturally heavy breathing. And things breaking; furniture, walls—

"Go, go, *go!*" H said, and now was the one pulling at Mal's arm, thrusting her forward. Mal hesitated for a full second, wondering why H insisted she go first, despite being unarmed.

And then it hit her.

That was precisely the reason.

Mal ran, but not like before. It was no half-assed jog or even a panicked scramble. She *sprinted*. Mal was in significantly better shape than H, but leaner and more robust, too. H followed nonetheless, her Torrent shouldered but only partially raised. She periodically glanced to her left at the townhouses as she trailed Mal.

Seconds before reaching the street, another quake

shook the earth and Mal could hear the armor plating on the skinny legs of the *Pluto* vibrate. She stumbled and caught herself on the mounted gutter at the front corner of the townhouse nearest the road.

She glanced over her shoulder.

H lagged, but kept moving.

A shadow fell over the *Pluto* and drew Mal's eyes up. Her throat swallowed dry and tears welled in her eyes. She was ready to accept her fate, despite all of the struggling and fighting.

A Hammerhead Titan's front right foot landed in the street a hundred feet away. One of its enormous claws halved an apartment building on the opposite side of the road. Its gigantic skull, which gave it its name, swung ninety feet over Mal's head. Its semicircular mouth cleared the top of the *Pluto* by maybe fifty feet.

The low, deep, raspy breathing of the behemoth reminded Mal of twenty Harleys pushing down the road. A particular memory from when she was five. Her father called them "choppers." Yet she grew up knowing only helicopters as "choppers," and that was before fusion-propelled thrusters were mass-produced.

Mal's mind and heart were forced back into present day as the Titan roared and her skull rattled under her scalp. She put both hands to her ears, grimacing, but was too spellbound to take her eyes off the Titan as it crawled on its four legs, right above them.

The fear of a back foot trampling them was gone from her mind in lieu of the awe.

Its enormous body started to turn, tail swinging out behind it, which suddenly swooshed above the townhouses where Mal and H had just been.

Something crashed and the sound of metal twisting drew Mal's eyes. She looked back, and her gaze lifted. A pair of vehicles were slung into the air, crashing into the rooves and windows of surrounding homes. Another quake wobbled Mal's legs when the Titan sidestepped, a clawed foot swinging above her, with no more than sixty feet of clearance. Her short hair whipped around her face and her eyes stung.

Three small fireballs—comparably small to the Titan, enormous for Mal and H—burst against the beast's left side, nearly a hundred feet away, above the other side of the road.

H arrived behind Mal, also gawking up.

The gargantuan mass and might of the Hammerhead was nearly lost to them in their Mechs. Especially to H in her "retired" *Fenrir*. Down here, everything was different. The terror was tangible and unparalleled.

There was also, unfortunately a guilty sense of wonder—being amazed at the Titans' immensity, and yet how agilely the Hammerheads could move at times.

Then came the pride—in themselves, as mere humans, with the right kind of technology, training, experience, and dedication…to be able to *kill* such a monster.

And the fear returned.

But not just theirs. The empathetic fear; they remembered for who and what they fought. All the unbelievably frightened civilians, praying that this would be over soon, and that they would live to see that day. Nevermind all the lives already lost, some in the blink of an eye, to this remorseless enemy.

It was the only motivation they truly needed.

H squeezed Mal's nape before walking past her, marching to the feet of the *Pluto*. Just then the Titan roared and still H ascended its bent, hocked knees. She kept the Torrent slung, dangling from her torso as she reached and stepped on various handlebars.

Below, Mal looked over her shoulder. She saw a Boar that had charged through the side of a townhouse, not even barging through the door, just a wall. White wood shards scattered around its bloody body, its snout riddled with bullet holes.

The faintest smile ever appeared on Mal's face, and she looked up at the *Pluto*. Finally, her mind kicked into gear and she followed H.

Mal was halfway up the *Pluto*'s crouched legs when she looked left and saw Eddie's *Adversary* stride partially into view. Its shoulder-mounted particle cannons lit up, stabbing the air with blue-white lightning that stole her eyes. She tried to follow their path, but it was out of sight.

"I promise we'll take the scenic route if you hurry the fuck up," H said from above, already hanging out of the cockpit hatch.

"You owe me," Mal grinned.

"If we survive this," H said, "I owe you shit. *You* owe *me*."

"What do *I* owe you?"

"A kiss."

Mal's brow furrowed as she hoisted herself up the *Pluto*, much faster than H had herself. She lent Mal a hand, nonetheless capably pulling her into the cockpit. H sealed the hatch door behind her, and then stowed the Torrent in the small arms compartment. She shut it and returned to her cockpit seat, donning her vest and connecting it to the coolant line.

"A kiss?" Mal asked, behind H's seat. "For you?"

H smirked, shaking her head as she secured her harness and scooted the seat forward. Mal practically fell as it slid out of her hands.

"You're pretty, but no, not for me."

H tapped at her control panel and brought the *Pluto* out of standby mode. While the fusion engine hummed out of hibernation, and all systems came back online, they saw Eddie's *Adversary* firing at the Titan to their far right. And behind him, maybe a mile away at most, were two more Hammerheads. They followed a low-flying Hawk.

"For who?" Mal asked, eyebrow raised.

H muted her comms while her HUD illuminated and synchronized.

"Eddie," she said, and peered over her shoulder, up at Mal. "Your engine could be white-hot critical, and he'd still dive in for you."

The corner of Mal's mouth started to curl.

"I'm sick of it," H said, looking forward. "We all are. If we survive this bullshit, you give that man a kiss."

"Deal," Mal said.

H smiled, unmuted her comms, and turned the *Pluto* in the opposite direction.

15

Eddie Locke had never been happier to hear Mal's voice than when she greeted the team just now. There was a grave tone to it that he had not heard in a long time, not since the Great Mech War, but there was more to it than that. There was relief, some version of excitement, and most importantly, determination.

"One of these days I'll have to pick you up in *my* Mech," he said without a second thought.

Some genuine laughter carried over their comms. He couldn't decipher Mal's among them, but he didn't regret saying it, even if it was received as a joke. He didn't care anymore.

God, he didn't care.

He just wanted to survive this.

And he wanted her to, as well, and H, and Nomi and Wally and—

He wanted everyone currently alive in the entire world to survive. An undue death was not this enemy's to give.

"Happy to hear your voice, Mal," Charly said. "Hope you're up to some sprinting, H. I've got company. No stalling 'em now."

"I take back everything I said about this planetoid," H said, propelling the *Pluto* forward and ably making sure its three-toed feet only stepped on asphalt or pavement. Meanwhile, Mal clutched the back of the seat and watched through the conical canopy, riveted.

"Max throttle if you aren't already," Eddie said. In the background of his transmission, an ACX rang out, the barrel clanging and reloading almost as noisily. "Still trying to keep this thing entertained, and at a safe distance, so you can catch up and we'll put it behind us."

"Likewise," Nomi said. "But Brick's helping."

Brick's Hawk was adeptly switching between targets while staying safely airborne: targeting both the Lumpy Titan to the Mechs' far left, and the Hammerhead that had previously only been focused on Nomi. The two Titans paid attention to his VTOL as if it were an annoying fly.

Nomi became background noise to the Hammerhead, which she didn't mind, so long as she could grab its "eye" once again.

Wally, still holding position close to the edge of Pacific Heights, occasionally sniped the two Hammerheads to keep them in check.

Both Eddie and Nomi were grateful.

"Passing!" H announced, as she nimbly piloted the *Pluto* to Eddie's far right. His *Adversary* twisted at the torso to glance to his three o'clock. He would miss seeing Mal's *Bandit*, but knowing she was with H gave him comfort.

"Copy. Let's take these dumb shits in for a hole-in-one," Eddie said.

"You just couldn't resist a golfing pun, could you?" Mal said. She and H exchanged head-shakes.

"Better than quoting Snow," Wally pitched in.

"He's got a point," Eddie said.

The Clanners smiled, from one Mech to the next. Up in the sky, Charly and Brick were not deaf to the humor, and appreciated the lightheartedness despite the intense situation. The irony was that their Mech teammates were in greater danger than they were, in the air.

Eight minutes ago, the bombers had requested an update from the Hawks.

"Give us ten," Charly's reply was sans hesitation. After closing the transmission with the bombers, Brick asked her if she genuinely thought H would have Mal by then—never addressing the possibility that they might not make it at all. Charly's reply was: "I think I've got their attention now."

She didn't even acknowledge Brick's question. She just focused on her task at hand, trying to lure the two Hammerheads out of the city.

As it turned out, they had two successes on their hands. And a third, the biggest one of the day, ahead.

"Permission to proceed to the exfil, boss?" Wally asked, his heart pounding. He watched the four Mechs luring the two Hammerheads his way, with three more being herded by two Hawks.

"Hop to it," Eddie said.

He was shocked Wally had not already been walking in that direction. He watched the *Mastodon* turn on its right foot and proceed past a large tree.

Eddie was throttling the *Adversary* at twice the speed Wally's max was, and he wasn't even topping out. He wanted to still try to watch his step, as much as he could, while avoiding making it look like he was in fact luring his enemy.

Finally, the Hammerheads no longer gave in to any suspect form of intelligence. They pursued the horde of heat signatures, not to mention ones that had made them bleed and been more than a nuisance.

"Mission accomplished," Eddie muttered.

All too constantly, he glanced at his spinal camera feed, and every time he did he was terrified at how close the Hammerhead was following. He was even more unnerved at how many houses its feet were trampling. The whole point of luring them out of the residential area and carpet-bombing them was to avoid further civilian deaths.

It would also simply be an easier way to kill the fucking things.

Supposedly.

"This thing's gaining on me, Wally," Eddie gulped. "Think you can give me some cushion?"

Wally stepped off to the side without reluctance, and targeted the nearest Hammerhead with his paired Lasers. A red triangle marked it on his HUD, the lower half through the bushy tree before him. He estimated its shape on the other side, and squeezed the trigger. Two red beams of concentrated heat split the canopy down the center, setting many branches on fire. The beams converged with pinpoint precision, emitted from the *Mastodon*'s left arm and chin. They caught the mobile Hammerhead close to the center of its skull, shockingly. They held for three seconds before phasing out, and made it falter for a breath.

"Shit, Wally, I didn't say kill it," Eddie laughed, and kept running.

"Sorry I'm such a great shot," he said with exaggerated

complacency, and pulled away just as the *Adversary* strode past him.

"Don't worry, it's still hot on your trail," Brick said, surveying from the sky. "Charly and I have backed off, now that our targets have officially taken an interest in you all. I think Wally just helped, too."

The size and extended-range capabilities of the *Mastodon*'s two Lasers had driven its heat levels just under yellow, from that shot alone. Simultaneous weapon discharging would do that, especially EBWs.

"Great. Need anymore?" Wally asked.

Charly laughed. "I don't think so, you madman. Just get your ass to the eighteenth hole. Confirming location now, unless you have any objections."

"Make that call," Eddie said. "We'll be ready."

"We'll take a dip if we have to," H said. She followed the *Adversary* on a hard left, advancing to the Presidio Golf Course. She passed the lumbering *Mastodon*, and to its left was Nomi in her *Rottweiler*, gradually catching up to Eddie.

"Bombers en route," Charly said, tenseness in her voice. "ETA fifteen seconds. Expect a four-second drop."

Eddie shook his head. "So much for that twenty-to-thirty second window, Major."

"Want me to abort, Princess?" Charly asked.

Eddie smirked. "Negative. Bring the rain."

"How you doing, Wally?" Nomi asked.

Her *Rottweiler* was on the *Adversary*'s heels, to the left of the *Pluto*. The three Mechs led the *Mastodon* by a couple of seconds.

"Ready to brace and hear these fuckers scream!"

They would have cheered if it wasn't for the next thing that came over their comms.

"Then your time is now," Brick said, his voice booming and mixed with ambivalence, as he watched the first payload deploy. "Bombs away!"

"Brace, Ember!" Charly shouted.

Eddie, Nomi, and H brought their Mechs to a dead stop as fast as they could. Nomi was able to stop sooner than the others, thanks to dropping to her *Rottweiler*'s heels and engaging its tank tracks. They absorbed her speed quickly, and then she crouched the Mech.

The *Adversary* followed suit.

H stopped a few paces later, past the golf course. She had been going so damn fast, and the *Pluto* wasn't designed for abrupt deceleration. Besides, H and Mal knew well enough that their lighter Mech would need more distance, as it was more likely to topple than the others. The *Rottweiler* was a couple of tons lighter, but structurally lower to the ground, and more robustly designed.

Wally could hear the deployed bombs whistling as they plummeted. He stopped in his tracks faster than any of the others, and crouched the massive Mech. The first bombs hit the Hammerheads less than two hundred feet behind him, seconds before he could achieve a full crouch. The detonations collided, forming a larger fireball that engulfed the top of the Hammerhead, from skull to upper back. The impacts of the blasts alone flattened its body against the turf.

The other Hammerhead took another payload, burying it beneath a blanket of explosions.

Carpet-bombing was called such for good reason.

Eddie, Nomi, H, and Mal barely felt anything more than a light tremor as the bombs hit their targets, far behind them.

Wally, meanwhile, continued to brace.

A third bomber fell in line, and dropped its payload as it flew into position, widening the targeted area below. It did this for good reason. There were only three bombers in the immediate vicinity. Two more were en route from a closer area, but from the pilot's perspective, the remaining targets needed to be hit before they wised up and turned tail.

Unfortunately, he could only hit two of the three himself. One of the remaining Hammerheads, and the Lumpy Titan. The payload exploded with a satisfying scatter, scorching nearby trees and golf turf.

Wally's teeth chattered in his skull as he tightly gripped his harness in the *Mastodon*. Even in standby mode, its heat levels rose. Yellow, and then orange. Alarms rang out. He shook his head and squinted, as flame flashed over the top of his canopy. He looked at his spinal camera, glimpsing a view of the explosions before the feed cut to static.

"Stay with me," Wally muttered, shutting his eyes. Not clamping them, but meditatively closing.

"Direct hits, fucking fireworks," Charly said victoriously.

"Scanners are reading two confirmed kills," Brick said. He tried avoiding a grin, or sounding too excited.

In his and Charly's restricted comms, one of the bombers confirmed an ETA on the second group. Thirty seconds.

"Tracking movement from one target, watch it,

312

Wally!"

Wally's eyes flung open at Charly's sudden warning. He reached for his controls, to take the *Mastodon* out of standby mode, and relinquishing it from a crouch at the same time. A sudden grinding sound occurred as a wounded Hammerhead's clawed hand grabbed the *Mastodon*'s right elbow. The dual-Railgun-mounted arm twisted backward, metal scraping in an ear-piercing fashion.

The fusion engine began to wake from hibernation. It would take a few seconds, but before that, a mechanical voice made an announcement in his cockpit.

"Weapons online."

Wally selected his Railguns.

"You want it, sucker!?" He grinded his teeth, blindly aiming, and then squeezed the trigger. "You can have it!"

The paired Railguns fired successfully, as they functioned independently from his torso. The eight-pound tungsten slugs discharged with the muzzle energy of twenty megajoules.

At two miles a second.

They penetrated the Hammerhead's skull at two different points, but the velocities sufficed to blast its head into pieces. Blood, brain matter, and mucus spilled into the air behind it.

"Headshot, baby!" Charly cheered. She almost lost control of her Hawk at the beautiful sight. And then her radar pinged. She bared her teeth in urgency as she made her next announcement: "Second bombardment, ETA ten seconds."

"Move your ass, Wally!" Brick shouted.

313

"Draw it farther out!" Eddie commanded, and had already rose back into a full stance, turned to face the city again, and targeted the remaining Titan.

A Hammerhead, which suddenly seemed reluctant to follow the others to a similar fate. It now skirted at the edge of the golf course, its tail swinging fifty feet above the rooftops of Presidio Heights.

At least it was a couple hundred feet to the left of, and behind, Wally.

Then he began moving, catching its gaze. The *Mastodon* was unmistakable, especially as a heat signature. He spun its torso, just as Eddie barraged the Titan with both PPCs, Lasers, *and* Autocannons. The onslaught violated the air in front of Wally, missing him by fifty feet or so. In the *Adversary* cockpit, heat warnings echoed. Eddie he rode it out and watched the impacts light up the Hammerhead. It staggered, one foot demolishing a house in the process.

Eddie was angered and feared that was his fault, but knew there was no other way to drag it into the open. At least, right after that, the Hammerhead took not one but two steps forward.

Wally's twin Autocannons flashed white-hot, but missed high. Deliberately. A split-second later, he launched four SRMs—into the turf twenty feet in front of him. The explosions rose but were neither close nor large enough to do any damage to his dense armor.

The added heat signatures, in addition to his own, sufficed to draw the Titan away from the homes.

"Clever, Wally," Eddie said, and started to backpedal. His teammates had already begun striding off the course, toward the tip of the Peninsula. "Now get the hell outta there!"

Wally ignored Eddie and engaged his target with both Lasers. A loud clanging sounded above his cockpit—his Autocannons reloading. Their display on his HUD changed from yellow to green; he scratched his itch, selecting them again.

And fired.

Both the Lasers and the ACX shots missed high.

It felt odd, for Wally, to be so enthusiastic about deliberately missing a target, especially with such imposing weapons.

The heat bloom, however…

Like fireworks.

The Hammerhead all but galloped, covering distance fast.

"Get outta there!" Charly shouted, as the first bomber arrived to drop its payload. There was no warning or hesitation. This was the plan.

The risks were known.

And proudly, viciously accepted by the Ember Wolves.

Wally leaned forward, both in his cockpit and the *Mastodon* itself. He peered up, through the canopy, and saw the bomber open its bay doors. From its dark belly poured a payload of Mk-85 bombs. Each one, capable of forming fifty-foot-wide craters with depths up to forty, penetrating twenty inches of steel or thirteen feet of concrete.

Four of them fell, two tons each, descending from a nine-hundred-foot drop.

Wally breathed through flaring nostrils and glared forward. The Hammerhead was all but upon him. He heard his teammates scream his name. He pulled the ejection handle, and shut his eyes.

This time, they clamped.

Charly and Brick, from their view, saw a pillar of amber-red explosions spread into a quilt of fire that buried the Hammerhead beneath it. Dense black smoke obscured their sight of the stooping *Mastodon*.

And no answer from Wally.

16

Ember Wolves and Hawks alike waited in a heavy silence for only so long. Eddie then piloted his Mech forward, radar scanning. Within a few seconds after the bomber departed, and Charly demanded the other one to stand-by, Eddie's systems highlighted the *Mastodon* on his HUD. It was still standing, and not critically damaged. According to its displayed chassis, it had suffered some heat damage to its legs and center torso, but was still above fifty-percent.

Unfortunately, the cockpit had been compromised. Eddie quickly tapped his controls, to scan the *Mastodon* for—

"Ejected, Wally ejected!" Brick cheered. "He's thrusting back toward you!"

"Eyes up, Clanners!" Charly said, elated.

Eddie stopped walking and pitched his torso back, so that he could peer straight through his canopy and scan the skies. Through a high cloud of black smoke that had begun to dissipate, a white bubble of canvas appeared.

Wally's parachute.

His seat, to which he was securely harnessed, descended less than a hundred feet in front of Eddie. A big grin appeared on his face.

"You fucking nut," he said quietly at first, and then laughed.

Cheering from his teammates spilled through their shared frequency.

"No sign of movement," Brick said. "I repeat, no sign of movement. All...targets...neutralized."

"Let's make sure of it, shall we, Brick?" Charly said, swooping her VTOL down.

"Thought you'd never ask."

Brick followed, but with the maneuvering flair reminiscent of the late and great Fox Kowalski.

Their original order from Major Reigart was to have the Mechs confirm kills, but for safety reasons this seemed more appropriate.

"See what I'm seeing?" Eddie asked, still gazing skyward, even after Wally soundly landed on the turf a few paces in front of the *Adversary*.

"What is it, boss?" Nomi asked, walking up next to him on the course.

"It'll be closed in maybe an hour, who knows, less, possibly." Eddie shook his head. "Call me crazy, but I want to go."

The three Mechs, H piloting the *Pluto* in behind Eddie, spectated the high heavens. Natural cloud cover was beginning to assemble once more in the atmosphere, partially obscuring their view. What they *could* see, however, was a glimpse adequate enough...

The rip in space above the planet was maybe a few miles from sealing altogether. A tiny gap up there, compared to the measurable distance on Earth.

Especially on foot.

Eddie had only known combat in his Mech, and as a

force of infantry. But to be flown into that crevice, and attack the enemy in its own realm, was a terrifying enthusiasm he couldn't shy from.

"Don't you even think about it," Mal said into H's mic, leaning over her shoulder.

Eddie realigned his Mech's torso and then turned on its feet to face H's *Pluto*.

They stood less than thirty feet away from each other. Their cockpits were vaguely visible from where they sat, although details such as facial expressions couldn't be discerned due to the glare.

"Yeah?" Eddie said, eyebrow raised.

"I've got a deal to make good on," Mal said.

"What deal?" Eddie was puzzled.

Mal and H exchanged grins.

"We'll tell you about it later," H finally said.

"What's the plan now?" Wally asked.

Eddie did a double-take, looking through his canopy. His eyes then narrowed on the source of that transmission. From Nomi's *Rottweiler*.

"Congratulations are in order, first of all," Eddie said. "For managing to survive that absurd call you made."

Wally shrugged, and looked down at Nomi, who struggled not to laugh. She was both disappointed in his recklessness, and impressed by his courage. Or had it been insanity?

Open for debate.

"Well, I appreciate that," Wally said. "Let's just say I was being looked out for."

"Farooq?" Eddie said, gently.

"And a few wingnuts," Wally nodded. "Three in particular."

"And a Clanner," Nomi smiled, tears beneath her eyes.

Wally clutched her shoulder in consolation. Nomi felt her heart swell, and was far from abandoning hope.

None of them had come close.

"Kills confirmed, Ember," Charly announced, her and Brick's VTOLs coming to a hover not far behind the still-standing *Mastodon*. In front of it, the smoke had cleared and the cratered remains of four Titans scattered the Presidio Golf Course.

"Happy to have you with us, Wally," Brick said.

"Delighted to be back," he replied.

"Operation Subterfuge is a success," Charly sighed, "but the mission is far from over. According to the Major's orders, Brick and I are to return and mop up smaller targets."

"You two have a much…lighter footprint than us," Eddie said. "I hate to abide by those orders, but I agree."

"According to our last flyby, most of the streets looked clear," Brick said.

H shook her head, grimly. "Negative," she said simply, and all the wrong emotions frothed within her. "Where Mal landed, there were Hounds and Boars alike, a fucking Gator in a *house*, and a tentacle thing giving *birth*, still."

She shook her head again and then laughed, madly. Her nose tingled with the sensation of encroaching tears.

"What we see up here, doesn't compare to what's really lurking down there," H said.

"So be thorough with your flybys," Mal added. "And

make sure any SAK and SAR teams the Major sends in are well informed. We'll do our part, too."

Eddie hated to hear H's voice tremble so much, and Mal's was not devoid of the same gritty emotion.

He couldn't fathom what exactly they encountered down there, but it made him even more fervent about returning to battle.

Not in space, either. But down here.

Where it really mattered.

"Charly, Brick…call Javelin Niner," Eddie said. "We need an immediate airlift back to base, for rearmament. We'll have the *Mastodon* picked up, too. Cockpit and canopy needs a quick repair, then we'll go where we're needed."

"Right back into it, huh?" Brick said.

"Fucking A," H nodded.

"Happy to hear we're all on the same page," Eddie said.

"Likewise," Brick added.

"Paging Javelin now," Charly chimed in. "We'll see you when we see you."

"Fly safe," Nomi said. "And kick ass."

"We'll do nothing less," Brick said, and punched his thrusters to jerk the Hawk vertically.

The Mechs gestured with their arms, in salute of the Hawks as they hooked around and thrusted back over San Francisco.

Their two airlifts loomed from above the Golden Gate Bridge. Behind them, the approach of a sunset.

Eddie could barely picture them battling such imposing enemies under the camouflage of nightfall. PPCs,

Lasers, and Autocannons scoring the darkness with blue, red, and white-hot light. It would be beautiful, and terrible, and worth every single risk.

"So, what's that deal you were talking about?" Eddie asked, thoughts of Mal, and the aftermath of this successful strategy creeping into his mind.

"I'll show you when we land at base," Mal said.

Eddie smiled.

Not just about Mal, and the survival of his Clan on this mission. His smile was pained at the thought of those that didn't make it, both on his team and other Clans world-wide, and the immense loss of civilian life.

However, Eddie's bittersweet smile was also a nod to the undying strength and tenacity of the human race. He would like to believe that even without such superior technology, humanity would still persevere against the worst odds.

At the absolute least, they would die in their struggle to endure.

And they would be damned if they did it alone.

At the end of the day—and the day had not yet seen its end—humanity's enemy, in all their vastness and violence, sought to conquer the planet…

But there was one thing they could not devour.

Unity.

Author's Note

Thank you to my friends and family, and even my coworkers. Many of you endured my ramblings during the planning and writing of this novel. Several even gave valuable advice, whether they realized it or not.

This has served as a sort of genre-shift companion piece to what I consider my first official novel, "Absolved of the Flesh." Also a Mech-driven story, albeit on a fictional planet and involving warring factions instead of aliens. Despite having only received one reader since its 2014 publication, that reader was my father. I miss him indescribably, and know that he is immortalized in my love, and others who loved him.

War, horror, and loss. This novel spans many themes. But in the end it's love that wins. Call it cliché, call it silly. If you read this book, and aren't just flipping to the back page (stop it! lol), you'll know that a central theme to the story was unity, not war. That, because of such fantastical, arguably unrealistic unity, the ending came to be what it was.

Not really an end. But a continuation.

Jacob Russell Dring
June 19, 2021